"How can you think of leaving, Kate?"

Alex had shattered her serenity. Why did he have to bring up the subject of her departure now? She didn't want to answer.

"You ran away once," he continued. "Don't do it again." He gestured at what lay before them, the meandering river, the far-off hills bathed in purple light and the plain below, where the Masai people were celebrating an ancient rite of passage. "This is where you belong. Here—with me."

There was such appeal in his eyes, such love. "Sometimes I believe that," she said, her heart breaking. "But then..."

"Then what?"

"All this can be so deceiving." She waved her hand. "There's not just beauty and peace here." Her voice broke. "There's darkness and violence and blood—" She stopped short.

"Doesn't my *love* for you mean anything?" he asked bitterly.

D0360665

ABOUT THE AUTHOR

Eleni Carr visited Kenya last year with her husband. Fascinated by the beautiful scenery and the wildlife, she decided it was the perfect setting for a love story. The result? The highly powerful *A Matter of Time*, a dramatic tale that touches on the spirit of the African people. When she's not traveling, Eleni makes her home in Florida. Fans will be delighted to know she's hard at work on her next book!

Books by Eleni Carr

HARLEQUIN SUPERROMANCE

Don't miss any of our special offers. Write to us at the following address for information on our newest releases.

Harlequin Reader Service
901 Fuhrmann Blvd., P.O. Box 1397, Buffalo, NY 14240
Canadian address: P.O. Box 603,
Fort Erie, Ont. L2A 5X3

A Matter of Time

ELENI CARR

Harlequin Books

TORONTO • NEW YORK • LONDON
AMSTERDAM • PARIS • SYDNEY • HAMBURG
STOCKHOLM • ATHENS • TOKYO • MILAN

Published September 1989

First printing July 1989

ISBN 0-373-70372-4

CHAPTER ONE

KATHERINE MARLOWE OPENED her boss's door, sniffed and
halted. "If you don't put out that cigar, I'm not coming in,"
she announced.

"This is good stuff," Harvey Blackwell growled. "Made
in Havana."

"I don't care if it was made in Shangri-la. It smells awful."

"Okay, okay. I'll put it out." Reluctantly he ground the
cigar into his ashtray.

Yellow smoke curled from the squashed cigar. Kate came
in, picked up the ashtray and moved it to the conference table near the door. "I thought your doctor told you to stop."

"He said to quit cigarettes."

"He meant all kinds of smoking," she pointed out as she
took the chair across from him.

"Don't lecture. I get plenty of that at home. You're as
bad as my wife. No—I take that back. No one's as bad as
Margo. But you're a close second." His bushy eyebrows almost met as he frowned.

Kate smiled. She'd worked for the public relations firm of
Blackwell Enterprises for nearly four years and knew that
Harvey's gruffness was all on the surface. He was one of the
most astute professionals in his field. More important, he
was a kind and generous man.

"I'm lucky you didn't marry my son," Harvey said.
"What a bossy daughter-in-law you'd have been."

Kate knew he didn't mean that. If anything, he'd been more disappointed than his son when she'd turned down Barry's proposal last winter. "So how come you're not grateful I spared you?" she countered.

"I am. That's why I'm giving you this easy assignment."

"But I've got an assignment." Kate was handling the publicity for a wealthy and flamboyant astrologer who periodically self-published her books of predictions about famous people. "I'm getting Elvira ready to go on tour."

"Reynolds can take over. Unless Elvira would object."

"Are you kidding?" Bob Reynolds was a handsome young addition to the staff. "She'll love it. Elvira thinks of herself as a man's woman. She'll be thrilled at the substitution. But you've never made this kind of change before." Kate shot her boss a curious look. "Why not give Bob the new assignment?"

"Because you're perfect for it."

"For what?"

"This." He rolled his chair back and took a heavy book from the shelf behind him. On the cover was a brilliantly hued photograph of three giraffes, their graceful necks crossed as they reached for the leaves of an acacia tree. In the foreground a small herd of impala grazed. Dark hills rose in the distance against a clear blue sky. *A Vanishing World*, the title read.

"Kenya," Kate said, the word escaping like a sigh.

"You lived there, right?" Harvey asked.

"Yes."

"For a long time, wasn't it?"

"Yes." She'd lived in Kenya from the age of six until she was fifteen. The information was in her personnel file, but she seldom talked about her life in East Africa.

"The photographer's Melanie Pearson," Harvey continued. "It's a great cover. I'm a sucker for wildlife. The book will be out in two or three weeks. Pearson did a book on Ireland a couple of years ago. It should have sold better than it did. The publisher didn't give it much of a publicity budget. For this book, Pearson got herself a collaborator to do the text and they turned out a good piece of work."

"Same publisher for this one?"

"Yeah. They've put out the usual prepublication releases and scheduled some appearances for Pearson, but she figures some extra hoopla will boost sales. Seems she persuaded the man she worked with to come to the States to help push the book. The guy's supposed to be pretty dynamic. Anyway, that's when her agent decided to go for some extra publicity. She wangled a deal to let the authors handle the promotion, with the publisher footing half the bill."

"I don't know, Harvey. With the book coming out in a few weeks, how much can we accomplish?"

"So you'll have to pull some fast deals, call in some favors. You've done it before."

"But why knock ourselves out? It doesn't sound like a very lucrative contract for us."

Harvey spread his pudgy hands. "It's not, but the book's good, and I'd like to help promote it. Besides, Rhoda twisted my arm."

"So you're twisting mine." He nodded. "Who's this Rhoda?"

"Melanie Pearson's agent. And my second cousin," he admitted sheepishly. "I couldn't say no. Anyway, I figured this might be fun for you . . . remind you of old times. Why are you frowning?"

"Getting radio and TV spots isn't going to be easy," Kate said with a sigh. "This isn't exactly a hot subject."

"Would you rather stick with Elvira?"

"Lord, no, though she's easy to place. Talk-show people seem to love her."

"Because she's a character." Harvey turned the book around to the photograph on the back cover. "Rhoda says these two are a pretty sharp duo." The picture showed a vibrant redhead petting a cub held by a tall, darkly handsome man.

Kate's breath caught in her throat. "Alex..."

She'd been so taken with the photograph on the cover that she'd failed to notice the author's name.

"Alexander Crane," Harvey said. "Don't tell me you know the guy?"

She struggled to keep her voice steady. "I knew him once...a long time ago."

Harvey grinned. "Great. I said you were perfect for this assignment, didn't I?"

She didn't answer.

"Why that funny look, Kate? You two weren't enemies or anything, were you?"

"No, we weren't enemies."

"Friends?" he inquired.

She hesitated. "Yes, we were friends."

Harvey looked at her curiously. "More than friends?"

She didn't know how to reply. A simple yes wouldn't explain what she and Alex had been to each other. They'd loved first with the simplicity of children, then with adolescent intensity. While still in their teens, they'd had to part, and had never experienced the maturing of their feelings. She'd often told herself that such bonds seldom survived into adulthood, but the sense of loss had stayed with her for thirteen years.

"We were kids. Growing up together, we were pretty tight, I guess. Then I left Kenya. Alex chose to stay. End of story."

Harvey raised his eyebrows. "Maybe not. Could be that when you meet again, there'll be a sequel—with a better ending."

Kate stood. "Not likely." Harvey meant well, but he didn't know the full story. She took the book and went back to her office. There was little she could do today, not at 4:45 on a Friday. She'd read the book over the weekend and make some notes on how to proceed. At her desk she found herself staring at the back cover. It would be strange seeing Alex again. What was he like now?

The telephone interrupted her reverie. It was Bob Reynolds. "I hear I'm taking over with Elvira," he said cheerfully.

"Do you mind?"

"No. She's kind of wacky, but fun, too."

"Want me to brief you?"

"Hey, Kate, it's quittin' time, Friday, getaway day, remember? I'm off for a little fun and frolic. You should be, too. Just thought I'd check about Elvira. Is it okay with you?"

"Sure. No problem."

"Harvey says you've got this special assignment you want to do for a friend."

Kate smiled. "Kind of." That was one way of putting it. "Enjoy your weekend, Bob. See you Monday."

After hanging up, Kate gathered her things to leave. Bob had recommended fun and frolic, but she had much to think about.

AT HOME THAT EVENING Kate was keyed up, unable to relax. Her apartment felt stuffy and confining. She opened the door off the kitchen and stepped onto the patio leading to her tiny back garden. It was this little bit of open space that had sold her on the overpriced ground-floor flat in the Gramercy Park town house. Amid the concrete skyscrapers and tunneled streets of Manhattan, she had a rectangle of earth and a patch of sky of her own.

Nothing like the vast savannas and endless horizons she'd known in Kenya, Kate thought with a sigh. Seeing that book with Alex's name on it had brought it all back. But, then, something always did. Why were all those memories so much more vivid than anything that had happened since she'd come to the United States? It was here that she'd finished high school, gone to college and established herself in public relations. She'd experienced friendship—and love, or what was called by that name in her social circle. But nothing with the intensity of emotion she remembered, nothing that had lasted.

She had to stop drawing on memories that made her emotional life today pallid by comparison. The hyped-up sensitivity of youth fostered emotional extremes that dulled with maturity. Rationally that's what Kate believed. Nevertheless she kept seeking what she'd lost, though she never found it in other relationships. She feared that the wildly happy love she'd known was unique to her and Alex, it couldn't be duplicated. But it had existed in another dimension, and had no relevance to her life now. It was time to let go. Perhaps seeing Alex again would do the trick.

She wondered when he would be coming to the States. Tomorrow she'd call Rhoda Field and ask her to set up an appointment with Alex and Melanie Pearson. Alex might even be in New York already. But surely he'd have gotten in touch with her. Though it had been years since they'd corresponded regularly, he'd always managed to keep track of her. Out of the blue would come a postcard whose picture had reminded him of something they'd shared. His few scrawled words never failed to evoke the same memory in her. There was no reason to keep these missives, she kept telling herself, but she'd added each one to the bundle in her lingerie drawer.

There had been no card this past year, however, not since before her move to this apartment. Alex had no way of contacting her—except through her brother, Derek. Kate went into the kitchen and dialed Derek's number in Washington.

"Hey, I was just about to call you," Derek said. He sounded excited. "Guess what?"

"You heard from Alex."

"How the hell did you know that?"

"ESP."

Derek's exclamation was a cross between a groan and a laugh. "Don't start with that. Elizabeth used to drive me crazy with that sixth sense of hers."

It had been three years since Derek's wife had died. For a long time, he'd been devastated and bitter about a fate that had taken his beautiful young wife from him and their four-year-old daughter. With time he'd learned to cope with his grief and his responsibility, but it was only lately that he could talk about Elizabeth without reliving the tragedy of her loss. He was raising Susan, now seven, and teaching undergraduate classes at Latham University outside of Washington, D.C. He'd finished all the course requirements for his Ph.D. and had only his dissertation to complete. Kate was proud of her younger brother.

"All right, so it's not ESP," Kate told him. "Just a lucky guess. I figured that if Alex was coming to the States, he'd be in touch."

"How did you know he was coming?"

Kate explained her new assignment.

"Talk about coincidences!" Derek exclaimed. "You know what Elizabeth would have said, don't you? That there are no coincidences. All this was meant to be."

"Sure, sure. When is Alex coming?"

"He'll be in Washington sometime tomorrow night."

"Why Washington?"

"For the reception Sunday."

"What reception?"

"That's what I'm trying to tell you. Your invitation was sent care of this address."

"What invitation? Derek, what are you talking about?"

"The Kenyan embassy is hosting a reception Sunday to herald the publication of *A Vanishing World*. Alex and the photographer—what's her name..."

"Melanie Pearson."

"Right. They're the guests of honor. I didn't even know about the book, so when the invitation came this morning, I called Alex."

"Where?"

"In Nairobi. He was getting ready to catch a plane to Frankfurt, then a direct flight to Washington. It's a grueling trip. I warned him he's going to be wiped out. It used to take me a week to recover."

After her father was killed, Kate had left Kenya for good, but Derek had been back several times before Elizabeth's death.

"He said to bring Mom to the reception, too. But I explained that she's remarried and she and Roger are away on business." Derek's voice became wistful. "We're all scattered now. We lived so closely once upon a time."

Once upon a time... That was how stories and fairy tales started, Kate thought. Their close-knit lives in Kenya had indeed been like a fairy tale. Derek's sigh echoed in her heart. Then she remembered how their fairy tale had ended and a tremor of revulsion shot through her.

"So when are you coming down?" Derek asked.

Her brother assumed she would come. He was right, of course. Even if it wasn't for her new assignment, she wouldn't pass up the chance to see Alex. "I guess I'll take an afternoon shuttle tomorrow."

"I'll pick you up at National."

"You don't have to bother."

"It's no bother. It'll be a treat for Susan. She loves to see the planes land."

"How is my favorite niece?"

"Growing like crazy. Here, say hello."

"Hi, Aunt Katie," a little voice said. "When are you coming?"

Kate smiled, picturing her sturdy, seven-year-old niece. Susan had her mother's brown skin and finely wrought facial features, but her gray-green eyes were like her father's. "Tomorrow afternoon," Kate answered. "Tell your dad I'll take the three-thirty shuttle."

"She's taking the three-thirty shuttle," Susan bellowed, though her father was still close by. "Would you like to bring me something?" she asked.

Kate heard her brother's fierce whisper. "Suzie, I told you not to ask Aunt Kate for presents."

"I didn't," Susan whispered back. "I asked her if she *wanted* to bring me something. I didn't say she had to."

"It's all right," Kate said laughingly. "What would you like?"

"A soccer ball."

"Soccer?"

"Yeah. I play after school."

"No more dolls?"

"Who said?"

"That was a question. I was asking."

"Oh. I still have my dolls, but they're for in the house. I'd like a soccer ball for when I play outside."

"That makes sense," Kate agreed. Susan's play area was a schoolyard or fenced public park, not the vast expanse of the Masai Mara, where her parents and aunt had lived. "I'll see what I can do about that soccer ball."

"Thanks. Here's Daddy."

"I think you've got a tomboy on your hands," Kate said when Derek took the phone.

"Tell me about it. Her coach says she's better than most of the boys on the team. And she's absolutely fearless."

"That's her Masai blood."

"Elizabeth was half Masai and she was so gentle."

"But strong underneath," Kate reminded him. Elizabeth's mother had married an Englishman, but her people had never trusted or accepted her white husband. The Masai were a tightly knit tribe, fiercely proud and loyal to their traditions. Elizabeth was bound to both worlds, her father's European culture and her mother's African heritage. At eighteen, she had married Derek and come to America, leaving behind all that she'd known, ready to embrace yet another culture. That took courage.

Elizabeth and Derek had been happy, a happiness that had increased when Susan was born. Kate recalled that her young sister-in-law had once said it was important to cram happiness into each passing moment because life was so short. At the time Kate had thought it just a general observation, not a prediction. Afterward, when Elizabeth had been diagnosed as having an inoperable cancer, Kate suspected that the young woman had known her life would be cut off.

Kate didn't exactly believe that the women in Elizabeth's family all had special powers, but she didn't discount the notion, either. Elizabeth's grandmother had been a medicine woman. As a child, Elizabeth had reported that when they went on visits to the Masai village, she and her mother were seated next to the revered grandmother during tribal ceremonies. Derek had teased Elizabeth about having inherited mystical powers, but his father, overhearing, had scolded him. Alastair Marlowe had had respect for African customs and beliefs. There were phenomena, he'd told the children, that couldn't be explained rationally. Though he himself had been educated as a scientist and he knew the value of the scientific method, he cautioned his son never to jeer at what couldn't be understood scientifically.

Kate had idolized her father. As a youngster, perched on his shoulders, she'd first seen the beauty of Kenya through his admiring eyes. She'd learned from him the fascinating lore of wild animal behavior and had come to have his curiosity and affection for the creatures who shared their environment. His death had been doubly devastating, for it had robbed her of a father and destroyed forever her image of the country she'd loved.

"I'd better go," Derek was saying. "I'll pick you up tomorrow. It'll be great seeing Alex again, won't it? Just like old times."

Kate hung up the phone. She sat staring into space. Like old times?

They'd been so close, four children growing up on the game preserve in the Masai Mara, the Kenyan stretch of the Serengeti Plain. Alex was the oldest, followed by Katherine, Derek and Elizabeth. Alastair Marlowe and Alex's father, Harold Crane, were friends and colleagues. They had come to Kenya to study the ecology of wildlife habitats and had stayed on at the request of the government to supervise the Mara preserve. Elizabeth's father, Patrick Sloane, a former hunter and guide, had acted as their majordomo. Patrick spoke Swahili and a half-dozen African dialects, and his wife,] ᵃ, daughter of a Masai chieftain, was an invaluable intermediary with her proud people.

Kate and Alex had been the most adventurous of the foursome, always pleading to accompany the men on safari. Derek, quiet and studious, had been content to stay behind to read or paint under a broad acacia tree. Elizabeth, who idolized Derek, was his willing companion. The pairing off had started early in childhood. When Derek was fourteen, he went away to prep school in America. Kate, however, had refused to go. Claiming that she got all the schooling she needed from her father and a resident tutor, Kate had persuaded her parents to postpone her formal education until she was sixteen. She couldn't bear the thought of leaving all that she loved—her parents, the vast Mara plain with its wild and beautiful animals, the fullness of each day that she shared with Alex. Alex had been the center of her being.

As soon as they were old enough to make choices, they had chosen each other. From dawn to dark, Alex and Kate were together constantly. Their parents used to joke about their closeness. Each seemed to know what the other was thinking. She remembered the time their mothers had sat them both down to caution them. Kate had just celebrated her fourteenth birthday and Alex, after a growth spurt, was a manly looking six-footer. Alex's mother had taken the initiative.

"This compound is so small that we're bound to get a bit interdependent," Jennifer Crane had said in her precise British accent. "And of course we're all happy you've been such good friends all these years. But things change as one gets older." She went on to talk about how Kate and Alex were bound to meet new people and form new attachments. They'd listened politely until they could excuse themselves. As soon as they were alone, they'd laughed about their mothers' concerns, scoffing at the notion of new attachments, unable to visualize a life separate from each other.

Alex had been almost seventeen then. Kate had sensed a difference in him, something that sparked a new awareness in her. Her body was changing, its angular form taking on the soft contours of a young woman. Her emotional responses were deepening, becoming turbulent. On her last birthday, Alex had kissed her for the first time, really kissed her. The following months were the happiest she'd ever known. There was a new intimacy and wonder in their friendship, leading to a physical hunger they were just beginning to explore. Their tentative caresses were sweet, yet powerful. She sensed that Alex was curbing his desire, and loved him all the more. "There's no rush," he told her. "We have all the time in the world."

Kate had believed him. When the time came, she would find some way of getting out of being sent away to school like Derek. Being separated from Alex was unthinkable.

Yet a few months later, the unthinkable had happened. And Kate had wanted to go.

It was several days after Christmas when her world had shattered. Kate's father and Harold Crane had gone out on a routine inspection tour, from which they never returned. They were found by a search party, their jeep overturned by a herd of spooked elephants. The men were dead, either killed in the trampling or later by predators. It was Alex who broke the news to her. She'd gone out by herself and Alex had come to find her. She remembered how, as he told her what had happened, the late-afternoon sun had blinded her vision and burned her skin, but her heart had been a block of ice and her blood had spread a chill that had frozen her being.

From that day everything had changed. Kate saw the landscape with different eyes, and its beauty was gone for

her. At night the sound of a lion's roar made her break out
in a cold sweat. After the funeral, when Ellen Marlowe had
decided to return to America, Kate had been relieved. The
Mara had become a threatening and brutal place. The only
wrenching pain she felt came from leaving Alex. She'd been
surprised and disappointed that he'd wanted to stay. Re-
sentful, too, since she was sure he could have persuaded his
mother to go. But Jennifer Crane had had no ties back in
England. She was offered a teaching position and chose to
stay in Kenya.

Kate and Alex had written often at first. Alex's letters
kept asking when she was coming home. He hadn't wanted
to understand. Her last long letter to him, right after she'd
graduated from college, gave a final and unequivocal reply.
Kenya would never be her home again. He finally seemed to
accept that, and their correspondence became sporadic. She
would never forget him. The boy she'd loved remained in
her heart, but the affection was based on a shared past. They
no longer had anything in common. Kenya was his world,
not hers.

As KATE'S PLANE made a bumpy landing at Washington's
National Airport the following afternoon, she wondered if
Alex's flight had arrived. It would be funny if they happened to meet right there at the airport. Not likely, though,
since international flights usually landed at Dulles. She
wondered what he might be feeling, and remembered a time
when she instinctively knew. She'd never again experienced
that kind of oneness with another person. Kate told herself
that what she remembered was childhood affection and adolescent love based on proximity. She and Alex had been
thrown together at a time when their newly felt yearnings
demanded an outlet and there were no other young people
around. Of course they had loved each other then. But

thirteen years had gone by. When she left Kenya, Kate had left those feelings and her childhood behind.

Derek was waiting at the gate. He grabbed her carry-on bag and gave her a kiss. Kate looked around. "Where's Susan?"

He pointed to where the little girl had her nose pressed against the glass as she watched a plane take off. "Suzie, come on," he called.

Susan turned and raced over, braids flying. Kate knelt to gather her niece in a warm hug. Susan planted a smudgy kiss on her cheek and stepped back, eyes searching until they fastened on the plastic bag her aunt had put down.

"If you can guess what's in here, it's yours," Kate said with a teasing smile, and picked up the bag.

Susan's eyes widened eagerly. "My soccer ball?"

Kate handed her the bag. "Right you are."

Susan opened the bag to look. "Wow! Thanks, Aunt Kate. Wait'll Arnold sees this."

"Arnold's her new best friend," Derek explained as they walked to his car. "Yesterday she announced that she'd rather play with Arnold than with Theresa Morella, even if he doesn't like her Cabbage Patch doll."

"Sounds serious."

"You never can tell. She probably takes after her mother. Elizabeth started following me around when she was six and never gave up. She claimed that she hooked me with a combination of mysticism and tenacity. I was powerless to resist."

"As I recall, you didn't even try." Derek and Elizabeth had married at eighteen, less than three months after his return to Kenya. "That was one whirlwind courtship."

They reached his car, where he paused before opening the door. His brow furrowed and he lost the youthful look. "Elizabeth said we had to make every minute count."

Kate guessed what he was thinking—that Elizabeth had known their time would be short.

"Time has a way of turning on you," Derek continued, "reminding you that life's not inexhaustible. That goes for you, too, Kate."

"Meaning?"

"Just that I get the feeling you've been marking time the past few years."

"I don't know why you should think that. I'm very satisfied with my life."

"Being satisfied is a wimpy state. What about being happy?"

"That, too—at times." Kate shrugged. "Happiness is elusive and temporary. One can make do with spurts of it as they come."

"You didn't used to think that way. I remember when you and Alex acted as though you owned the world and would be happy together forever."

A rush of nostalgia mingled with pain tore through her. "We were children, and the world we owned was destroyed."

"Not for Alex. He never wants to leave Kenya."

"That's his choice," Kate said coldly.

Derek studied her thoughtfully but dropped the subject until they were in the car, heading into the city. Susan sat in the back, watching for out-of-state license plates she could read aloud.

"Aren't you looking forward to seeing Alex again?" Derek asked.

"Of course. It'll be great."

"Do you think you'll recognize him?"

The question startled her. How could she not recognize Alex Crane? His image was indelibly etched in her mind. Sometimes he appeared as the vibrant youth of her teen years. At other times, she pictured the man he had become, a man she knew only from the pictures Derek always brought home from his trips to Kenya.

"He can't have changed much from three years ago," Kate said, referring to the photographs Derek had taken on his last visit.

"You know, Kate, every time Elizabeth and I went over, Alex hoped you'd be with us."

"He knew how I felt." Kate refrained from adding something she'd often thought—that Alex could have been with her long ago, had he so chosen.

As Derek concentrated on making his way through the heavy traffic heading over the Potomac, Kate let her mind slip back. Once again she remembered the numbness that came over her right after her father's death—it had been a protective encapsulation that she'd feared losing. She'd welcomed her mother's decision to leave. The impact of her separation from Alex didn't hit her immediately. Their leave-taking was cluttered with chaotic details and many people milling around them. There were only a few moments when they were alone, when the dark pain in Alex's eyes pierced her self-absorption and she realized that the unthinkable was happening: they would no longer be together. He'd reached for her, and Kate had clung to him. In their kiss she tasted bitter tears. "How can you leave me?" was his anguished question.

Hers was more like an accusation. "How can you stay behind?"

Later, as she tried to adjust to the unfamiliar routine of suburban life in America and the structured atmosphere of a public high school, the reality of being without Alex sank in. There was a void deep inside her, as if she'd lost a vital part of herself. She wrote Alex long letters, and bemoaned his much briefer replies. When he mentioned some adventure they'd shared, she would cry for hours. After a while, however, resentment began to build. Alex still enjoyed the things they had done together, as if there were no horror lurking behind the beauty.

In her loneliness, she blamed Alex for not being with her. He couldn't have cared for her as deeply as she'd thought. But it had been more than caring—like being a part of each other. When she was older, Kate decided that the bond between her and Alex had been due to the restricted life on the compound. She convinced herself that their close relationship wasn't meant to survive.

In college it was easy to make friends. People—men especially—were attracted to her vivid good looks and her vibrancy. Though others were intrigued by her exotic background, Kate was reluctant to talk about her former life. Unlike Derek, whose affection for and interest in Kenya remained strong and who was always voluble on the subject. He'd managed a combined major in anthropology and art history, and had recently published two articles on the traditional art of East Africa. Kate had thought that Elizabeth's death would weaken Derek's ties to Kenya, but it hadn't. If anything, he was determined that his daughter not lose that part of her heritage.

Derek pulled up in front of the town house in which he had a second-floor flat. He cut the engine and turned to his sister. "You should come with me the next time I go," he said, as if continuing their earlier conversation.

"No, I shouldn't."

"I think it'd be healthy if you did."

"Healthy?"

"To get rid of that mental block of yours."

"I don't have a mental block."

"What would you call it, then?"

Susan interrupted before Kate could reply. "Hey, we're home. Aren't we getting out of the car?"

"A good question," Kate said. She exited and pulled back the seat so her niece could scramble out.

"Wait," Derek cried. "I almost forgot your dental appointment. Back in the car, Suzie."

"Aw, Daddy..."

"No arguments, please. Hope you don't mind, Kate, but Suzie's due for a checkup, and appointments are made way in advance. The office isn't far...right by the university," he explained. "You don't have to come unless you want to meet Dr. Mooney."

"Dr. Mooney has a white beard," Susan informed her.

"I'm not big on beards," Kate told them. "I think I'll pass on Dr. Mooney."

Derek took her bag out of the trunk. "Can you manage this?"

"Of course."

He handed her his keys. "Make yourself a drink or some tea or whatever. You know where everything is. We won't be long."

"Not to worry." She turned to her niece. "Want me to take your soccer ball upstairs?"

Susan hugged the ball to her chest. "No. I want to show it to Dr. Mooney."

"I'm sure he'll be thrilled," her father said with a smile. "Okay, back in the car. See you later, Kate."

When Kate let herself into the apartment, she marveled as she always did at how neat it was. Kate's cleaning woman came once a week and grumbled that she spent half her time picking up after Kate before she could get to the real cleaning. Ellen Marlowe had always despaired of her daughter's sloppiness. "I thought girls were supposed to like tidiness,'' she complained to her husband. ''Derek's so good about it, but Katie leaves such a mess.''

Alistair Marlowe had been unperturbed. ''She's got better things to do.''

It had seemed that way then, that there was always something beckoning her and Alex. The days were never long enough, and only the beauty of the sun spreading its tones of orange and crimson as it sank below the horizon kept them from sadness that another day had ended.

Kate put her bag on the sofa bed in the room that doubled as a guest room and Derek's study. The throw over the bed was an African print in orange and purple and black. Kate wandered into the living room, and here again was Elizabeth's touch in things she'd brought with her from Kenya—in the framed batiks on the wall, the soapstone elephant figures atop the television console, the huge carved table in front of the couch. Derek was comfortable living with these reminders of another world. Kate's apartment, on the other hand, was decorated with a mélange of furniture she had bought, mostly on the spur of the moment, over her working years. It held not a hint that she had ever lived in Africa. Except for that one item, hidden away in a drawer, the only keepsake she'd been unable to part with.

Kate noted the framed photographs all around Derek's living room. Right after Elizabeth's death he had put away all the pictures. But eventually he moved beyond his grief, and the pictures were put back.

There were many of the four of them as children—Alex at ten, clowning for the camera, while Kate, in the background, egged him on. Another in which he proudly shouldered his first rifle. He was thirteen then, and Kate had been indignant that she wasn't allowed to have one, too. Two years later, her father and Alex taught her to shoot. She

hated guns now, never wanted to see or touch a rifle again—
or to live where they were needed.

She picked up a picture of her and Alex with the baby elephant their fathers had found and brought to the compound. Its mother had died. Usually an orphan was cared
for by the other females in the herd, but somehow this one
had been left behind. Derek had wanted to name the baby
"Dumbo," as in the Disney cartoon, but Alex had said that
animals in the wild didn't need cute names. They'd ended up
calling the elephant "Baby." When their fathers took Baby
away to what they hoped would be a welcoming herd of female elephants, the children were heartbroken. Kate had
cried until Alex made her stop. Baby wasn't a pet, he told
her sternly. He was meant to live with other elephants. Alex
had made her ashamed of her secret wish that the herd
would reject Baby and they could have him again.

Kate remembered that she was nine that year. Soon after
that, Alex stopped explaining things to her. He didn't have
to. They didn't need words. She always seemed to know
what he thought and how he felt—and it was always the
right way to think and to feel. That was what she had believed. But she had been wrong.

Kate picked up another picture, a photograph of herself
in a frothy white grown-up dress, laughingly trying to feed
a piece of birthday cake to a little donkey. Rusty had been
her special pet, practically a member of the family, and Kate
had insisted that Rusty should have some cake. The others
had all laughed at how funny Rusty looked. No one knew
then how much pain the little donkey would later cause.

That fourteenth birthday had been a turning point for
Kate and Alex. She'd been so acutely aware of him that
night, conscious of something different between them. For
the next few months they had reveled in what was happening, not labeling it love, not needing any word for the won-

der they felt with each other. They'd been so happy—until that morning in December when the wonder had clouded over.

Kate shook her head as if trying to shake off that memory. She put down the picture and turned away. Derek couldn't understand what he called her "mental block." But, then, how could she expect him to? He'd been in school in America at the time and hadn't had to go through the ordeal of the funeral. His grief had been cushioned by distance from the actual event, and so he'd escaped Kate's disillusionment.

Alex had been with her, but unable to penetrate her grief. His own loss had affected him differently, and he'd never shared Kate's need to escape. As a consequence, Kate had felt isolated and alone.

She wondered what would happen when they met again. So many years had gone by. Would she be able to read his thoughts, his heart, as she had when they were children?

CHAPTER TWO

ALEX LOOKED AROUND the crowded ballroom and was intrigued. The people came in all sizes, shapes, colors and costumes. But that was to be expected at an embassy function in Washington. There were a number of people in the native dress of their countries. Alex smiled to himself when he recognized a Kenyan member of parliament bedecked in a vividly colored robe. At home in Nairobi, the gentleman usually wore Brooks Brothers business suits.

Alex's memories of America were dim, since he'd left with his parents when he was only nine. His impressions of life here were based on the television programs he occasionally had time to watch and the stories he heard from others. The vicarious was never as exciting as the firsthand experience. The excitement he felt at this moment, however, was based on one thing, one person, actually—Katherine Marlowe.

These past few years, whenever he'd thought of visiting the States, Kate had been the main temptation. Such a costly trip was an extravagance he felt he couldn't allow himself. Alex had followed his father's career, specializing in wildlife and environmental preservation. He was part of a government think tank concerned with conserving Kenya's natural resources. By Kenyan standards, his salary was high, and he supplemented his income by arranging special tours for visiting VIPs and groups of foreign scientists. But every penny he earned, outside of what provided for his own modest needs, went to Jambo Youth Safari, his project for giving young people from all over the world a true safari experience.

For a long time, Alex had continued to believe that Kate would come back. In his letters, he'd asked when. She'd finally sent a long letter in which she made it clear that the answer was never. That had been almost six years ago and should have signaled an ending. In a way it had. After that their correspondence dwindled to infrequent brief notes. Their lives had diverged, and Alex had been forced to accept Kate's resolve that she would not return to Kenya—or to him. But in his heart he'd never let go of her. They had shared so much and dreamed of what they would do together. Kate was part of his life, not the one he lived at the moment, but an idyllic past that had shaped his emotional life, and a future they had planned for themselves as children. This future was still real to him, despite the intervening years. In the independent American careerwoman Kate had become, would he find the tempestuous, spirited girl he had loved? Alex hadn't wanted to face his fear that if they met again, there might be nothing left between them.

This fear was still with him, but he'd decided it was time to test his dream. That's why he'd let himself be persuaded to take time off to come to America and promote his book. When he saw Kate, he would know if the dream had survived. He hadn't had a chance to call Derek to ask if Kate would be at the embassy party, but he was certain she would be. He *willed* it. Scanning the room again, he spotted Melanie Pearson waving frantically at him. She was with a stocky woman and beckoned him to join them.

"Alex, you should've called me when you got in," Melanie said. "I wanted us to make a grand entrance together."

Melanie wore a long saffron-colored dress that looked vaguely African and around her neck hung a heavy choker of multicolored beads. Her cropped brown hair stood away from her head in a spiked halo.

"I'm sure you managed just fine without me," Alex said with a smile. It had taken him a while to get used to Melanie's flamboyance, but as they'd worked together, he'd come to appreciate her professional expertise and her high-spirited good nature.

Melanie introduced the stocky woman as her agent, Rhoda Field.

Rhoda had a firm handshake and a brisk smile. "Nice to meet you finally, Alex. Actually, I'm representing both of you on this book, so I'm your agent, too."

The notion of needing another person as intermediary in any kind of transaction was new to Alex, but publishing a book was unfamiliar territory for him, so he accepted the guidance.

Rhoda cast a speculative eye around. "It's a good turn-out. I hope we get some decent press coverage out of this shindig."

"Whose idea was this?" Alex asked.

"Mine," Rhoda said, "but don't tell the ambassador. I figured some kind of fanfare when the book came out would benefit us and them. You know, draw attention to what Kenya has to offer American tourists and publicize what is being done over there to save the environment. I had to sweet-talk my way through a receptionist, a secretary and a cultural aide, but when I finally got to speak to the ambassador, he'd been briefed and made like this was his idea from the beginning. So here we are."

"It's not quite as grand as I'd hoped," Melanie said with some disappointment. "I'd pictured us standing next to the ambassador in a receiving line..."

"Hey, this is a reception, not a state occasion," Rhoda said.

"Thank God," Alex said.

"Look. Isn't that Elijah Waring?" Melanie pointed in the direction of a tall, black man with a trim goatee.

Rhoda squinted. "Is it? I'm not that familiar with local talk-show honchos."

"I met him at a party last year. He's aching to be a male Oprah Winfrey or a black Phil Donahue. I caught his show once or twice. It's not bad."

"So what are you waiting for, girl? Go make points with the man," Rhoda urged.

Melanie grinned and darted off.

"I assume that making points has something to do with publicity," Alex said to Rhoda.

"Oh, yes. Waring's show doesn't pack a lot of clout, but a spot on one of the network shows can shoot up the sales of a book overnight. I've seen a book go from relative obscurity to the *New York Times* best-seller list."

"I doubt our book has that kind of potential."

"Maybe not best-seller, but it should do well. It's a gorgeous edition, and with the ecology hook, we might bring it out of the coffee-table book category."

Alex knew what a coffee-table book was and winced at the idea that his work would be used for decorative display. "'Ecology hook'?" He smiled ironically. "Is that what my text is?"

"Don't take that the wrong way. Every book needs something to hook the reader. People today are into this save the environment stuff. Jacques Cousteau's an international hero."

"I'm not Jacques Cousteau."

"No." Rhoda gave him an appreciative onceover.
"You're younger and a helluva lot better looking. You'll do
all right on tour."

" 'Tour'?"

Rhoda disregarded his frown. "Which reminds me, did
Melanie tell you about the firm that's going to handle your
publicity?"

Alex's frown deepened. "No. Melanie and I haven't
talked since I got here."

"I cut us a good deal." Rhoda grinned. "Blackwell's the
best in the business and we're being charged family rates
because Blackwell's my cousin. He even took one of his best
people off another job because—"

Alex stopped listening. A young woman had come into
the room. Her head was turned away, but he knew it was
Kate. She walked in his direction, then paused to wait for
someone. Alex caught a glimpse of Derek, but his eyes
didn't veer from Kate. He issued a silent command, which
she seemed to obey. She turned and looked directly at him.
Everything, everyone else, fell away. How wrong he had
been to be afraid. She was so beautiful, tall and slender, her
blond hair cut in unfamiliar bangs that curled over her
forehead. She wore a dress of some frothy, wispy material
whose color matched her eyes. But could anything really
match those blue-violet depths?

"Excuse me," he murmured without looking at Rhoda.
"There's someone I know." Quickly he made his way across
the room. This was a woman, not the girl he'd last seen
thirteen years ago. But he felt he knew her. There was
something deep inside each of them that was known only to
the other. Time couldn't change that. Surely she had to feel
it. Kate extended her hands. In taking them, Alex felt he'd
bridged the years of separation.

The noise and chatter around Kate dimmed. In the hush she heard only Alex's voice. "Hello, Kate" was all he said, but the remembered timbre of his voice transmitted so many unspoken messages. They'd never needed many words.

"Alex." Saying his name brought home the reality of his presence. "It's been a long time."

"Too long."

The boyish contours of his face had hardened into strong, bronzed features. He was older, of course, thirty-one now. When she'd caught sight of him a moment ago, his gray eyes had narrowed, as they used to when he squinted into the sun to peer across the savanna. Now they widened, encompassing her, drawing her into their depths.

Kate didn't know how long they stood like that before Derek's voice intruded. "Is this an exclusive reunion, or can a third party break in?" Reluctantly Alex released her and turned to greet Derek.

The woman Alex had been talking to came over and was introduced. Conversation flowed around Kate, but she felt removed from what was going on, preoccupied with the flood of feelings that seeing Alex had aroused. Then a striking young woman with spiked hair and an African necklace joined them. Alex introduced her as his collaborator, Melanie Pearson. When Melanie put her arm through Alex's in a proprietary manner, Kate was jarred into being attentive. Melanie gave the impression that theirs was more than a professional partnership. Kate wondered at the sharp, unpleasant stab of jealousy this thought produced in her. Surely she hadn't expected Alex to lead a monastic existence—any more than she had.

"I feel like I know you two," Melanie told Kate and Derek. "Alex is always talking about you and all the good times you had as kids."

Kate wasn't pleased. Childish frolicking—that's what Melanie was making the past sound like. But it hadn't been that way....

"And the thousands of pictures he has all over his apartment."

"Melanie's prone to exaggerate," Alex said.

Kate noticed that he'd gently extricated himself from Melanie's grip.

"Okay, then, at least a dozen," Melanie conceded. She turned to Derek. "And that cute little girl he's godfather to. That's your baby, isn't it?"

"Yes, Suzie's mine. But you'd get quite an argument if she heard you call her a 'baby.' She's seven now."

"I'd love to meet her."

Melanie flashed Derek a smile that clearly intrigued him. The young woman confused Kate. She'd given the impression there was something between her and Alex, but now she seemed interested in charming Derek, who appeared to welcome her attention. Melanie was undoubtedly very different from the reserved academic types Derek usually met.

"Maybe we can all get together sometime," Derek said. "How long are you staying, Alex?"

Kate felt Alex's eyes on her. "I'm not sure," he answered.

"Hopefully long enough to get this book of theirs well launched," Rhoda Field said.

Suddenly the woman's presence registered with Kate. "Rhoda Field?"

"That's my name."

"I'm sorry. I must have been in a daze when Alex introduced us." Her excuse wasn't far from the truth. "I was going to get in touch with you in New York to set up a meeting. I'm with Blackwell Associates."

"And you're a friend of Alex's. Well, how about that?" Rhoda said with a grin. "Harvey said he knew the perfect person for this assignment."

Kate laughed. "I don't know about perfect, but I should be able to get things moving for you. We need to talk about budget and—" She halted when she caught Alex's perplexed look.

"Is there something I don't know about?" he asked.

"Apparently you're not aware that I'm going to be handling your publicity," Kate replied. "To supplement what your publisher's doing."

The perplexity remained. "You?"

"No cause for alarm," Derek offered. "Kate's a dynamo at her job. You're in good hands."

"Didn't you know I was in public relations?" Kate asked Alex.

"I guess I did," he admitted. "Derek said something about that the last time he visited. He described you as a high-powered New York career woman, but the details never registered."

"You don't object, I hope."

"On the contrary." He smiled. "I might even enjoy it."

"Well, I've started the ball rolling with Elijah Waring," Melanie announced.

Rhoda beamed. "Good girl."

Kate knew Waring. She'd occasionally gotten her clients on his show. But his program dealt with trendy issues of interest to the local Washington area. "*A Vanishing World* doesn't sound like Waring's type of subject," she said dubiously.

"Did I hear my name taken in vain?" Elijah Waring had sauntered up behind her to join them. "You're Kittie Marlowe, right?"

"'Katherine' or 'Kate,' please—not 'Kittie'." She had never liked Waring's easy familiarity and ultrasuave mannerisms.

"Close enough. I never forget names or faces, especially not the pretty ones."

Melanie introduced Elijah Waring to the others.

"I think I got a spot for you," Elijah told Alex.

Alex indicated Melanie. "You mean for both of us, don't you?"

"No, just you. Not that the little lady wouldn't dress up the show, but this program is on black male teenagers. I thought it might spark things up if you were there to talk about their African counterparts. You know... family life, school, sexual habits."

Alex frowned. "What does this have to do with the subject of our book?"

"Nothing," Elijah happily admitted. "But I'll let you get in a couple of plugs, maybe even bring a copy to hold up. No problem."

"I think there is," Alex told him. "You see, I don't know anything about the sexual habits of African teenagers."

"I thought you grew up in Africa."

"I did. Now if it's *my* teenage sexual habits you're interested in, that's another story, though a dull one. On the other hand, the sexual habits of the endangered rhinoceros are very much within my expertise and quite an exciting subject. If you ever decide to do a program on rhinos..."

"Wise ass," Elijah muttered, and stalked off.

"I don't think you should antagonize the media," Rhoda said, but when the others all started to laugh, she couldn't help but join in.

"I'm sorry, hon," Melanie told Alex. "I guess that wasn't such a great idea."

"Damn right it wasn't," Alex agreed, but without rancor. "I'm here to help sell this book and what it stands for—nothing else. I can talk about what I know and what I believe in. I'm not going to huckster someone else's line."

Huckster? It was a word Kate didn't like. Was that what Alex thought of her kind of work?

The festivities took on a formal tone when the Kenyan ambassador appeared at the podium. He held up a copy of *A Vanishing World* and praised it for its marvelous photographs and enlightening text. "It is fitting," he said in flawless English, "that this work is the product of a collaboration between an American photographer and a Kenyan scientist. When I say Kenyan scientist, I know that many of you will expect to see a black man on the back cover." He turned the book around, pausing for effect. Then he continued. "It is often overlooked that Kenya has many white citizens. Alexander Crane spent most of his childhood in our country, received his education in our schools and chooses to remain and pursue his career in Kenya. This book is called *A Vanishing World*, but our government is determined that will not happen. With the dedication of people like Alexander Crane, the beautiful world Miss Melanie Pearson has captured in her pictures will remain one of the world's wonders."

He went on to describe and extol his government's enlightened policies and the vastly improved facilities for tourism Kenya offered. He then introduced Melanie and Alex.

Melanie gave an amusing little speech about how she'd grown up as what she called "a zoo groupie" and had started her African safari with only a vacation in mind. After being in Kenya and meeting and talking to Alex Crane, the idea for the book developed. "Alex didn't think of himself as a writer, so I had to do a little arm-twisting." She looked over at Alex with a mischievous smile. "I'm good at that. Turns out we make a good team. We produced a book we're both proud of. We hope you'll buy it and enjoy it."

Alex picked up on what Melanie had said. "I admit I was coaxed into the project...."

Kate didn't want to speculate on what Melanie's coaxing tactics might have been.

"But I realized," Alex continued, "that the book could help our work. The preservation of life and the environment should be important to all of us, regardless of geographic boundaries. The destruction of any piece of this earth affects us all."

Kate remembered how Alex's voice always took on a thrilling intensity when he felt deeply about something.

"We have to preserve and replenish the earth's resources, and if we don't prevent the extinction of endangered forms of life, mankind itself will be endangered."

Alex went on to thank the ambassador for hosting the reception. His conclusion was brief and gracious. "Thank you all for being here. Like Melanie, I hope you buy our book. Perhaps it will whet your appetite to see in person what Melanie captured with her camera. Your interest and support can keep that beauty from being a vanishing world."

"Bravo," Derek said when Alex rejoined them.

"You two'll do okay in interviews," Rhoda told them. She turned to Kate. "Don't you think so?"

"They'll do fine," Kate agreed.

"But you know, Alex, it wouldn't be a bad idea to slip in a personal anecdote or two," Rhoda suggested. "You don't want to sound like you're on a soapbox. Preaching doesn't sell many books. Tell a funny little story about being chased by a lion...something cute."

Though Kate knew the woman had meant nothing hurtful in the remark, she stiffened. Keeping her voice even, she said, "There's nothing cute about an attacking lion."

"A monkey, then. Whatever.... You catch my meaning. Especially on the tube, it's the personal note that's effective."

"I'm not sure I'm ready for this," Alex said warily.

"Not to worry" was Rhoda's breezy reassurance. "Blackwell's the best in the business. Kate will prime you—you'll be ready." Rhoda's attention was diverted when she saw someone she knew. Her gaze sharpening, she announced, "I've got to check out a potential client."

"Who's that?" Melanie asked.

"Waldo Avery." Rhoda indicated the rugged-looking Southern senator who had just come into the ballroom. "Seems like half the senators now fancy themselves writers. Rumor has it Avery's got a pretty hot thriller in the making. Excuse me while I check him out," she said, and ambled off.

"I'm for checking out that buffet," Derek said. "How about it?"

"Good idea," Melanie agreed.

Kate started to move with them, but Alex took hold of her arm.

"You two go on ahead," he told the others. "Kate and I have a lot to talk about, a lot of catching up to do."

Melanie's eyes swept from one to the other. Then she shrugged and put her arm through Derek's. "Derek, my love, it seems we're being shunted off. Let's go stuff our faces and exchange life stories."

"Sounds good to me," Derek said, and led her away.

"You didn't ask if I was hungry," Kate said when she and Alex were alone.

"Food's the last thing either one of us is thinking of right now."

"How do you know?"

"I know."

His smile wasn't arrogant. It reflected a sureness that had always been part of the way they related to each other. But she had to stop searching for signs of the past in what was happening now. "We do have a lot of catching up to do," Kate told him. "After so many years we really don't know each other anymore."

"I don't believe that."

Again she glimpsed that deep intensity she found so stirring.

But their catching up had to be put off.

"Alexander...don't run off. There are some people who want to meet you." The ambassador was closing in on them, with a group following behind him.

Kate stepped back, removing herself from the small crowd that quickly surrounded Alex. He shrugged helplessly and gave her a smile that signaled "Wait...I won't be long."

For a while Kate stood and eavesdropped. The most vociferous people in the entourage were a bejeweled woman bent on getting Alex to come to a dinner party she was giving and an aggressive South African who tried to engage Alex in a debate about politics.

After some time, Kate walked over to the buffet table. Derek was helping himself with great relish. "Try some of this stuff," he told his sister. "It's great."

"Judging by the amount of food on your plate, you must have been starving."

"I'm always starving for this kind of food. My culinary repertoire consists of fish sticks, beef stew and spaghetti. Luckily Suzie doesn't gripe as long as I bribe her with occasional splurges at McDonald's. It's not easy being a single parent.''

"You do just fine," said Kate with a fond smile.

"If you want to take over my kitchen while you're visiting, feel free," he offered magnanimously.

"Sure. I wouldn't mind. I don't cook much for myself."

"I guess it's no fun cooking for one, is it?"

"Do I detect a not-so-subtle hint in that comment?"

"All I meant was that it'd be more fun if you had someone to cook for."

"Has this something to do with Alex being here?"

Derek became serious. "It has everything to do with Alex being here."

"Don't make too much of it, Derek. Alex's mission is to promote his book."

"And to see you. I caught the way you two looked at each other... closing everyone else out just as you used to do."

"You're a romantic, Derek."

"What's wrong with that?"

"The real world doesn't nurture romantics."

"I think you're wrong. I hope you're wrong."

There was nothing more to say. Kate changed the subject. "What happened to Melanie?"

"She's holding forth over there." Derek pointed.

Melanie was near the bar, surrounded by people. As Derek and Kate walked closer, they heard her enthusiastically describing her African adventure.

"She sure is something," Derek remarked.

The admiring tone surprised Kate. "Care to define that 'something'?" she asked.

The question startled him. Then he grinned. Derek had his father's coloring, sandy hair and brown eyes, and Kate was gratified to see in him their father's honesty, intelligence and compassion. He'd lost his youth too quickly in the wake of Elizabeth's death. Although a year younger than Kate, Derek's usual serious, professional look made him appear older. Kate preferred seeing him like this, a glint in his eye, a smile on his lips.

"The woman gives off sparks," Derek said. "The way she dresses and the way she talks...she has a kind of verve that's ...well, very appealing."

"So it seems."

"Jealous?"

"Don't be ridiculous."

"You needn't be. I can't picture Alex with anyone else but you, Kate."

Maybe that was the problem, Kate thought. She and Alex had never had a chance to grow out of their childhood passion, so it still existed in everyone's mind. Alex's, too? She didn't know.

Melanie was gesturing at them to join her. "You go on over," Kate told Derek. "I'll wait for Alex."

No sooner was Derek gone than Alex appeared at Kate's side, smiling. He grabbed her hand. "Come on."

"Where?"

"Out of here."

"But the reception..."

"They'll never miss us."

"You're the guest of honor."

"Melanie can carry on." He glanced over to where Melanie was entertaining her audience. "She's doing fine."

"But don't you have to take her home?"

"No. Melanie never has any trouble finding an escort." He grinned. "I think Derek will be more than happy to volunteer." He pulled her toward the door.

"Where are we going?"

He paused and turned to her. "Someplace where we can be alone. Any more objections?"

She couldn't think of a single one.

This reminded her of so many times in the past when they'd ached to get away from the others and schemed for an excuse to race away together to one of their favorite places.

"Then let's get out of here," Alex whispered.

Kate held his hand tightly, and they raced away.

CHAPTER THREE

OUTSIDE THE EMBASSY the streets were quiet, dimly lit by lamps on the corner and light filtering through curtained windows. This was a residential section of Washington, an area of stately homes and diplomatic offices and dwellings. The only people they saw were two chauffeurs indolently leaning against their parked limousines. No strollers were about. In this neighborhood, life was conducted indoors.

"Where are we going?" Kate inquired again when they were outside.

"You never used to ask."

"Because I always knew."

There had been a hill in back of the compound. Because it was within the enclosure, it was considered safe, though Alex always had with him a short Masai sword and stick, the kind the young tribesmen carried when they grazed their herds. Kate had thought it more an adornment than a necessity. That was before she'd learned to be afraid.

"Pambazuko," Alex said. "Our place." They'd given their hill the Swahili name for sunrise because that was where the sun first made its appearance each morning. "Do you have such a place here?" he asked.

She shook her head. "This is a city, not the Serengeti."

"I wish we were back there right now."

"I don't," Kate said. She remembered their last time together at Pambazuko, and the painful news Alex had brought. She shook off the memory, not wanting to spoil the magic of their reunion. "What's wrong with where we are? Look—" Kate pointed to a small park on the corner "—nature."

Alex laughed. "Your definition of nature has been sadly modified. But this will have to do." The park was deserted. Alex led Kate to a bench, and they sat down. He put his arm around her and looked up at the sky. "How different the sky is here. Don't you miss the vastness . . . all the stars?"

"I don't think about it."

"Do you remember that night we counted the stars? You said they appeared so close you could reach up and grab one. Are you going to tell me you don't think about that night, either?"

The pressure of his arm around her and the intimacy of his low voice spurred her memory. Kate gazed up into the dark sky and fixed on one bright star. She let her mind drift back. . . .

"I THINK OUR GUEST OF HONOR is sneaking out," her father said.

Kate and Alex paused at the French doors. "Just for some air," Kate explained. "It's so hot inside."

"You blew out your candles, ate your cake, opened your presents, and now you're running off," her mother said, but in a teasing, not critical way.

There was still one present Kate hadn't received—Alex's. His whispered promise that he would give her his gift when they were alone had stirred in her the trembling excitement she'd begun to feel with him lately. They'd been waiting all evening for a chance to get away. A minute ago he'd given her a look from across the room. They were used to interpreting each other's silent signals. Kate had immediately moved toward the door.

"Help with the cleaning up first," her father said.

"Can't it wait until I get back?" Adults had such ridiculous ideas about what was important, Kate thought impatiently. She had her chores, as did everyone else on the compound, and she never shirked them. But they could wait when something more exciting beckoned.

"I'll help," Elizabeth offered.

Kate shot her a grateful smile. She knew how lonely Elizabeth was with Derek away at school in America. Kate and Alex made it a point to include the twelve-year-old in some of their activities. But the younger girl also had a marvelous sensitivity about when the other two needed to be by themselves—that curious sixth sense Derek used to tease Elizabeth about.

"Okay, go on," Ellen Marlowe said, "but not out of the compound."

"Mom, we're going for a walk, not on safari," Kate said exasperatedly. She was fourteen now, not a child.

As soon as she and Alex were outside, he took her hand. "Come on," he urged her softly. It was pitch-black out, and her eyes weren't accustomed to the darkness yet, but when they started to run, she felt no hesitation. Every path, every structure, every tree on the compound were familiar.

The air was laden with moisture, signaling that the rainy season was imminent, but their running created a breeze that molded Kate's white party dress against her body. Her mother often told her to slow down and stop wearing herself out, but she couldn't hold back when there was something great to see or do. That was the feeling she had that night, that she and Alex were racing toward something wondrous.

At the clearing some distance from the houses, Alex slowed. There were many rocks here, including some large oddly shaped ones. Over the years the four children had given some of these shapes names and characteristics. One resembled a table, where they would picnic, and one was shaped like a chair, which had become Alex's when he was the only one tall enough to climb onto it. Kate had teasingly dubbed it "Alex's throne." This was their destination. Kate usually had to reach a bit to scramble onto it, but before she could, Alex put his arms around her and lifted her up. He'd helped her like that before, yet tonight the gesture seemed more intimate.

Things were changing between them. They hadn't discussed it, but it was something they both felt. Alex took his place next to her. By now her eyes had adapted to the darkness and she could see the huge profilelike monolith nearby that they had christened the Oracle. Derek and Elizabeth had been reading Greek mythology at the time. As children they'd all played a game of asking the Oracle questions, then making up crazy answers. They hadn't done that for a long time.

Kate leaned back, shivering when the coldness of the stone pierced her filmy dress. Alex put his arm around her to warm her. Kate let her head fall against his shoulder, then nestled comfortably closer. "Look at the stars," she said in a hushed voice. "Millions of them."

"It's a beautiful sky tonight, special for your birthday."

She felt his cheek against her hair.

"Look." He pointed. "There's Orion."

She extended her arm, reaching up into the velvety darkness. "They seem so close, as if you could touch them."

"Want me to pluck one . . . give you a star for your birthday?"

She laughed softly. "No, leave them in the heavens, where they belong." She waited. It was the perfect time for him to give her the present he had for her, but he said nothing. Finally her impatience surfaced. She sat up and faced him. "Did you forget to bring my present?"

"Maybe."

She knew he was teasing. "No, you didn't." She pointed to the bulge in the deep pocket of his khaki shirt. "Aren't you going to give it to me?"

He grabbed her hands and smiled. "I was waiting for the right moment."

"What's wrong with this one?"

"Nothing. In fact, it's just perfect."

Alex pulled out a small tissue-wrapped package, which she took eagerly. Whatever it was wasn't boxed and she could feel the hard contours of something heavy. Smiling, she ripped away the paper and ran her fingers over the cold smoothness of the carving. "Ohh..." She held up the small soapstone sculpture of two figures embracing, their arms entwined, their bodies touching. It was an abstract piece that used form and space to depict the unity of the two, rather than delineating their features.

"Do you like it?"

"It's beautiful," she said softly. "Where did you find it?"

"In the market at Nanyuki. A woman was selling Kikuyu carvings, mostly animals, but she had a few different pieces. This one reminded me of you...of us...so I bought it."

"Nanyuki? But that was months ago."

"I know."

"You bought this for me months ago? Why didn't you give it to me then?"

"Because it wasn't your birthday." He reached over to touch her face and she rubbed her cheek against the roughness of his palm. "And I didn't think it was the right time," Alex added in a low voice. "I was waiting for you to grow up a little."

"Alex, I've grown up a lot," she protested. "You're not much older, you know."

"Sometimes I feel as if I am."

"But not tonight." Her voice became a silky plea. "Not tonight."

"No, not tonight."

He lowered his head, gently touching his mouth to hers. It was the first time he'd ever kissed her like that. What began to stir deep inside her made the gentleness inadequate. Kate kissed him back, her mouth moving under his, eliciting a fiery response that thrilled her. Still clutching her statue, she wrapped her arms around his neck. She had a moment of conscious wonder at the warmth and magic of Alex's lips, at her own fervent response, and then she gave herself up to the sweet pleasure of it all.

Breathless, they finally drew apart.

"We belong together," Alex said.

Kate knew it was true.

KATE WAS STARTLED by the deep sigh that escaped her. "That was a long time ago," she told Alex.

"You keep saying that."

"It's true."

"I know, but the years aren't important. Some things are never meant to change. I feel now as I did that night, Kate, that we belong together."

She shook her head with confusion. How could he deny the passage of time? The past was a dream. They were being seduced by the darkness and the sky and the stars. But when Alex tilted her chin, turning her face up to his, she closed her eyes and welcomed his kiss. For a moment, she would let herself relive the sweetness of that dream.

She got more than she bargained for. The passionate demand in Alex's kiss was shattering. This was not a tentative youth in his first romance, but a man reaching for her with sexual urgency. His probing lips beseeched and promised, expressing his need, delving into hers, pledging fulfillment for them both.

Kate sensed the danger and pulled away. "I don't think we should be doing this."

"Why not?"

"We're acting like teenagers."

"I wasn't. I was acting like a thirty-year-old man who wants you very much."

"You're thirty-one."

Surprised, he looked at her, then broke into laughter. "So I am. I sometimes lose count." He shook his head, stood, took her hands and pulled her up. Then he planted a brief kiss on her forehead and said, "Okay, you win—for now."

Kate was relieved. "Do you want to go back to the reception?"

"Not on your life. You don't want me to kiss you, but we can still talk. Or are you afraid of that, too?"

"It's not fear."

"What then?"

"You can't just walk back into my life."

"I think I have."

"You're only here for a short while."

"Then we'd better make the most of it." He took her hand. "Come on. Let's walk. You can show me the city."

"It's nighttime."

"So much the better. Cities usually look better at night."

Alex made walking down Massachusetts Avenue an adventure. He commented on everything he saw, the buildings, the people, the cars. Kate realized that she'd lost that ability to make a visual sweep of her surroundings and clearly note the minutest details. "There's a saying we have," Kate told Alex, "about not being able to see the forest for the trees."

"I've heard it."

"You still have the faculty for seeing both."

"Don't you?"

"Not anymore," she admitted.

As they walked toward Dupont Circle, they passed some impressive embassy mansions. Alex could identify each by its flag.

"How on earth did you memorize the flags?" Kate asked.

"It wasn't a conscious effort. At the university there were students from all over—mostly from other African countries, but we had some from Europe, Canada, even Russia. One of the history professors organized round-table discussions, and each participant would have a tiny national flag in front of him. I couldn't always pronounce the foreign names," he said with a rueful smile, "but I got to know the flags."

"I'd have lost track long ago, especially with all the third world countries."

He halted and turned to face her. "Third world? That label always bothers me."

"Why?"

"First . . . second . . . third . . . as if there were three separate worlds—that's crazy. Kate, you must have seen pictures of the earth taken from space."

"I can guess what you're driving at."

"Of course you can. Those global pictures bring the point home. There's only one world. This earth is what we all have in common, its beauty and its creatures and its bounty. We'll lose it if we're not careful."

"I think I'll have to get you a soapbox," she teased.

Alex had to smile. They had reached Dupont Circle, which was, as usual, filled with people. "This looks like a good place for one. Do you think I'd attract a crowd?"

"Probably. There's a great mix of people here—yuppies, students, artists."

"At the moment I'm interested in an audience of one. Let's find a restaurant, someplace we can sit and talk."

"How about the Café Max?" Kate suggested. "It's across the circle and up a block. They have wine and cheese, crepes, light fare like that. Does that suit you?"

"Sounds good."

Max's was the kind of place where students brought books to read and others nursed cups of cappuccino while they played chess. The small booths provided privacy, and culinary clattering was minimal.

The waiter led them to a semicircular booth, lit the candle on the table, took their order for crabmeat quiche and a half-liter of Chablis and left.

"Is this all right?" Kate asked quietly. Sitting next to each other like this on the curved banquette suggested a comfortable intimacy.

"Perfect. Not a soapbox in sight. It's designed for conversation, not oratory."

"Actually, I love to hear you talk. I always have."

"If I remember right," he said, "you were the talkative one. I had to fight to get a word in."

"What an exaggeration!"

He laughed. "Have you forgotten what an independent firebrand you were?"

"As I recall, it didn't bother you a bit."

He grinned. "That's true, until you stopped being a tomboy and started wearing dresses. That's when I was bothered, but not the way you mean. I liked the change in you. You became . . . different."

"In what way?"

Her hand was resting on the table. Alex covered it with his. "Sweeter," he said. "Aware of yourself as a young woman."

"Because I was responding to something different in you," Kate told him softly, acutely conscious of his closeness, of his fingers caressing the back of her hand.

"It doesn't matter how it started...who fell in love first."

"In love? Is that what you call it?"

"What do you call it?"

"I don't know. We loved each other as friends, companions..."

"That part continued, but something new was added, and you know it, Kate. At least you did then."

"I'm almost twice as old now."

"What's that supposed to mean?" Alex asked with a frown.

"That what happened a long time ago isn't relevant now. We've chosen different lives. We can't recapture what was lost."

"Was it lost?"

The question sounded innocent enough, but his eyes darkened with compelling intensity, and she turned away from their scrutiny. Kate had no answer and was grateful when the waiter chose that moment to serve them.

Alex didn't persist. The intensity faded and he appeared content to enjoy his wine and quiche and her conversation. He confused her. She didn't know how to react to this man—a stranger really—who had seemed to be making claims on her, but who then gave up when she didn't respond. Perhaps this was only an ego trip for him, with no important stakes, win or lose. She'd encountered that kind of male mentality before. Yet she didn't want to believe that of Alex. He couldn't have lost the honesty and directness she remembered.

It was more likely that he shared her own ambivalence, attracted to the idea of renewing a lost love but afraid to let it happen because of the differences between them now.

Kate had hoped that Alex's appearance in America signaled a change that he might be ready to leave Kenya. Hearing him describe what he was trying to accomplish there, she knew that wasn't the case. He was talking about the venture he'd mentioned in his brief speech at the reception: bringing to Kenya young people from all over the world to live and travel together on safari.

"But why not use the facilities that are available?" she asked. "There are tour operators who are doing that kind of thing."

"You don't understand, Kate. This won't be the usual tourist vacation. This is a true camping safari—with an international flavor. Everybody has to pitch in and help with the work at each campsite, but there will be plenty of time for game drives, informal lectures, getting to know one another... all that."

"A learning experience?"

"In the best sense. Not an academic chore, but something to be enjoyed. That's why I want the book to succeed. I'm not going to limit this to kids whose parents can afford to pay their expenses. What I want to do takes money."

"You could try for some foundation grants, or even private donations."

"That takes time and an expertise I don't have yet. I've got to concentrate on getting this project going the way I want it. After that, I'll see. Maybe I'll get myself some help."

"This is really important to you, isn't it?"

"Important enough to get me to parade myself around in order to drum up interest in *A Vanishing World*."

His tone bothered her. "You won't be 'parading' yourself around. An author's tour isn't like that."

"Just what is it you do with authors?"

"Book signings, interviews, sometimes talks on college campuses. I help authors get exposure to the public."

" 'Exposure'? Sounds unhealthy."

Testily Kate said, "It makes for some pretty healthy royalties."

"You've got a point," he conceded. "I guess I'm just more comfortable with game wardens than talk-show hosts."

"They're not all that different," Kate pointed out with a smile.

"Your usual clients are probably pretty sophisticated about this whole publicity business," Alex remarked.

"Some are." Kate had Alex laughing as she described Elvira and her avidity for the limelight.

"She predicts the future? Like our oracle?" he asked, reminding Kate of the monolithic stone they'd imbued with supernatural powers when they were children.

Kate had to smile. The comparison was apt. "They've got about the same batting average."

"Do people really believe Elvira reads the future?"

"Probably not. But it doesn't seem to matter. She chooses famous people for her subjects, and since they can be pretty predictable—there's always a new love affair or imminent breakup—she's sometimes right. She's really an entertainer, both in her book and in personal appearances."

"Are all your clients like that?"

"Oh, not at all. Last year I worked with Cindy Lorimer."

The name didn't register with him. "The movie actress?" Kate prodded.

"I'm afraid I don't keep up with cinema personalities."

"Cindy was a pleasure to work with, a real trouper."

"What was her book about—diet or exercise?"

"Both, as a matter of fact," Kate admitted with surprise. "How did you know?"

"I sometimes glance at the *New York Times Book Review*. Actresses are always writing that kind of book."

His expression was one of pleasant interest, but Kate sensed his real opinion, and it bothered her. "Did you also happen to notice that they make the best-seller lists?"

"I did. There's always an exercise book, a diet book and a self-help treatise on those lists. Oh, yes, and a guide to good sex. Although," he added with a grin, "one might include that in the self-help category."

"Another of my firm's clients happens to be a noted sex therapist." The statement came out belligerently.

Alex's expression changed. "I'm making you angry. Kate, I'm sorry. I don't mean to belittle your profession."

"Perhaps you don't mean to, but that's how it sounds."

"As long as you believe in what you're doing..."

"I believe in doing a good job on every assignment I take on, which at the moment means you and Melanie Pearson. I assume you consider your book worthy of my endeavors." She couldn't help the sarcasm, or the hurt it masked.

"Kate, I apologize," Alex said. "I must sound like a pompous ass."

"Close," she answered, but the sincere regret in his voice had begun to soften her.

"Actually, I admire what you've accomplished," Alex said. "Rhoda Field says you're one of the best in the business. It's just that I can't help thinking of the plans we made together. Do you remember how we used to talk for hours at Pambazuko? About all the things we were going to do?"

Kate stared down at the wineglass she was holding. She didn't want to be drawn in.

"The habitat?" he went on eagerly. "You must remember the habitat we swore we would have."

It had been after they'd had to give up the baby elephant. Kate and Alex had decided that one day they would establish their own habitat for orphaned wild animals. Their fathers tried to care for the occasional stray they came across, but the available facilities were inadequate.

"You wanted to have a huge place where the babies would grow up and stay with you forever," Alex reminded her.

Kate looked at him, remembering. "And you insisted that would be unfair to the animals and no better than a zoo, and that I'd have to let them go when they were ready to return to the wild."

"You finally agreed."

"I knew you were right."

"We always ended up agreeing."

"Not always," Kate said sadly. "Not at the end."

A grimace of pain tightened his mouth.

"There should never have been an end, Kate."

"I couldn't stay and you wouldn't leave."

"Things can be different. Some of our plans . . . the habitat . . . we can still make them happen."

Kate felt a twisting deep inside, as if there were a knotted cord being stretched in opposite directions. "I could never live in Africa again," she said in a low voice. "Surely you know that." Her voice strengthened. "Not after what happened. Alex, your father was killed, too. How can you be forgiving about an environment that permits such brutality?" she asked accusingly.

"For God's sake, Kate!" he exclaimed. "Do you think you have a corner on grief? What happened fills me with pain even now, but the pain doesn't destroy all that I love about Kenya. That's where I was raised. It's the home my father chose for us. He loved his work, the life he led. Your father did, too. Don't you remember how dedicated they were, what enthusiasm they had?"

Kate shook her head. She wanted to remember, but a darkness kept getting in the way. She looked away. The flame from the candle on the table was magnified and reflected by the wine decanter. Kate gazed steadily into the light.

Alex felt deeply disturbed. Kate had withdrawn from him. He sensed a darkness in her. Was she trying to penetrate that darkness, or was she hiding behind it? He put his arm around her. "Kate..."

She closed her eyes and leaned against him. The spell was broken.

"I know how you feel," he murmured.

She opened her eyes and turned to face him. "Then you have to know that I could never be happy in Kenya."

"You were once."

"I was a child. The risks weren't real."

"There are always risks."

"Not here, or not the same kind. Why should I take those risks when my life here offers a better alternative?"

"Is it really better?" His eyes held both demand and appeal. "I think there's something missing. You're cheating yourself, and you're cheating us."

What did he know about her life, her needs? Alex was relying on impressions of her that were no longer valid. She wasn't the girl he remembered. He couldn't erase the years that had come between them.

"There is no *us* anymore," she said.

"Are you trying to convince me—or yourself?"

Kate didn't answer.

CHAPTER FOUR

"AREN'T YOU GOING TO ASK me in?" Alex wanted to know.

"I don't think that's a good idea," Kate told him. They were talking in whispers outside the door to Derek's flat. After leaving the restaurant, they had walked all the way to Georgetown. Kate wasn't sure how long it had taken. Alex absorbed her attention, and she'd lost track of time. She glanced at her watch. "Alex, do you know what time it is?"

"Does it matter?"

"It's almost two in the morning. I think we'd better call it a day."

"You used to hate to see the day end."

She had that same feeling now, but wouldn't admit it. "Susan's asleep. Derek, too, probably."

"Do you have a key?"

"No. Maybe Derek left it unlatched for me." She tried the knob, with no success. "I'll have to ring and wake him."

"Wait. Someone's coming."

Kate hadn't heard a sound. At one time she could rival Alex in picking up even the slightest rustle around them, but she was out of practice. To her surprise, the person who opened the door was Marie Petrucci, the teenage baby-sitter from upstairs.

"Hi, Miss Marlowe. I heard you jiggling the doorknob."

"My brother's not home yet?" Kate asked in surprise.

"No. He called and said he'd be a little late, if it was okay. There's no school tomorrow because of teacher conferences or something, so I don't mind." As Kate and Alex entered the apartment, Marie gazed curiously at Alex. "Hey, you're Derek's friend from Africa, aren't you? I've seen pictures of you in the living room. It must be real neat living in the jungle."

"Where I live isn't exactly a jungle," Alex said with a smile.

"Whatever. I bet it's more exciting than here. Well, I gotta go." At the door, she paused and flashed Alex a toothy grin. "You're better looking than your pictures. G'night." She closed the door behind her.

"Looks like you've got a fan," Kate told Alex.

"But will she spend $29.95 to buy a copy of my book?"

Kate laughed. "She just might. Maybe we should look into the teenage market. You seem to have a way with that age group."

"That's the group I'd like to reach, the ones who come to Kenya expecting to see Tarzan in a loincloth, swinging from tree to tree." He stopped. "Why are you looking at me like that."

"I'm trying to picture you in a loincloth."

He arched his dark eyebrows. "And?"

Pretty terrific was what she was thinking, but what she said was "Not bad. You could play the part."

"Not interested, thank you. I have my hands full just playing myself."

"I'd never have thought so."

His look sharpened. "Meaning . . . ?"

"Just that you always seem to know exactly what you want out of life."

"You don't anymore?"

Kate realized she was revealing more than she wanted him to know, more than she herself understood. "We weren't talking about me."

"I'd like to."

She turned her head to avoid his eyes. "I have what I want for this stage in my life."

"I think you're begging the question. What about the next stage . . . and after that?"

"Please, Alex, let's not get into that again. Don't spoil things."

He hesitated, then said, "I'm sorry. I don't mean to spoil anything. Quite the contrary." In a jaunty tone, he proposed, "Why don't we forget whatever differences we have, make believe they don't exist? We've got this time together, so let's make the most of it. What do you say?" He took her by the shoulders.

His touch was light, so the pressure she felt was coming from within her. "Sounds good to me," she answered, seeking to match his lightness.

"Great. How about tomorrow? What time should I pick you up?"

"Tomorrow? I'd planned to get back to New York tomorrow."

"Why?"

"I've got a job."

"*I'm* your job, remember?"

She thought about it. "You've got a point. You and Melanie are my clients, and since you're here . . ."

"Exactly."

"We should probably all get together."

"All in good time. This is my first trip to Washington. I want to see the sights. I need a guide, and you're elected." He hesitated. "Why the smile?"

"The thought of you being guided. That's a switch."

"This is unknown territory. I need you."

Kate felt an increase in the pressure of his grip. The physical hold she could handle; it was the emotional pull that concerned her.

"Maybe Melanie would like to join us," she said, but the suggestion was half-hearted. Kate was curious about Alex's attractive collaborator, but right now she didn't want to share Alex with her, except for business purposes.

"I doubt it," Alex said. "Melanie will be sleeping in until noon."

"If you say so. I'm sure you know her sleeping habits better than I do."

He smiled. "We sometimes shared a tent, but never a bed, if that's what you mean."

Kate's relief overshadowed her embarrassment.

They decided that whoever was up first in the morning would call the other and they would get an early start.

"Good night," Alex said.

Kate tensed, waiting for his kiss, wondering if it would arouse the same rush of desire—and knowing that it would. When Alex's lips met hers, the tension quickly melted in the heat that suffused her. Their kiss was long and deep. Neither pulled back as the kiss softened, becoming a tender tasting, a feathery exploration. Kate felt her mouth curve into a smile traced by Alex's tongue.

Finally he whispered, "I'd better go."

"Yes."

There was acceptance, but also disappointment in that one word. Alex chose to tune into the disappointment.

"We could go to my hotel."

"Is that a lascivious offer?" she asked, trying to lighten the mood.

"It's a loving one," Alex said, but didn't protest when Kate pulled away from him. "All right, we'll do it your way."

His parting words stayed with her after he'd gone. It had been a strange reunion for both of them, with the undeniable reminders of the past and the equally strong attractions of the present. "We'll do it your way," Alex had said. *Her way....*

Kate walked to Derek's room at the end of the narrow hallway. Her brother had insisted that she use it. He was sleeping on the sofabed in the study. She took off her clothes, leaving them where she'd dropped them, a childhood habit she kept vowing to change, and slipped into a silky green nightgown. She had always loathed nightclothes that stuck to her skin, preferring to sleep nude or in something as minimal and satiny as this. She touched the smooth fabric, letting her fingers glide over her body, aware of the lingering sensitivity Alex had aroused. *Her way....* Kate knew she would have to keep a check on their passion. She wasn't sure she liked that role, or could play it.

After she'd washed up, Kate looked in on her niece. Susan was sleeping soundly, her dark head flanked by two Cabbage Patch dolls. Kate smiled when she noticed that one doll was fair and the other dark skinned. Derek made sure that his daughter was aware of both sides of her heritage, though Kate thought he sometimes made too much of the issue. Susan had her mother's affectionate nature and acceptance of people, together with Derek's curiosity and sharp intellect. The little girl also had her mother's coloring and beauty. But she was uniquely herself, with a toughness and honesty that would serve her well.

Kate heard the door to the apartment open, then Derek appeared. He came up to stand behind her. "Is Suzie all right?" he asked in a whisper.

Kate nodded and gently closed the bedroom door. "She's fine," Kate assured him. "How about you?"

"Great."

"You enjoyed the party, did you?"

"Yeah. It was great."

"Well, isn't that just great."

Derek recognized her teasing, but didn't care. "Actually, it didn't last much longer after you left," he said. "As soon as the food was gone, people started to take off, so we did, too."

" 'We'?"

"I offered to take Melanie home."

Still teasing, Kate made a point of looking at her watch. "That was some long trip. She must live in the boondocks."

"Don't be cute. As you probably already know, Melanie and Alex are staying at the Mayflower. It was early, so Melanie suggested we take in the show at the Comedy Club. Have you ever heard of Franny Fagan?"

The female comic from New York was a sensation, a gritty combination of earthiness and sophistication. "Sure I have, but I didn't think you'd even know the name."

"I didn't. Going to the show was Melanie's idea. It was terrific. I haven't laughed like that in years."

Kate gave him a curious smile. Derek's taste didn't usually run to bawdy comedy.

"Franny joined us for a drink afterward," Derek said. "Melanie knows her from college. Franny dropped out after a year. She says her jokes were too raunchy for the Radcliffe girls."

"I wouldn't have typed Melanie as a product of Radcliffe," Kate said with surprise.

"She defies type, doesn't she? At first I thought she was fun but, you know, a lightweight. Was I ever wrong. Underneath that weird hairdo is a sharp mind. Which I should have figured, since she's such a close friend of Alex's."

"Are they close?"

He shrugged. "How could they not be?"

That was no answer, but Derek couldn't be expected to have a more definite one.

"Where did you and Alex go when you left?" he asked.

"We walked for a long time, and stopped for something to eat at Max's. We did a lot of talking about old times."

"How did you feel?"

"What do you mean?"

"It must have been strange to be together after such a long time. You two used to be so close it was uncanny, as if you shared one mind."

"That's an exaggeration."

"It's not. I've sometimes wondered if Elizabeth and I would have been so drawn to each other, if you and Alex hadn't closed us out," Derek said pensively.

"That's preposterous. We didn't close you out."

"You sure did. Not intentionally, but you two used to close out the whole world when you were kids."

"Well, we're not kids now, and the world is very much with us." *Two separate worlds,* Kate added to herself, *Alex's and mine.* "Speaking of work, what's your schedule tomorrow?"

"Up at seven to take Susan to school, and then I'll head straight for my nine o'clock class at the college."

"Wake me when you get up."

"You're not leaving tomorrow, are you?"

"I was, but since Melanie and Alex are here..."

He seemed relieved. "That's what Melanie said, that you might as well get together now. I thought we could all have dinner together before you take care of business—or after—if you meet earlier in the day."

"Have dinner out?"

"No, here. I don't like leaving Susan two nights in a row, so Melanie and I decided—"

"You and Melanie?"

"Yeah. She thought it would be cozier if we ate in."

"So she's into coziness. Is she also into cooking?"

"I didn't ask. I figured you'd volunteer to make your special lemon chicken." He smiled ingratiatingly. "Suzie loves it."

"Okay, okay, I know when I've been conned." She really didn't mind, since she did have to meet with Melanie and Alex. Besides, Derek's enthusiasm about Melanie made Kate especially curious to see her again....

Derek's bed was narrow, not like her king-size bed at home. Kate found it difficult to fall asleep. So many memories had been evoked these past few hours, yet the image that dominated was the most recent, that of Alex as he'd appeared tonight, mature and more compelling than ever. Time had hardened his body and strengthened his features, but he still had the idealism and zest of youth. Tonight he'd exerted a powerful sexual attraction. When Kate finally drifted off to sleep, erotic fantasies filled her dreams.

KATE WAS VAGUELY AWAKE when she heard sounds and knew that the others were up. She had a habitual way of getting up every morning. She'd lie in bed for a few minutes, allowing consciousness of the new day to seep into her mind. Then she'd leap out of bed, immediately charged with energy. A cup of strong instant coffee provided her with her caffeine fix, after which she showered, dressed and was on her way in twenty minutes. She could never understand why people needed more than half an hour to get themselves ready for work.

This morning, however, Kate allowed herself an extra few minutes to think about the day ahead.

The door opened a crack. "Auntie Kate, are you up?" a voice called.

"Sure am. Come give me a hug."

The door opened wider and Susan appeared. "I can't. I'm making breakfast."

Kate smiled at how serious the little girl was. Susan was dressed for school in a plaid jumper and white blouse, with red bows fastening her braids. Kate got out of bed, went over to her niece and knelt down. "Just a little hug?" she asked.

"Okay." Susan gave her a squeeze and a kiss. "What do you want, oatmeal or farina? The rest of us are having oatmeal, but you can choose."

"I don't eat breakfast," Kate said, but when she saw Susan's disappointment, she quickly added, "except on special occasions when my favorite niece is the chef. I'll have oatmeal."

Susan brightened. "Cinnamon apple or plain?"

"Plain."

"Okay. It'll be ready right away, so you gotta hurry up."

"I will."

Susan opened the door, paused, then said, "Daddy says no dawdling on school days."

"I get the message. I'll wash my face and be right in."

Susan left. True to her word, Kate washed quickly, put on slippers and a satin wraparound robe and headed for the kitchen. She was smiling with the anticipation of seeing her niece preside over breakfast. Susan was kneeling on a chair at the round kitchen table, emptying a packet of instant cereal into a bowl. When the little girl went to pick up the kettle of hot water, Alex helped her hold it and pour.

Alex!

He smiled at her surprise.

"What are you doing here?" she asked, joining them at the table.

"Having some cereal."

"The apple cinnamon," Susan said. "Here's yours, Aunt Kate. Plain, like you said."

"It was my idea," Derek explained. "I called Alex this morning to nail him down for tonight. When he said he was waiting on you to show him around town, I told him to come on over and have breakfast with us."

"I hope you don't mind," Alex said.

"Of course not." *Quite the contrary,* she reflected. "It's just a surprise to find you sitting here."

"Aren't you going to eat your cereal?" Susan asked.

"Sure." Alex took a big spoonful, Kate a smaller one.

"Is there coffee?" Kate asked.

"Sorry," Derek said. "It's not on our usual menu. But Alex brought some Kenyan coffee. I'll make it."

"Don't bother," Alex told him. "You two are on a tight schedule. Kate and I can fend for ourselves. We'll have it later."

"Sorry, Kate," Derek told his sister. "Next time I'll remember."

"And next time I'll make toast," Susan promised. "Oatmeal and toast are the only two things Daddy lets me make myself. He won't let me flip pancakes anymore."

"Because the last time, you flipped two of them right onto the floor," her father reminded her.

"They weren't really dirty. We could've ate them."

"We could have 'eaten' them," Derek said.

Susan was confused. "Then how come we didn't?"

"Daddy was just correcting your grammar," Kate explained with a smile.

"Huh?"

"Never mind," Derek said. "I'll give you another shot at flapjack flipping next time."

"Tomorrow?"

"Pancakes take too long on a school day."

"Saturday?"

"Okay."

Susan was appeased. "Will you come, Uncle Alex?"

"If I'm around. I'm not sure what your aunt has in store for me." He looked at Kate expectantly.

"I haven't decided yet," Kate said, aware of the double message in her words. She noticed that Derek and Susan had finished breakfast. "I'll clean up," she offered.

Derek went to get his briefcase and Alex helped Susan into her schoolbag backpack. "Thanks, Uncle Alex." She started for the door.

"Wait," Alex called, hanging on to her. "You've got a white mustache."

She swept her tongue across her upper lip.

"You got most of it," Alex said.

Susan gave him a wet kiss on the cheek.

"Now you got it all."

The little girl giggled and they smiled at each other.

"You have a way with young girls," Kate teased when her brother and Susan had gone. "The baby-sitter and now Susan."

"A seven-year-old and an adolescent—I'd hoped for more."

"I don't mean to limit you."

He grinned. "I'm glad to hear that, because I don't intend to be limited."

"Is that a warning?"

"You'd better believe it."

This kind of verbal sparring came naturally, as it always had. Kate got up to clear the table.

"You didn't finish," he said.

She made a face. "You know how I hate cereal. Remember how you would eat mine sometimes?"

"I remember everything."

"Your mother wouldn't let us leave the table until we'd eaten our porridge."

"I didn't like it much, either," Alex admitted.

"Then why did you eat mine, too?"

"As a means to an end. So the two of us could be excused."

Kate met his gaze, feeling again the connection between them. Alex cleared the table while she filled the dishwasher. "Such a domestic scene," she commented. She was in her robe and slippers, and Alex was informally attired in chinos and an open-necked sport shirt.

Alex walked over to her. He didn't actually touch her, but he caressed her with his eyes. "Feels right, doesn't it?"

"I'm not sure." She moved away. "I'd better get dressed." At the door she paused. "I have a confession. I always knew you weren't wild about eating my porridge."

"Why did you make me do it, then?"

"I didn't make you—I *let* you."

"There's a difference?"

"Sure. If I'd made you, I'd have felt guilty."

They both laughed, and Kate started for her room.

"I'll make the coffee while you're dressing," he called after her.

"Fine. I can use it."

Kate dug out clean underwear. Not expecting an extended stay, she had only her cocktail dress, the suit she'd worn for traveling and denim jeans with a patchwork denim overblouse. Alex was dressed casually, so the denims would do. In the shower, Kate turned on the water full blast and almost cried out at the shocking coldness. She recalled that on one of her previous visits, Derek had warned her about the building's limited supply of hot water. She endured the cold blast for about fifteen seconds, then gave up. Rubbing herself vigorously to get the blood flowing, she noticed her skin had puckered into goose bumps.

Just then she heard Alex calling her from the hallway. "Yes?" she answered.

"Coffee's ready. Want it in there?"

A provocative thought. "No, but if you put a cup in my room, I'll be eternally grateful."

"Will do."

She finished drying herself, toweled her hair and put on her robe. Then she padded down the short corridor to her room. Alex was standing near the bed, a coffee mug in hand, looking at the arrangement of framed photographs on the wall. "Do you remember when that one was taken?" he asked, pointing. He turned to face her, his smile intimate and warm. His presence in her bedroom seemed completely natural.

"Yes," she said, going over and standing beside him to look at the picture of the four children making up a live totem pole. Alex, a sturdy ten-year-old, had Kate sitting on his shoulders, while she supported Derek, and Elizabeth was on top. "We were doing fine until Elizabeth sneezed and threw us off balance."

"And we all came tumbling down."

"And laughed so hard we couldn't get up."

"It was fun. I didn't know Derek had all these old pictures."

"Mom was the original custodian. When we went out on our own, she offered them to us. I wasn't interested, so Derek and Elizabeth took most of them."

"I see."

There was a disturbing quality in the way he looked at her. Kate wasn't sure he understood. For a time, all reminders of the past, even the happy ones, had brought back the pain of those last weeks in Kenya.

But she didn't want to think of that now. "You promised me coffee," she said. "Are we sharing that cup?"

"If you like."

Kate reached for the coffee, but when he didn't let go, she put her hand over his and guided the cup to her mouth. "Mmm, strong and hot. Just what I need. But you already drank most of it."

"Yours is on the dresser."

She turned and saw the other mug of coffee. "Why didn't you say so?"

"I like the idea of our sharing." He smiled. "I always have."

Kate went over to get her coffee. She leaned against the dresser, warming her hands around the mug, then took a sip of the richly satisfying brew. Kenyan coffee was the best in the world.

Alex sat down on the bed. He gestured around the room. "I see you still haven't mastered the art of neatness."

Kate's clothes lay strewn where she'd dropped them the night before. Her carryon sat open on the bedside table, and the contents of her cosmetic bag were in a jumble on the dresser.

"Your room was always the messiest," he said, more with indulgence than criticism.

He always used to tease her about that. As children, they had barged in freely on each other. Many a time, Kate recalled, she'd shaken Alex awake in the morning, then sat on the bed, as he was doing now, waiting for him to dress so they could be off somewhere. Privacy to them had meant privacy from other people, never from each other. Perhaps that was why she felt so completely at ease with him now.

"Neatness," Kate proclaimed, "is overrated. Being one of the lesser arts, I deem it unworthy of my attention."

"A fancy excuse if I've ever heard one," he said with a grin. "What you used to say was 'I can't be bothered.'"

She had to laugh. "It's what I mean. I just found a more intellectual way of saying it. I still can't be bothered." But not for the same reason as before, Kate thought to herself regretfully. Back then the prospect of a joyful day with Alex had always lured her from any mundane chore. Now her disdain for orderliness was little more than a habit.

She took another sip of coffee, savoring the taste and the aroma. "I should make time to brew coffee for myself. Instant doesn't compare." She sniffed appreciatively. "Without the aroma, you miss half the pleasure."

"You shouldn't have to settle for half pleasures." Alex rose, put down his cup and walked over to her. "That was never your way."

"With my busy schedule, I need shortcuts. I make do."

"Is that what your life is here—making do? Kate, you always wanted it all, every bit of excitement and beauty and wonder that was out there."

He reached to brush back her damp hair and let his hands drop to her shoulders. The comfort of remembered familiarity took on a different dimension as Kate felt the stirrings of desire. His touch was sending a flood of warmth cascading through her. His voice, vibrant with feeling, was having the same effect.

"You never wanted to wait for the future to happen." Alex brought his head close to hers, and Kate felt on her face the warm breath that carried his words. "You *made* it happen, rushing headlong. That's what I loved in you, what I still love. That's the essence of you, Kate."

Something soared within Kate to meet his emotion. Wrapping her arms around his neck, she pulled his head to her, her parted lips ready for his kiss. She didn't want to question the validity of his vision of her. What he saw was what she felt right now. For the moment, it was what she wanted to be. In grasping Alex to her, Kate sought herself in him.

She found passion and need and a wish to erase all the dividing years. Alex's mouth was warm with desire and a promise of fulfillment, but when the kiss ended, Kate drew back. She wasn't ready to trust his promise, afraid of the price it would carry.

"I'd better get dressed," Kate murmured.

Alex frowned, was about to protest, then released her. "Once I thought we had all the time in the world," he said lightly. "And then I lost you."

"But now you've found me again. We don't have to rush."

"Are you so sure?"

She nodded, giving him a sparkling smile, feigning a sureness she didn't feel.

CHAPTER FIVE

THEY WERE ALMOST OUT the door, when the telephone rang. Kate was surprised to hear her mother on the other end of the line. "I called Derek at the university to let him know I was back, and he told me Alex was in town," her mother said.

"Yes. In fact, he's here with me. I thought you were traveling."

"Roger's San Diego meeting was canceled. He's finishing some business in St. Louis, but I got bored so I decided to come home. I'm glad I did. How long is Alex staying?"

"I'm not sure. Do you want to talk to him?"

"Of course, but in person, not on the telephone."

"Well, why don't you start with the telephone?" Kate handed the receiver to Alex.

His pleasure at talking to her mother was apparent. Their conversation ended with his agreeing to stop by for a short visit that afternoon.

"It's already ten o'clock," Kate pointed out when he'd hung up. "We're not going to have much time for sightseeing."

"That's all right. People are more important than monuments and museums. What's your mother's name now? I almost called her 'Bibi Ellen.'"

"Her name's Hutchinson, but she'd probably still answer to 'Bibi Ellen.'" The children had affectionately used the Swahili title for 'madam.' "So we're adding Chevy Chase to our day's itinerary."

"Do you mind?"

"Of course not. I haven't seen Mom in a while."

"Then we're on our way."

Outside on the street, Kate paused and looked around. "Hold on a second while I get my bearings. We've got a lot of territory to cover, so it'll take some strategic planning. Fortunately the metro system in this city is pretty good."

"We won't need it." He pointed to the red Camry parked across the street.

"That's yours?"

"Temporarily. I rented it this morning. But you'll have to be my navigator. I'm used to driving on dirt roads and open plains."

"And on the left side of the road."

"That, too. I expect you to supply directions and keep me out of trouble."

"That's a tall order."

"You can handle it."

Kate smiled up at him. At this moment she felt she could handle anything.

"I THINK WE'VE DONE MORE sight-seeing in one day than most people do in a week," Kate said as they neared her mother's home in Chevy Chase. It was almost three o'clock, and they'd been on the go for five hours.

"It was a good day. I hope I didn't tire you out."

"You're the one who should be bushed from all that rowing." Alex had decided that seeing the skyline of Washington from a rented rowboat on the Potomac was vastly preferable to driving around. This was after they had visited the main sites.

"I'm fine."

"No calluses?"

"Just the ones that were there before." He took hold of her hand. "I enjoyed every part of the day. This is a beautiful city. I'm glad you weren't bored doing the tourist route with me."

"Seeing the city through your eyes made it different this time." Sharing Alex's reaction had restored beauty and majesty to what had come to appear merely scenic. His curiosity had prodded hers, and their tour had become an adventure. Alex had had no compunctions about asking the guards all kinds of questions, and he struck up conversations with perfect strangers. He'd made jokes on the steps of the Capitol Building, stood awesomely silent at the Vietnam Memorial and been amazed in the National Gallery by the primitive look of some modern sculpture pieces, which he likened to Kikuyu native art.

"Maybe that's the way you need to see Kenya again—through my eyes," he said.

Kate experienced a sinking feeling. "Alex, don't spoil things. We said we wouldn't talk about that."

"All right."

He agreed, but Kate could see that he wasn't satisfied. She was glad they'd reached their destination. "Turn here," she told him. "Mom's house is on the next block."

Kate's mother gave Alex a warm tearful welcome. She held him in a long, hard hug. Kate wasn't surprised at the affectionate display. Ellen Marlowe and Alex's mother had been closer than sisters and had often joked that with the exception of their husbands, the women on the compound shared everything, including their children. The two women still maintained their friendship through letters and phone calls, and Ellen was planning a trip to London later in the summer, expressly to see her old friend.

"Mom, why are you crying?" Kate asked.

"Because it's like seeing a long-lost son after so many years. Do you remember what your mother and I used to say?" she asked Alex, but didn't wait for an answer. "That we were lucky to have two sons and two daughters without having had to give birth four times." She paused and her eyes brimmed with tears again. "Now there are only three of you." Alex put his arms around her. She brushed away her tears. "But you're home now, so this is a happy occasion."

Her mother's use of the word "home" startled Kate—and gave her something to ponder.

In the comfortable family room downstairs, Kate's mother served coffee and hot Danishes and plied Alex with questions. She was most concerned about Elizabeth's mother. "How is Kama?" she asked. "Do you see her?"

"Whenever I get up to Lake Naivasha. That's where she lives most of the time."

"I tried to call her last month."

Kate's mother had mentioned to her that she'd made an attempt to reach Kama Sloane on the anniversary of Elizabeth's death.

"It took ages to get through, but no one answered."

"She probably went to the Mara to stay in the Masai village for a while," Alex said.

"Patrick never liked it when she went there," Ellen remembered.

"He still doesn't, but he's not around much these days. Patrick's an old-timer, right out of the pages of Hemingway. If he could, he'd turn back the clock to when men like Teddy Roosevelt came for extended hunting safaris. Working with my father and Mr. Marlowe was probably the longest he ever stayed in one place. The past few years he's been taking guide jobs that keep him away for months at a time. And not just in Kenya. Patrick's a restless man."

"How does Kama manage when he's gone?" Kate's mother asked.

"Patrick sees that she's well provided for, but even if he didn't, she'd never have a problem on that score. The Masai would see to it that she has all she needs. Her family has high standing in the tribe. Her mother is a *mganga*."

"Doesn't that mean witch doctor?" Kate asked.

"More than that. A *mganga* is also a healer and a prophet," Alex explained. "Very important to the tribe. Kama is expected to take her mother's place one day."

"You don't really believe all that business about special powers, do you?" Kate wanted to know.

Alex frowned. "I believe there are things that happen that go beyond normal ken, and that some people have extraordinary powers of perception. I also respect the Masai and their right to live according to their traditional ways. Your father used to preach that all the time."

"Alastair loved the people and the work he did," Kate's mother said.

Kate choked back the bitter observation that her father's love had been no match for the violence that killed him.

There was no way Alex and her mother were going to run out of conversation, so Kate finally reminded them that she and Alex had to leave. The two women were alone in the kitchen for a moment after Kate helped her mother clear the dishes.

"You know, darling," her mother said with a fond smile, "I've never seen you this radiant."

"Meaning?"

"Meaning that if Alex has this effect on you, I'm glad he's come."

"Don't get carried away, Mom. When we came in, you welcomed him home, but Alex's *home*, as he keeps reminding me, is in Kenya, not here. This is just a visit."

"Oh." Ellen Marlowe's eyebrows rose. "Too bad."

Kate gave an exasperated laugh. "Mom, you're making too much of this. Of course I'm happy to see Alex . . ."

"It's much more than that."

The sureness in her mother's voice annoyed Kate, just as it had when she was a child, when her mother's opinions and judgments were contrary to Kate's emotionally charged assertions. It had been hard for the volatile girl to concede that her mother was often right. She still had that problem.

"I think you're projecting," Kate said.

"Nonsense. You two were always inseparable. I hadn't thought about that for a long time—until I saw you together again today. It seemed so right." Her mother frowned, groping for the right words. "It's as if something's been missing in your life . . . as if you've been incomplete without Alex."

"Come on, now. You make it sound as if my life's been empty."

"I want you to be happy."

"I am. I've got my work, friends. . . ."

"Love?"

"Sure, when I want it."

Her brazen assertion didn't fool her mother. "Don't let him go."

"I can't keep him here." It was an admission of frustration.

"Then go with him."

Kate was shocked. "How can you say that after what happened to you?"

"Because you belong with Alex."

"Not in Kenya. I can't go back there."

Her mother gave a deep sigh, then a hopeful smile. "Alex seems to like it here. Maybe he'll decide to stay."

"I doubt that."

"You never can tell."

Kate didn't argue. She didn't want to destroy her mother's optimism, or the echoing flicker she herself felt.

WHEN KATE AND ALEX returned to the Georgetown apartment, Derek greeted them with relief. "You're here. I wondered if you'd eloped or something."

"Why didn't I think of that?" Alex asked, giving Kate a joking smile. He was carrying two bags of groceries.

Of course he'd meant to be frivolous, so Kate didn't reply. "Come on," she ordered. "We've got a dinner to prepare. I wasn't sure what you had on hand," she told Derek, "so Alex and I stopped at the market and bought whatever we're going to need."

"Great."

Susan came into the kitchen. Alex put the groceries on the table and scooped her up, lifting her high in the air as she giggled with glee. "Hi, there. How was school today?"

"Fine," she answered breathlessly when he put her down. "Where did you and Auntie Kate go?"

Alex spread his arms expansively. "Everywhere." He took Susan's hand. "Let's go into the other room and I'll tell you all about it."

Kate had started taking out the groceries. "Oh, no, you don't. You're not leaving me in the kitchen by myself. Everybody helps. This is going to be a communal effort."

"What a tyrant," Alex said. "I guess we're stuck, Susan. You'd better find us four aprons."

"Uh, make that three," Derek told his daughter. "I told Melanie I'd pick her up." To Kate, he said, "You don't need me. You've got two very able assistants here."

Kate eyed her brother curiously. There was a nervous elation about him. She wondered if Alex perceived it. When

Derek had gone, she said casually, "Derek's really on a high."

"I think Melanie's gotten to him," Alex said with a knowing look.

So he had noticed, and fathomed the reason.

"I think Daddy likes Melanie," Susan announced.

Kate was startled. "Have you met Melanie?"

"No, but I heard Daddy talking to her on the telephone before. I could tell. He kept smiling, and sometimes he laughed."

"Ah, the sagacity of children," Alex said.

"What's that mean?" Susan asked suspiciously.

"It means," Alex said, patting her on the head, "that you're a pretty smart kid."

"Okay." Susan gave him a happy grin.

For the next half hour, the three of them worked diligently. Kate put the cut-up chicken pieces in a bowl to marinate in a mixture of olive oil, lemon juice and seasonings.

Alex and Susan were in charge of the salad. They kept up a running conversation while they worked. Alex described all the things he and Kate had seen. "Did you go to the zoo?" Susan asked.

"No. I'm not big on seeing caged animals."

"My mommy didn't like it much, either. I remember when I was little we went. She bought me a balloon. We saw monkeys and elephants. But then she started to cry and said we had to leave. She was homesick for where she grew up. I held her hand when she cried."

Kate had been listening. Susan couldn't have been more than four at the time she was describing.

"You're very like your mother," Alex said softly.

"My dad says I look like her, but that I'm my own self, too. I like to hear him tell about the things you all used to do together. Then I can pretend I was there. Sometimes I make up a dream about it, and when I go to sleep, I see it like it was on television."

"You make your dreams happen?" Alex asked.

His expression revealed curiosity, not the skepticism that most adults would have shown.

"Once in a while," Susan answered.

"That's a neat trick," Kate said.

"It's not a trick. You just gotta think hard." Susan reached for a cucumber. "Want me to peel this?"

"From the mystical to the mundane," Alex observed with a smile.

"Huh?"

"Nothing. Can you handle a paring knife?"

"No." Susan got down from her chair, went to the cabinet and took a utensil from the drawer. She came back and waved it at Alex. "Daddy lets me use this vegetable peeler. Then when I'm done you get to cut up the cuke."

"Right on. You peel and I'll cut. What a team."

"Yeah, what a team."

Kate felt a welling of affection for both of them, the little girl with the imaginative mind and boisterous spirit and the man who could communicate with the child so easily.

In a half hour they'd finished their preparations. Kate smiled with satisfaction. "This is a great no-fuss menu. The salad's ready, the broccoli's in the steamer and the chicken and potatoes are baking nicely in the oven. In forty-five minutes, voilà—nouvelle cuisine. Too bad dessert's only store-bought pound cake."

Susan had an idea. "We can put ice cream on it—strawberry swirl and rocky road. We got both."

"Good thinking. It'll be delicious."

"Yeah!" Susan's agreement was practically a yell.

Laughing, Kate echoed, "Yeah!"

The outside door opened and Derek called, "What's all the cheering about?" He and Melanie came into the kitchen.

Melanie had dispensed with the spiked hairdo. Her short brown hair framed her face in a gamin style. There was nothing boyish, however, about her full-bosomed figure in a blue silk shirt and pleated pants. Last night she'd looked wonderfully outré and very sexy. Today, with little makeup except to highlight her eyes, she was the friendly all-American type—and still very sexy.

"Hi," Melanie said, and immediately went over to the little girl, who was standing on a chair next to Alex. "You must be Susan. My name's Melanie." She put out her hand. "I'm real pleased to meet you."

Susan smiled and shook hands. Shaking hands was a nice gesture, Kate thought. Melanie apparently knew how to appeal to children.

"Me, too, I'm pleased," Susan said.

"I brought you something."

"What?"

Melanie dug into the huge woven straw bag she had slung over her shoulder. "Your dad says you're into soccer." She extracted a thin package. "So I brought you a game, Soccer Video."

"Oh, wow!"

"We'll play after dinner, okay?"

Susan nodded, bobbing her head eagerly. But before she took the present she looked at her father. His expression gave her the approval she sought. Remembering her manners, she said formally, "Thank you very much."

"It was my pleasure," Melanie assured Susan. Then, giving Alex a head-to-toe survey, she said, "My, don't you look domestic." She went up to him and lifted the hem of the chef's apron he was wearing. "This is a side of you I've never seen before."

He was unperturbed. "I'm a man of many talents."

"I can vouch for that."

The innocent remark bothered Kate. She'd believed Alex when he'd said that romance had no part in his collaboration with Melanie. Yet Melanie seemed to know more about Alex than Kate did. In a sense, Kate and Alex had just met the day before. Their childhood bond had no relevance now.

Melanie turned to Kate. "Whatever you're cooking smells great. Can we help?"

"We're ready," Derek offered.

"Sure. Just when everything's done," Alex said. "Perfect timing, Derek. We managed just fine without you."

"Uncle Alex and I did the salad," Susan told them. "We're a team."

"Lucky you," Derek said. "He's a great partner to have. Right, Kate?"

"Right." Kate ignored her brother's knowing grin. "Derek, how about you mixing the dressing?"

He rubbed his hands. "That's my specialty."

"And setting the table," Kate added.

"No problem."

"I'll do that," Melanie offered. "But you'll have to show me where everything is," she said to Derek.

"You and Daddy can be a team," Susan said.

The idea seemed to appeal to Melanie.

By the time they sat down to dinner, a camaraderie prevailed among all of them. The dinner was good, the conversation lively, and Kate was enjoying herself.

"That was fabulous," Melanie said when they'd finished. "I can't cook to save my soul. Alex is a better cook than I am."

"That was part of our training as kids," Derek said. "Cooking was one of the survival skills we all had to learn.

Unfortunately I never progressed beyond the rudimentaries. Thank God for microwaves and frozen foods.''

"I'm with you." Melanie gave Derek a big smile. "We're two of a kind."

It was just an expression. Kate thought Melanie and her brother were very different, but it didn't seem to matter. Their interest in each other was very obvious. Derek was all attention as Melanie amusingly described some of her adventures taking the pictures for *A Vanishing World*.

Susan was especially delighted by the story of how a monkey had run off with one of Melanie's cameras. "Did he take your picture?" she asked.

"He looked like he was ready to," Melanie answered, "and he could have. It was an Instamatic that I use for fast shots. I took a picture of the monkey aiming it at us. It's in the book." Melanie got up from the table to get the autographed copy of the book she'd given Derek. "See, here it is. Too bad he didn't press the right button. I'd have put the picture of us on the opposite page."

"It might have been a better picture than yours," Derek teased.

Melanie broke into a laugh. "I never thought of that."

"Daddy, can I have a camera for when I go to see *Ayah*?" Susan asked. *Ayah* was what she called her grandmother Kama.

"When you're older."

"Susan can probably handle one of those little automatics," Melanie suggested.

"Yes, I can. I can handle one of those little automatics," the little girl mimicked eagerly.

"If you like, I'll help you pick one out," Melanie told Derek.

"That would be great."

"You're not planning to take Susan to Kenya, are you?" Kate asked. Derek had not returned since Elizabeth's death.

"I think it may be time."

Kate knew her brother was determined that his child not lose touch with her African heritage. It was his obligation to Elizabeth and to Susan. "Wouldn't it be better to wait until she's older?" Kate suggested.

"Why?" The question was Alex's.

"She's a little young to be subjected to..."

"To what?"

Kate hesitated. "I'm not sure."

"Your fears are unreasonable," Alex said quietly.

He was probably right, but Kate couldn't help her fears. What she could help, however, was projecting her apprehension onto others.

Melanie, who obviously didn't understand the undercurrents of the conversation, turned to Derek. "When were you planning to go to Kenya?"

"This summer, I think. There's some research I need to do for my doctorate, and Susan can visit with her grandmother."

"Sounds super. I wouldn't mind another trip myself," Melanie said. "Hey, why don't we all go? Wouldn't that be a blast?"

"Yeah." Susan liked the sound of it.

"Right now, I think you and Alex should concentrate on this publicity tour," Kate warned.

"What tour? Do you have it all set up?" Melanie easily transferred her enthusiasm to this new topic.

"Partially. I'll be coordinating with your publisher, of course, but that should be no problem. There's kind of a set procedure. I'll be contacting all the radio and television production people who might be interested. They usually work way in advance, so we have to find out their scheduling needs."

Alex frowned. "How far in advance?"

"It depends. Sometimes months, sometimes weeks."

"I don't have months, or even many weeks, for this kind of thing."

"'This kind of thing' is what's going to sell your book." Again she suspected he was disparaging her work. "How long were you planning to stay?"

"I hadn't thought about it. There were other things on my mind."

"If you don't want to do this—"

"Of course we want to do this," Melanie interrupted. "Alex, what's with you? That's what we're here for, isn't it?" She didn't wait for a reply. To Kate, she said, "Hey, whatever you set up is fine with us. Rhoda says that if this promotional push pays off in increased orders, the publisher's likely to up the advertising budget."

"It helps fire up their sales force, too," Kate said.

"Any chance of getting on one of the network shows?" Melanie asked.

"It's tough, but it's possible. Occasionally the big story doesn't materialize, or something unexpected can louse up a schedule. I'll certainly try. You can do yourselves a lot of good on local shows, too. We'll work all the angles."

"How about that, Susan?" Melanie said, preening a bit. "Your uncle Alex and I are going to be on television."

"Maybe you can be on *Sesame Street*," Susan said.

"Hey, why not? We're game for anything. Right, Alex?"

He shrugged and smiled. "Sure." Then he looked at Kate and added, "We're in your hands. What's the next step?"

"I'll get back to New York tomorrow and set things up."

"When do you want me there?" Melanie asked.

"Let's see. Tomorrow's Tuesday. How about the end of the week? I should have a partial itinerary by then. Say, Friday?"

"Fine with me." Melanie glanced over at Derek. "I wouldn't mind a few more days here."

Judging by his smile, Derek wouldn't mind, either.

"Maybe you want to go to New York with Kate," Derek suggested to Alex.

The idea appealed to Kate. But was her brother playing matchmaker, or simply trying to keep Melanie to himself? Alex's reply disappointed her.

"I wish I could, but there are some people I have to see before I leave Washington."

Alex had mentioned that while he was here, he would be trying to gain support for an international conference on ecosystem conservation.

"I probably won't get to New York before Thursday," he said to Kate.

"Whatever you like," she replied, the casualness of her remark at variance with the intensity of her desire to have Alex with her.

KATE TOOK an early flight home the next morning, then stopped by her apartment to drop off her suitcase and change clothes. Anxious to get to the office, she was ready to leave again in ten minutes. At the door, she paused, then returned to her bedroom. She rummaged through a drawer in her bureau and extracted a velvet pouch. Opening the drawstring, she took out the small soapstone sculpture, running her fingers over the two embracing figures. She started to put it back, then changed her mind and thrust the empty bag into the drawer. The sculpture she placed gently on the bureau.

As soon as she got to the office, she called Beth in and kept her assistant busy with a barrage of memos and a list of phone calls to put through. "First get me Rhoda Field. Her number should be listed. If not, get it from Mr. Blackwell. Ask if I can see her this afternoon, tomorrow at the latest. Oh, and ask her whom to call at the publisher's to coordinate their efforts with ours. Get in touch with whoever it is and arrange an appointment ASAP. Then—"

"Kate, slow down," Beth pleaded. "Why don't I take care of the first hundred items before you get going on the next batch? After your extended weekend, I figured you'd come in all mellowed out, but you're going like a steamroller. When did you have time to plan all this?"

"Coming in this morning on the shuttle. The planning doesn't take long. I know exactly where I want to place Pearson and Crane. The rough part is setting it all up fast. That's where you come in."

"I get the message. Let me start with what I have. I'll get back to you this afternoon."

"Okay. While you're doing that, there are a couple of people I can call."

After Beth left, Kate got busy on the phone, with good results. Not a hundred percent, but she had yeses from an Atlanta radio host, a Miami talk-show producer and a local public television channel in Chicago. Plus several promising maybes. Now she could work on other media outlets in the same cities.

She was eating lunch at her desk, when Bob Reynolds came in for his briefing about Elvira's publicity tour. "I met with her yesterday," Bob told Kate. He spread a sheaf of photographs on her desk. "She just got this new set of pictures for her publicity folder and wants your opinion. Mine wouldn't do."

"Problems? Was she upset at the change?"

"Not really. Elvira likes the idea of having me around as escort on her tour, but she relies on your judgment 'as woman to woman,'" he said, mimicking Elvira's high-pitched voice.

Kate laughed, looked over the pictures and selected the best poses. She reviewed the tour with Bob and gave him some hints about handling Elvira and the media people.

After he left, Kate leaned back in her chair and stretched the stiffness out of her neck. She'd been bent over her desk all day. Bob would be good with Elvira. Kate had figured that the woman would like having him tour with her. That was a chore she herself hadn't relished.

But accompanying Alex...that was a different story.

Kate reminded herself she would be with him in a professional capacity. But would she be able to sustain the role? Did she even want to? In Derek's room that first morning, Alex had wanted to make love to her. He'd held back, but that was bound to change. Kate wasn't sure how she would react. The sexual attraction was strong, but so was her apprehension about surrendering to a love that couldn't last.

Beth came in with the information Kate had requested, and she got back to work. When Alex arrived on Thursday, she would show him what she could accomplish. He kept thinking back to the girl she had been; Kate wanted him to admire the woman she'd become.

ON THURSDAY AFTERNOON, Alex called from Pennsylvania Station. Kate had come to the office before eight and had been busy every moment, but there was the constant underlying anticipation that he would call. He was here now, and she felt a soaring rush of happiness. "How come you're at Penn Station?"

"I just got off the Metroliner."

"You came by train? The shuttle flight's only an hour."

"By rail I can look out the window and see something besides clouds. I want to see the country."

"You'll be seeing plenty." In two days of incessant long distance calls, persuading, cajoling and reminding producers of past favors, Kate had set up an enviable itinerary for Alex and Melanie. She'd managed good spots for them on popular programs in several major cities, and there was a strong possibility of a midmorning network talk show. "Atlanta on Monday afternoon, then Boston, Chicago and Miami. Sorry about the zigzagging route, but that's the best I could do on short notice. Right now, I'm trying to keep all the West Coast stops together so you won't be crisscrossing the country."

"I'm used to long treks."

What Alex was used to was different from the whirlwind jet travel that awaited him, but Kate didn't want to discourage him with a detailed description.

"With you along, I might even enjoy it," he continued. "Remember how we used to go exploring?"

He assumed that Kate would be accompanying him. "I probably won't catch up with you until Chicago," she hedged. "There's still too much to do here. Besides, you won't have much time for exploring."

"I thought part of your job was to do a little hand-holding with your clients."

"Only if they need it. Melanie's done this before. She's a pro."

"I'm not talking about Melanie."

"You won't have any problems."

"I'm having them already. When's that first date you mentioned?"

"Monday afternoon . . . Boston."

"That doesn't give us much time here."

"I know. Where are you staying?"

"With Andrew McLeod, a friend I went to college with. He works at the U.N. and has an apartment in Manhattan. Problem is, I haven't been able to reach him."

"Did you try his office?"

"They said he's away but expected back later today or tomorrow morning. He didn't know for sure when I'd be here. In Nairobi there'd be no problem. I'd just have the concierge let me in."

"New York's not like that."

"So I gather."

"What are you going to do?"

"I thought we could spend the afternoon together. I gave Andy's secretary your number at home. If he gets back today, he'll call me there."

And if he doesn't? Kate thought, but didn't pose the question out loud.

"How about it?" Alex asked. "Take the rest of the day off."

"I shouldn't. I've still got a thousand things to do."

"Let nine hundred and ninety-nine wait."

Alex didn't have the key to her place, and she couldn't expect him to wander around the city, waiting for her to get home. Kate looked at her watch. "It's after one. I guess I could take a long lunch break and finish up later."

"Good thinking."

Kate gave him her address and directions and hung up, then called in her assistant. "Beth, can you handle things? I have to go out."

"Sure. Where are you going?"

"Home."

"What for?"

Kate was used to Beth's outspoken curiosity, but had no intention of satisfying it. "It's personal."

"How personal?"

"None of your business."

Beth grinned. "Oh, like that, is it? Well, have fun. There's nothing wrong with a romantic interlude in the afternoon, I always say. Don't rush."

Kate never made it back to the office that afternoon. She got to her apartment a few minutes before Alex. He walked in the door, drenched from a sudden downpour, put down his bag and gathered her in a bear hug. "You're all wet," she protested. But when his lips touched hers, sweetly tasting of rain freshness, nothing else mattered.

The hours flew by. When the brief storm passed, they made sandwiches and ate outside on her little terrace. They talked about everything, their experiences during the long years apart, their work, their memories. Their hands touched, accidentally at first, then deliberately, seeking physical confirmation of their deepening emotional intimacy.

In the late afternoon, the sun disappeared behind the tall buildings, and they went inside. While Kate was busy in the kitchen, Alex explored the apartment. He discovered her stereo, and soon the throaty voice of Karen Carpenter sang of love and promise. Alex came up behind Kate and put his arms around her waist. She leaned back against him. He gently turned her to face him. In his dark eyes was the pent-up desire that could shatter her resistance.

He held back, however, content with a light kiss on her forehead. "Let's take a walk before it gets dark," he said.

"If that's what you want to do."

"What do *you* want to do?"

The telephone rang before she had to answer. It was Andrew McLeod. Alex took the phone. Andy was home and wanted Alex to come right over. Alex hesitated, looked searchingly at Kate, then told his friend, "I'm on my way."

A half hour later, the cab he'd summoned came and he was gone. Kate looked around her apartment. Never had it seemed so empty.

CHAPTER SIX

THE TOUR WAS GOING WELL. Alex's dynamism coupled with Melanie's quirky sharpness made them a talk-show hit, and it became easier for Kate to schedule additional bookings. Rhoda Field was ecstatic, and Melanie loved every moment. Though less enthusiastic, Alex was bearing up. Kate had been a little apprehensive about this afternoon's show, which had been taped at Tampa's Busch Gardens. Alex had been reluctant to do it, but they'd just watched the tape at the studio, and it was good. For the past few days, he and Melanie had had separate schedules in order to cover more territory, so he'd done this show alone.

"You've developed a stage presence," Kate told him. It was the third week of the tour, and she'd just flown down to Florida that morning. Kate couldn't travel with Alex the whole time, but managed to join him for a day or two every week. It became harder each time she had to leave him. She felt that Alex was focusing less on what they had been to each other and more on the here and now. Being with him was exciting—mentally, emotionally and sexually. Though Alex still let her set the guidelines, Kate sensed a growing intimacy that she couldn't stem.

She had called from New York the night before and he'd asked her to meet him here in Tampa. Kate knew he'd had misgivings about this afternoon's program. Dan Farragut, who did a weekly travel and vacation segment for the local Channel 4 station, had seen a copy of *A Vanishing World*.

For his feature on the Tampa Bay area, he was highlighting Busch Gardens and its popular attraction, a facsimile of the Serengeti Plain. Dan thought it would be a great gimmick to interview Alex on the monorail from which visitors viewed the animals that roamed there. A wildlife expert and guide from the real Serengeti commenting on this Florida version of it. After some persuasion, Alex had finally agreed.

"You were terrific," Kate said. Alex gave her a skeptical smile and settled into an armchair in the elegant sitting room of his hotel suite. He'd balked at wearing a safari outfit for the filming, but in chinos and a plaid sport shirt, he still looked ruggedly out of place in the Queen Anne chair. "Dan was very pleased with your performance."

"I don't like to think of myself as a performer," Alex said, "and pleasing people like Farragut is not one of my burning ambitions."

"Come on. He's not that bad."

"Better than most," Alex conceded. "At least he'd read the book and understood what I was talking about. But," he added with a wry smile, "the guy's convinced that Busch Gardens is Utopia for wildlife."

"What's wrong with it?"

"It's set up well, but it's still a contrived, manufactured experience."

"An experience that thousands of people enjoy. Isn't it better than the alternative—seeing animals in cages or as circus performers?"

"There's another alternative."

Kate knew what he meant. "Alex, traveling to Africa is not possible for most people. A visit to a place like Busch Gardens is. And there, at least, the animals have space to roam."

"I know, but I still hate to see animals in captivity."

Kate shook her head impatiently. "Would you want to just release all captured animals?"

"Yes, now that you ask." His mouth curved in an ironic grin. "But I'm pragmatist enough to realize that's not possible."

"But idealist enough to wish it were."

"Exactly."

His eyes narrowed and darkened, and she knew his thoughts were turning in a personal direction.

"Living creatures may be able to survive being transplanted from their natural environments, but I doubt that they can thrive elsewhere."

"There's a hidden message here."

Alex rose and walked over to Kate, taking her lightly by the shoulders. "Not hidden at all."

His hold wasn't confining, but his penetrating gaze caught and enveloped her. "Kenya isn't my natural environment," she told him. "I was born here in the States. So were you."

"Birthplace doesn't necessarily determine a person's natural home. Kenya was ours, Kate. You know that." He pulled her closer.

"That's not true anymore, not for me." Those were the words she spoke, but another thought filled her mind. Here, in Alex's arms...*this* was her natural environment. She felt the force not of his desire but her own. Something unfolded deep inside her and warmth radiated through her body.

Alex tightened his hold and his gaze intensified. "I don't accept that." He compelled her to look at him.

"Alex, I don't want to argue. Not now. I just want to..." She couldn't finish the thought.

"Kate, you're a lovely, desirable woman. Don't deny yourself. Don't deny me."

He brought his lips to hers and felt a surging joy as her mouth quickened in a heated response. Passion spread through him, tightening his muscles and firing his blood. Their kiss was long and deep. Lifting his head, he saw desire filling her eyes, deepening their color to turquoise, and his breath caught in his throat. His hand filtered through the silky luxury of her hair, and he tasted her sweetness as he ran his lips over her eyelids, her cheeks, down to the pulsing arch of her throat. Her arms were around him, her fingers warm and caressing on his neck. Her body yielded to the pressure of his hands and molded to him. Alex's desire was a thrusting command, but he craved from Kate a passion equal to his own.

Kate could not deny him, or herself.

She helped him lift the loose blouse over her head, then allowed him the pleasure of sensuously peeling off the rest of her clothes. Kate heard his sharp intake of breath, then gave herself up to the warm envelopment of his arms, the sinuous caress of his fingers on the bareness of her waist, her hips, her breasts. In their kiss, Kate's lips transmitted a message she'd never before been able to send, a silent *I'm yours—love me.*

The buttons of his shirt pressed into her skin. Kate pulled back and started to undo them. He gave a small laugh and helped, quickly shedding his clothes. There was nothing awkward in his movements, no embarrassment, no panting haste. When he was naked, he took and held her hands as they stood apart, unabashedly enjoying the vision of each other. Kate reveled in the admiration and wonder in Alex's eyes and in her own similar reaction to him. How taut and lean his body was! There was that scar just below his shoulder on the right side, not as pronounced as she remembered. He'd been fifteen when it had happened. Urged on by Kate's dare, Alex had dived into the river from a high ledge. He'd grazed a jagged rock, and the gash had required fifteen stitches. The scar had faded into a light-toned line against his darker coloring.

His tanned skin ended just below his waist; the paler tones of his flat belly were bisected by a shadowy line of curling hair that widened at the pelvis. Alex was no longer the youth she'd wanted to love her many years before. He drew her to him, and she gasped at the hardness of his erection. But his gaze was tender and promised more than sexual release.

Alex led her to the bed, where they quickly made themselves comfortable. His hands roved over her body, claiming what was his. Kate allowed, then abetted his exploration. She seemed to anticipate what he would do, where and how he would touch her. For a while, she allowed herself to be captive to her own sensations, but then roused herself to tune into his. When Kate permitted herself the same freedom with his body, Alex's eyes sparked silver fire. This dual concentration, on his arousal as well as her own, intensified her passion. Kate touched the top of his scar.

"Do you remember how I got that?" he asked, knowing that she did.

She'd been responsible for that scar, and she had felt his pain. Kate let her lips glide down the length of the scar, then traced a path upward with her tongue, ending with a kiss. She felt the flesh under the skin, the bones that supported it, the blood that coursed through him.

She moved closer, touching the length of her body to his. His arms tightened around her, moving her against him. Her skin felt hotly sensitive as her body strained into his. Within her rose a spiraling clamor for more.

Alex understood, but he hesitated a moment. "Kate, we should have protection."

"It's all right," she told him softly, appreciative of his concern. "I'm on the pill." She reached for him, and Alex positioned himself over her. For a moment, he held himself above her as their eyes locked. Kate relished this pause, this shared awareness of the deep sensual experience they had willed into happening and the trembling anticipation of fruition.

What followed was a harmony of mounting excitement. Kate lived both her passion and Alex's, meeting his thrusting body with pleasure. She felt the coalescing warmth that signaled climax and welcomed it, without the tightening fear of going over a brink. Joyously Kate moved to instinctual rhythms. Alex lifted away from her, gave her a smile of tender triumph, then drew from her the deep, undulating orgasm that fused with his own.

Afterward, while their bodies stilled, he held her quietly. No masculine platitudes or questions or claims. Kate felt suspended in a rosy euphoria. Then Alex moved to lie beside her, resting on his elbow, gazing at her. "This had to be, you know," he said. "I've been waiting for such a long time."

She, too, had been waiting, Kate realized. Long ago, she and Alex had barely tasted the sweetness of love. She'd been eager for more, but Alex had heeded caution. This was where they had been heading, this act of love that should have happened in the natural course of things. But the natural course had been violently thwarted.

Kate had searched elsewhere for love, but had never found the fulfillment it was supposed to bring. Her involvements with men were characteristically intense—but temporary. Of late, she'd given up on intimacy and kept things companionable and light.

Making love with Alex was everything she'd been seeking. Being with him renewed the bond that had always connected them. In a way, she'd been subject to that bond even during the long years of absence, unconsciously comparing every other promise of love to what might have been with Alex.

She wondered if those invisible knots that had kept them tied might now unravel. There had been that feeling of something unfinished, yearning for culmination. Could giving herself to Alex have freed her from the past?

Kate sensed that Alex had different ideas. His eyes had a far away dreaminess. "What are you thinking?" she asked.

"You used to know without asking."

"Maybe I still do. You were imagining us back ho—" Kate paused and corrected herself. "Back on the compound, weren't you?"

"Yes, but not as children. As we are now."

His lips curved in a smile. She ran her finger over them. How finely etched his mouth was. She wanted to trace its contours, committing every detail to memory. "What's wrong with this," she asked, "an elegant suite in a deluxe hotel?"

"Like the fake Serengeti, it's a manufactured setting." His voice deepened. "I want to make love to you at our place, at Pambazuko. The rains are almost over now. Soon the grass will be tall enough to cover us. Remember how we used to mat it down to make a bed?"

"I also remember that I wanted you to make love to me there, but you refused."

"We were too young. That wasn't the time."

Kate looked up at him, her faint smile tinged with sadness. "Maybe our time has passed. We're different people now. There's too much between us."

"There's nothing between us," he said, and made it true by pulling her close again. He planted a soft kiss on her forehead, then traced a path to her lips. "Isn't it enough that we make each other happy?" he asked, his lips touching her mouth.

At this moment, for Kate it was enough.

FOR THE NEXT TWO WEEKS, Kate was happy. The remaining schedule for the tour was all set. She was able to make herself available when Alex had free time, and they'd had fun exploring Philadelphia and Denver and San Francisco together. Melanie, when she was around, often made other plans for herself. She seemed to know people everywhere. "She also knows we need time to ourselves," Alex had told Kate.

"How does she know that?" Kate asked.

"I told her," he admitted with a smile.

With commitments in the metropolitan New York area for the past two days, Alex had been staying at Kate's. How quickly she'd gotten used to having him with her, waking up with him in the morning, having breakfast together, meeting again in the evening, making love when they wanted. There was one subject, however, that they both avoided—the future.

Kate almost resented the time she had to go to the office. She'd just gotten her budget for a publicity campaign that had been commissioned by a group of practicing acupuncturists. It should have been a challenging assignment, but she was finding it difficult to concentrate on her work, so absorbed was she with her personal life. Harvey Blackwell noticed. He called her into his office one afternoon.

"Want some time off?" he asked, taking her by surprise.

"What for?"

"Whatever. I noticed you weren't quite with us at the staff meeting this morning."

"I'm sorry. I guess I was daydreaming."

"So take a vacation. Do some more daydreaming. You're entitled. How long's your boyfriend going to be around?"

"If you mean Alex..."

"Who else?"

"His last interview's the week after next. At least until then." And beyond, Kate hoped.

"Okay. When he's done, you can both take off...go to Acapulco."

Kate smiled. "I don't think Alex is the Acapulco type."

"So go to Atlantic City. What's the difference? As long as you're together."

Kate hesitated. "What about the acupuncturists?"

"Don't worry about them. Maybe I'll take over that campaign. If you want the time, Kate, my dear, it's yours. Think about it."

She thanked him and left. As the day wore on, her boss's suggestion appealed to Kate more and more. She and Alex had spent a good deal of time together, but in short intervals. The prospect of a long, uninterrupted stretch with nothing to do or think about except their pleasure in each other was tempting. She couldn't wait to broach the subject to Alex.

But she never had the chance.

WHEN KATE GOT HOME that evening, Alex wasn't in yet. All week, he'd been doing book signings around the city. She decided to surprise him by having dinner ready, something special. The little Greek restaurant around the corner provided the meal and a bottle of white wine. Kate showered, brushed her hair into a gleaming swirl and put on a sapphire-blue silk blouse and pants. Then she set the table, put the wine in the ice bucket, lit the candles and waited for Alex. She waited a long time.

By the time he arrived, it was almost eight. The ice was melted and the candles almost burned down. Having fancied all kinds of dire accidents, Kate felt only relief when he first walked in. "Are you all right?" she asked. "I was beginning to worry."

Alex looked at his watch and was surprised. "I didn't realize how late it was. I should have called." He noticed the candlelit table. "What's all this?"

"All this," Kate said, holding out her hands palms up, "was supposed to be a romantic dinner for two."

"I'm sorry, but something important came up."

Kate had a foreboding that made her want to forestall what he had to tell her. "Well, you're here now. That's what counts. I've got a special dinner for you." She spoke in a rush of sentences to keep him from breaking in. "I hope you like Greek food. We're having moussaka, as soon as I heat it up in the microwave. That's eggplant and spiced meat in a marvelous creamy sauce. Why don't you get some more ice for the wine cooler while I—"

He grabbed her arm to keep her from darting off. "Kate, hold it."

"You must be starved. I know I am."

"No." He held her firmly. "Dinner can wait."

"It has, for two hours."

More gently he said, "Then a few minutes more won't hurt." He propelled her over to the sofa. "Please sit down. I need to talk to you."

Kate complied. She sat stiffly facing him, aware of a hard knot forming in her chest. "What's up?" she asked with forced bravado.

"I have to leave."

The words seemed to assault her, and she drew back. "You can't." She was surprised by her vehemence.

"I must."

"But the tour's not finished."

"I'm sure Melanie can cover for both of us."

"She shouldn't have to. You're both in this. And things are going so well. According to the figures from your publisher's West Coast distributor, the orders are way above what was projected."

"I'm glad, but . . ."

"That's what you came for, isn't it?"

"That was one reason. The other was to see you."

"All the more reason to stay," she cried.

"I can't. Kate, I got a call from Nairobi this morning. I've spent all afternoon at the embassy office. Steven Ngelindi is dead." He hit his knee with his fist. "I knew Steve had a heart condition, but I didn't realize it was so serious."

Kate could see how troubled Alex was, but she still didn't understand why he had to leave. "Was he a close friend?"

"He was a colleague, and a fine man. We served together on the president's council for administering the national game preserves." Alex rubbed his brow. "Steve was my mentor. I'm a Kenyan citizen, but there are still those who regard all whites with suspicion. I have the technical expertise, and Steve has—had—the political influence. Joining forces gave us more clout than either of us would have had individually."

"Alex, I'm so sorry, but there's nothing you can do for him now. Surely your appearance at the funeral isn't mandatory."

"No. I probably won't even make it in time. That's not why I have to go. You see, Ngelindi was also chairman of the President's Advisory Council for Development. He held the line, but now there's going to be a real push by developers to encroach on the game preserves."

"Do you have to get involved?"

"Yes. Kate, try to understand. The president has to select a replacement. There's going to be a lot of behind-the-scenes dealing. It's started already from what I hear. Whoever heads that council will have a hell of a lot of power. We need a man like Steve, not someone who's out to line his own pockets."

"What can you do about it?"

"That's what I'm going to find out." Suddenly his steely look softened into an appeal. "Kate, come with me."

"What?" He couldn't be serious.

"Come with me."

"I can't." The knot in her chest had risen to her throat, constricting her voice. "I made that decision long ago."

"A girl made that decision." He reached over and took her hands. "You're a woman now, the woman I want to share my life."

"That's one of the problems. What about my life? Alex, the things I value are here."

"In New York?"

"Why is that so unbelievable? Oh, it's no use." She tried to pull away, but Alex held her.

"Don't say that. We can work it out."

"How?"

"I love you, Kate," Alex said. "I can never be completely whole without you."

Kate was afraid of the corollary that immediately sprang to mind—that she, too, was incomplete without him. "Then stay," she cried.

"I can't. Come with me."

"I can't."

The look they exchanged was fraught with anguish. Recognizing the futility of further argument, Alex pulled her to him. The desperation of imminent parting was in their embrace, and their kisses were bittersweet. The candles sputtered and died; the food and wine went untasted. Alex carried her into the bedroom and closed the door. Their lovemaking all that night was fiercely demanding, as if they sought an ultimate consummation that would have to last them... how long? Perhaps forever.

In the morning, Alex said goodbye.

KATE FELT DESOLATE. The balmy weather of late May was no solace. Her job and the social life she resumed consumed her time, but did not fill her emptiness. She told Harvey Blackwell she wouldn't need that vacation he'd offered. With nothing else on which to focus her creative energy, she immersed herself in her work. The public relations strategy she devised for the acupuncture group was brilliantly innovative. However, her former satisfaction in her work was somehow lacking.

Kate thought of Alex's fervency when he'd talked about what he wanted to accomplish. She couldn't help comparing her work to Alex's, her life to Alex's. He hadn't denied the dangers that came with living in Kenya, but he preferred them to the sophisticated savagery of life in New York—the craze for success and money, the competition, the loveless sex and the loneliness. Kate knew what he meant; she'd never felt so alone before. She spent more and more time at the office.

Melanie was handling the balance of her tour quite successfully, so there were no problems there. Kate knew from Derek that Melanie often stopped at Washington on her travels. From the sound of it, the friendship between the two had deepened. Kate wondered what would happen when Derek and Susan left for Kenya in late June. Then Derek surprised her. He called her at the office one afternoon to say he was catching a flight from New York to Nairobi.

"I'm coming to New York tomorrow to meet with one of the curators of African art at the Metropolitan Museum.

How about I stay at your place and then you take me to the airport Saturday morning?"

"Sure, but I don't understand." Kate looked at the calendar on her desk. "You're leaving June 3?"

"You got it."

"I thought you were going to wait until Susan's school was out."

"I was until this came up." Excitedly Derek described recent new discoveries of cave art in Tanzania, the country bordering Kenya to the south. He was going to join the field team there for a few weeks. "I had to knock myself out to mark finals and get the grades in early, but it was worth it. I can't pass this up. My transportation's being paid for, and I'll have access to great new material for my thesis. Plus that impressive addendum to my résumé when I apply for a tenured position."

"But what about Susan? A field camp in Tanzania's no place for a child."

"I know that. I wouldn't want to take her out of school, anyway. She's staying with Mom until June 17."

"And then?"

"Then she'll join me in Kenya."

"Traveling alone! Derek, that's crazy. She's only seven."

"Seven going on seventeen," he said with a chuckle, "from the way she talks sometimes. I think Suzie could handle herself."

"Derek . . ."

"Simmer down. She won't be traveling alone. Mom's taking her."

"Oh." Kate was caught by surprise. "Is Roger going, too?"

"If he can get away." Their stepfather seldom took vacations.

"What if he can't?"

"Are you volunteering?"

"Of course not."

"Then I guess Mom will go."

"I guess so," she said with unnecessary defiance.

AFTER SEEING DEREK OFF, Kate found herself wandering aimlessly through the main terminal of Kennedy Airport. It was swarming with purposeful people heading someplace. The crowds made her feel more alone. She passed a series of phone booths. On impulse, she took out her credit card and dialed her mother's number in Chevy Chase.

"Did Derek get off all right?" her mother asked.

"After a slight delay. I'm still at the airport." Kate hesitated, then said in a rush, "As long as I'm here, I thought I could catch a flight to Washington and spend the weekend." She'd had no such conscious intention when she'd picked up the phone, but why not? "Got a spare nightgown and toothbrush?" she asked.

If her mother was surprised, she didn't show it. "Sure, come ahead," she replied.

Kate was grateful that her mother asked no questions, but she felt a twinge of guilt that prompted her to say, "It's kind of short notice."

"Since when does a mother need notice? I'm glad you're coming. Shall I have Roger meet you?"

"No. I'll take a cab. See you in a couple of hours."

Kate felt better when she hung up. Going to Washington was a spur-of-the-moment decision, but after seeing Derek off, she'd felt so lonely, and the thought of returning to her empty apartment depressed her. She felt the need to be with people she loved.

When she got to Chevy Chase, her mother was alone. "Roger took Susan and her soccer ball to Rock Creek

Park," her mother told her. "They'll be back around three. We have plenty of time to talk."

They sat at the kitchen table with steaming mugs of coffee. Her mother said nothing, just waited. Other than awareness of her malaise, Kate hadn't consciously acknowledged what had been on her mind, but now realized that a thought had been gnawing at her all day. When she'd seen Derek board his plane that morning, she'd had the unsettling feeling she should be going with him. Alex was going to meet Derek in Nairobi. Kate pictured Alex at the airport, striding forward with a welcoming smile. But in her mind, *she* was the one Alex should be greeting.

Her mother sipped her coffee patiently as Kate sorted out her thoughts. Finally Kate broke the silence. "It didn't seem right somehow."

"What?"

"My staying behind while Derek was on his way to Kenya."

Ellen Marlowe put her cup down and reached out to pat her daughter's hand. "I understand."

"Do you? I wish I did. It's not that I *want* to be there."

"It's because Alex is there."

"That's the problem." Kate's voice showed her frustration.

"It doesn't have to be."

"I was thinking," Kate said slowly, as if the idea were just taking shape, "that I could save you the trip...I could take Susan to Kenya." Kate realized, once she'd made the suggestion, that she'd been building up to this all day.

"That's a wonderful idea. Can you get away?"

"Before Alex left, Blackwell offered me a long holiday. I'm sure the offer's still good. I haven't taken a real vacation in years."

"Marvelous. It'll do you good."

"You don't mind?"

"Not a bit. Roger can't get away now, and I'd much rather make the trip with him later on."

"You really want to go back there, don't you?"

"Not permanently," Ellen said, her smile without rancor or regret. "That part of my life is over, but it was a good part."

"You're not bitter?"

"No. I prefer to remember how happy we were."

Kate hadn't forgotten the happy times, but they were always clouded by her father's death. That event was like a dark curtain that she had to penetrate to get back to her earlier feelings. Often she couldn't get beyond it. "I can't help thinking that Dad would still be alive if he'd chosen another place, another kind of life."

"Perhaps. But as you said, your father chose his life."

"But he didn't choose to get sent to his death."

Her mother looked puzzled. "Alastair wasn't *sent* to his death, Kate. It was an accident, a tragic accident."

"Which never would have happened if he'd stayed in America."

"Kate, it's over. Don't keep dwelling on the way your father died. Think of how he lived, of how happy he was in his work. There were safer, certainly more comfortable careers, but not for him. That was the man he was, Kate, and that was the person we loved. I think Alex is like that. To love such a man, you must accept what he is."

"I'm not sure I can."

When Roger and Susan returned, Kate told her niece they'd be traveling together. Susan was gleeful. "We're all gonna be there, just like Melanie said—Daddy and Uncle Alex and Melanie and me and you."

"Well, I don't know about Melanie," Kate said.

"She's going. She told me so."

"When?"

"When she came to tell Daddy goodbye."

Kate looked questioningly at her mother, but she, too, appeared surprised. "Derek brought Melanie around the last time she was in town," her mother said, "but neither one of them said anything about it. Why do you suppose she's going?"

Kate shrugged. "I guess we've each got our own reasons." She wished she were clearer about her own.

ON MONDAY, Kate got the okay from Harvey to take three weeks' vacation starting mid-June. When she got to her own office, her assistant was waiting.

"Guess what?" Beth asked excitedly.

"Good news or bad?"

"Great news. Ike Paulsen wants Melanie for a spot on *A.M. New York.*"

Kate called Ike, got the details and immediately telephoned Melanie. "It's this Thursday. Short notice, but can you do it?" Kate asked.

Melanie was ecstatic. "Are you kidding? Of course. But how come?"

"They're doing a series on women in adventurous occupations, and the woman scheduled for Thursday can't make it."

"Who was she?" Melanie asked.

"Trixie Beckworth, a drag racer. She broke her leg."

"What a break for me. Oops! No pun intended. I don't mean to sound callous, but I'd sell my soul for a spot on that program. What a great way to end up my tour. Kate, you're fabulous."

"Lucky this came up before your trip."

"How'd you know about my trip? I haven't had a chance to call you."

"Susan mentioned it."

"Look, I've got to run, so I can't talk now. I'll tell you more when I see you. How about I stop by your office after the show Thursday, and you tell me how it went? I'll bring a bottle of champagne to celebrate—that is, if there's anything to celebrate."

"Don't worry. You'll be great."

"Keep that thought," Melanie said.

Kate hung up. Melanie had been a good client, easy to work with, reliable and able to handle herself smartly in all the appearances Kate had arranged for her. Kate had no doubt that she'd do well on Thursday.

MELANIE ARRIVED a little before noon, smiling, still excited and waving a bottle of champagne.

"Did you see the show? What did you think?"

"You were terrific," Kate told her. "It was a good interview, really lively. You obviously hit it off with Graham." Doug Graham had cohosted the program.

"Yeah," Melanie agreed. "What a neat guy! I was afraid they'd stick me with what's her name—the one who comes across like little Mary Sunshine. That would never have gone as well. I'm better with men, don't you think?"

"I'm sure of it."

Melanie put the bottle on the desk and popped the cork. "So let's celebrate. The secretary outside gave me some paper cups." Melanie dug them out of her shoulder bag. "Not elegant, but they'll do. What a day! Everything went just perfectly. I couldn't believe it. I was good, wasn't I?"

Kate laughed. "You know you were."

"Too bad Alex and Derek couldn't have been here to see it."

"I've got it on tape."

"Great! Why didn't I think of that? Okay if I take it with me when I go?"

"Or I could."

"You?" Melanie was obviously surprised. "You're going to Kenya? You never said . . . But, then, I haven't seen you in a while. Still, Derek didn't say anything, either."

"Derek doesn't know yet. I just decided." Kate was making it sound like a casual decision.

"How about that." Melanie raised her cup. "Well, here's to a gala reunion. This is going to be fabulous. When are you leaving?"

"As soon as Susan's school is out, June 17. Maybe you can get on the flight with us, and we can travel together."

"No, I can't wait that long." Melanie took a sip of her champagne. "Otherwise I'd have offered to take Susan. I'm wait-listed for Sunday."

"This Sunday?" Melanie nodded. "What's the rush?" Kate asked.

"That's the way I am. Once I decide on something, I've just got to get to it."

"Then this isn't just a pleasure trip?"

Melanie grinned. "Oh, I hope there'll be some pleasure involved."

"But that's not your main purpose?"

"Pleasure's always one of my main purposes. Work and pleasure make a great combination. I want to do a follow-up book, this time focusing on Tanzania. My agent thinks it's a good idea, since this one's doing so well. But we should get moving on it, so there's not too big a gap."

"A sequel?" Kate was surprised. "Has Alex agreed to do it?"

"I'll find out when I see him. You know who gave me the idea originally? Derek. He suggested that Tanzania would be a fascinating study, and why didn't I go while he was there. That's when I thought about maybe coaxing Alex into another book.''

"That's probably not what Derek had in mind.''

Melanie frowned. "I'm not always sure what's on Derek's mind. He runs hot and cold on me.''

"Maybe he's jealous of Alex.''

"He doesn't have to be.'' Melanie gave her a speculative look. "I'll level with you, Kate. When I first met Alex, I had some romantic notions. He's one helluva guy, and there we were, working together in an exotic setting. Alex was like the romantic hero every woman imagines for herself. But I soon realized I wasn't the heroine in his love story. We're friends, that's all. Lucky for me I didn't have a real case on him, because it wouldn't have done me a bit of good. The way he kept talking about the past, when you'd all lived together, I finally figured it out. He was hung up on someone he hadn't seen in thirteen years.'' She gave a short laugh. "Me—I can't even remember the names of my college boyfriends. I figured that unless Alex could get you out of his system, he'd never be able to let another woman into his life.'' She gave Kate a meaningful look. "He needed to see you again for that to happen.''

"And you think it has?'' The evenness of Kate's voice came from a surface control. Inside, her emotions were churning.

Melanie shrugged. "Well, he did cut his trip short. He did leave.''

Something deep inside of Kate cried out, *no, that's not true. It's not over.*

"But maybe I'm wrong,'' Melanie said. "Do you want me to be?''

Kate didn't answer.

"What a crazy situation!'' Melanie exclaimed. "It's like the convoluted plot in a Shakespearean comedy—you, me,

Alex, Derek." She paused, wrinkling her forehead into worry lines. "Derek's another one who's dragging around heavy baggage from the past."

"Everybody does."

"Not like you three. There must have been something about growing up in Africa, something elemental that makes for fierce loyalties."

"We were very close."

"That's an understatement. God, you paired off practically from infancy, Derek and Elizabeth, Alex and you. Derek told me how you all were. He made it sound as though everything that happened had been inevitable."

"Including the way it all ended? Did he say that was inevitable, too?"

"No. He said it was a horrible accident."

"He wasn't there."

"That's why you've never gone back, isn't it?"

"Yes."

"But you're going now?"

"Yes."

"This is going to be quite a reunion," Melanie said. "We've all got such different agendas."

But with interesting and confusing interconnections, Kate thought. "What will you do if Alex says no to another book?" she asked.

"Oh, I'll do it, anyway. Derek may be able to help me make arrangements in Tanzania. I'm prepared for all eventualities," Melanie declared with a breezy smile. "How about you?"

Kate hesitated, then said, "I'll take it as it comes."

That was the way she used to feel, eager for each day's happenings and ready to deal with whatever occurred. Could she recapture the spontaneity of that long-ago time? She might discover that there was no going back, that those feelings were buried in the past. Melanie had suggested Alex had needed to see Kate again to get her out of his system. Perhaps Kate had to make a similar pilgrimage, to be with Alex on his home territory in order to free herself. It would be ironic if making this trip proved, once and for all, that she could never go back. The finality of that realization would enable her to get on with her life, to break the bond that she had allowed to tether her to the past and to Alex.

Kate took a deep breath. "I have a feeling this is going to be a very eventful trip for all of us."

"And a happy one," Melanie added, sounding more wistful than sure.

"Let's hope so."

CHAPTER SEVEN

"LOOK! THERE'S NAIROBI. I can see it. Aunt Kate, look."

Susan couldn't contain her excitement. After they'd changed planes at Frankfurt, the exhausted child had slept for most of this last segment of the long trip. However, as soon as the pilot announced they were approaching the Jomo Kenyatta Airport, she was wide-awake. "Yes, I see, darling," Kate said.

It was just after daybreak, and as the plane circled, the city below was bathed in golden light. "The city in the sun," Kate said softly, remembering the phrase from some long-lost time. During most of the seemingly endless flight, Kate had nervously oscillated between the two extremes of apprehension and anticipation. Now, with the Kenyan capital in sight, she felt suddenly calm.

When they were on the ground, Kate heard an exclamation from the woman who was seated behind her. "What a grueling trip! Boy, am I glad it's finally over."

Kate knew that her own journey was just beginning.

As soon as they deplaned, a tall uniformed man greeted them. "Miss Katherine Marlowe?"

"Yes."

He inclined his head toward Susan. "And this must be Miss Susan Marlowe."

Susan was delighted to be addressed thus. "That's me."

"Please come this way," he said. He led them to a quieter area and into an office. The first person Kate saw was

Alex. Propelled by a rush of joy, Kate was headed straight into his arms, when she noticed Derek and Melanie behind them. She halted self-consciously. Derek, with a whoop of happiness, lifted up his daughter and gave her a bear hug. Melanie was chattering her greetings and asking about the trip. But as Alex took Kate's hands, his welcoming smile lighting up his face, all else faded for Kate.

"You're here," he said. "I can't believe it."

"I'm not sure I do, either," she replied. "It doesn't seem real yet."

"We'll make it real," he promised. "You'll see."

His welcoming kiss was perfunctory, but his eyes promised a warmer embrace later.

Alex's friend, the man who had brought them through the lines, quickly stamped their passports. "I hope you enjoy your stay with us. Is this your first visit to our country?"

Kate didn't know how to answer. "In a way it is," she said. She'd lived here long ago, but had now come as a visitor. Alex gave her a curious look.

"Let's go," Derek said. "Our driver's outside."

"What about the luggage?"

"It'll be sent to the hotel. Alex made the arrangements."

Susan was thrilled to see that their vehicle was not a taxi but a safari van. The driver, a tall robust black man, welcomed them with a cheerful *"Jambo."* Kate smiled. It was years since she'd heard that familiar greeting. Alex introduced him as his friend Richo. Richo spoke excellent English, but with an intonation that Kate recognized as Kikuyu.

The van was white with zebra stripes. "Do you know what animal is striped like that?" Richo asked Susan.

"The zebra."

"Right. In Swahili we call it *punda milia*. Can you say that?"

"Punda milia," she repeated carefully.

"Very good. We'll have you talking like a native in no time. Now how would you like to sit up front with me?" he asked, and immediately captured her affection.

"Oh, can I? And with the top up like that one?" She pointed to another van.

"Of course."

They stood outside the van while Richo raised the top. The air still held morning freshness, but the sun was increasing in intensity as it rose above the horizon. Kate felt its warmth enter her body and soothe her tiredness. Derek started describing the cave art that had been found recently in Tanzania.

"It's fascinating, Kate." Melanie chimed in. "I've never seen anything like it. You ought to see it."

"So you got the material you wanted for your research," Kate said to Derek.

"Not yet."

"You're going back?" Kate was surprised.

"There's a seminar I've been asked to attend. The biggest honchos in archaeology and art history are going to be there. Kate, this is one of the finds of the century, a marvelous break for me."

"What about Susan?"

"We have that all figured out," Alex said. Before he could explain, however, his attention was drawn to a huge, ponderous-looking man heading their way.

"Alexander, what a coincidence," the man said. His formal, British-accented speech matched his appearance—impeccably tailored business suit, starched white shirt, striped tie. "Are you traveling? I do hope you've changed your mind about attending that conference in London."

"I haven't changed my mind. But I see you have another traveling companion." With a grim expression, Alex gestured toward another man, who stayed back and waited.

"Harry Lunt? No, he's not going with me. He kindly offered me a ride to the airport. That's all."

"Is it? Lunt isn't known for his kindly gestures."

"Rumors...rumors." The man dismissed them with an impatient wave of the hand. "Nothing proven. Harry is anxious to be a part of the new Kenya."

"I'll bet."

The portly man ignored Alex's sarcasm. "Sorry you're not coming to London, Alex. It might have been productive to travel together and talk further about our mutual concerns."

Alex's expression remained grim. "I doubt there's anything further to talk about. Unfortunately our concerns are far from being mutual."

"Progress should be everybody's concern," the man replied with a cold smile. "Since you are not traveling, I presume you are here to welcome visitors." The smile became more benign as it took in the others.

Kate sensed Alex's reluctance as he made the introductions. The man's name was Peter Bazeek. After a flowery speech of welcome and an invitation to dine with him on his return, Mr. Bazeek departed.

"Bazeek? Isn't he some big shot in Parliament?" Derek asked.

"He is. He's also angling to replace Steven Ngelindi on the President's Advisory Council for Development."

"I gather you two do not see eye to eye," Derek said.

"That's putting it mildly. At best we've been cordial enemies. I suspect that cordiality is at an end—especially if he's teaming up with a snake like Harry Lunt."

"Does that mean trouble for you?" Kate asked.

"I'm not sure." Alex shook off his seriousness and smiled at her. "But there's going to be a hiatus for a couple of weeks at least. The president's leaving tomorrow for an extended goodwill tour to North America and western Europe, so political shenanigans are on hold for a while. Perfect timing, isn't it?" His dark eyes filled with warmth. "We don't have to think of anything else..."

Except being together was the way Kate's mind completed his sentence.

"We're ready to go," Richo called. They climbed into the van and were on their way.

Kate was quiet on the drive into the city. She slid back the window and gazed out. There was nothing especially picturesque about the countryside here, but she was acutely aware that this was Kenya—the distinctive flavor of the air, the heat of the sun, that spreading acacia up ahead and the amazing vastness of the sky. When they got into Nairobi, however, the sights and smells and sounds changed. The city had all the bustle of any large metropolis. Most of the people in the streets wore Western clothes, and the store signs were in English. But then they passed a market square where the myriad colors of various native costumes brightened the scene.

"Where are we staying?" Kate asked.

"Where else?" Alex answered.

Kate smiled. Their parents had always taken them to the Norfolk, preferring its old-fashioned decor and ambience to the newer high-rise hotels.

When they pulled up in front of the hotel, Kate marveled at the new buildings on the university grounds opposite. The hotel, however, looked endearingly the same. A few people were having a late breakfast in the outdoor café. Kate and Derek and Alex glanced at one another and almost in unison said, "Ice cream sodas," at which they broke into laughter.

"I gather this is another little reminiscence," Melanie said dryly.

"That's what we always had first thing when we came here," Derek explained.

"Can we have one now?" Susan asked.

Alex grinned. "Sure, why not?" He asked Richo to join them and the six of them settled around a large table. Alex ordered. "One strawberry and two chocolate ice cream sodas." He didn't have to ask Kate and Derek.

"I want the same like Daddy," Susan said.

"Make that another strawberry soda," Alex told the waiter.

"I think I'll pass," Melanie said, and she and Richo ordered coffee. Kate sensed that Melanie felt left out.

"Elizabeth and I used to come here once in a while when we were at the university," Derek said. "We'd splurge and have dinner, then live on porridge and toast for a week."

"Did you have strawberry sodas?" Susan asked.

"Sometimes. Your mother liked vanilla."

"I'll have that next time."

He leaned over to kiss her cheek. "Sure."

Alex started to talk about his own experiences at the university. Kate suspected he deliberately changed the subject for Melanie's sake.

They finished and were about to go inside, when Kate noticed that a small truck had pulled up and was unloading luggage. "I think our bags have arrived."

"Which ones are yours?" Richo asked.

"The two gray ones on the end there."

"And yours?" he asked Susan.

"I'll show you. Come on."

With Richo following, Susan ran down to where the bags were being piled on the street. She pointed to a green duffel bag. "That's mine," she told Richo.

A porter grabbed it and placed it next to Kate's. *"Moja?"* he asked Susan.

Richo repeated the man's question in English. "Only one?"

Susan held up two fingers.

"Two is *mbili*," Richo told her. Susan dutifully repeated the word and pointed to her second suitcase.

The others had been watching from the porch. "I think Suzie's got her mother's gift for languages," Derek said. "Remember how Elizabeth could pick up any dialect? And not just to mimic the sounds—she understood what was said."

"Elizabeth claimed she didn't have to translate words because she could read people's minds," Alex recalled.

"She was joking," Kate said.

Alex shrugged. "Maybe."

"Daddy," Susan called, "Richo's going to show me the birds in the courtyard, okay?"

"Okay. We'll be along in a minute." He watched the little girl skip off with Richo. "She seems to love it here already."

"What's not to love?" Melanie said. "She's having a holiday."

"I want it to be more than that for her," Derek said.

Kate felt a stab of uneasiness. Each of them had his or her own expectations about this trip, and she already sensed the conflicts ahead.

DEREK KNOCKED on his sister's door from the bathroom connecting their rooms. "Susan's asleep," he said. "She was out like a light the minute her head hit the pillow. I've got some business at the university that'll take about an hour. Can we leave these doors open in case she wakes up?"

"Sure. I probably won't sleep much. I just need to shower and change. I feel I've been in these clothes for a week."

"You should get some rest. Your system's still on New York time."

"Which is why I'm better off staying up, then crashing tonight."

"No jet lag?"

"Mind over matter. I refuse to give in to it."

Derek shook his head and laughed. "You always were a stubborn cuss. See you later."

When he'd gone, Kate stripped and got into the shower. She turned the water on full force, enjoying the impact of the heavy stream, then the flow of it over her. She felt a heightened sensitivity. She closed the hot water and finished off under an icy shower. As she toweled herself dry, her skin felt cool and tingling, but her blood spread warmth through her body. She put on a light cotton robe and went to check on Susan. Fully clothed, the little girl was still fast asleep.

In her own room, Kate unpacked her suitcases and put away her things. Then she propped herself up against the pillows and relaxed on the bed. She turned on the radio, and smiled to hear Frank Sinatra singing "My Way." So far there had been nothing traumatic about this visit, but she was aware of the reservoir of apprehension she had inside. The airport, the city, this hotel room—they were not the Africa she feared. People she loved were here, protected by the trappings of civilization. But only a three-hour drive to the west was the vastness of the Masai Mara....

Kate closed her eyes. Pictures flooded her mind. Awake...asleep...somewhere in between, a kaleidoscope of images flashed on a screen as if someone had programmed her past and were playing it in fast forward. There were lovely scenes that she wanted to keep from hurtling by—a picnic, riding the baby elephant with Alex, the sunset from Pambazuko, herself and Alex racing up the hill, the two of them on safari with their fathers—but each quickly gave way to the next. Then the final picture approached; Kate moaned and shook herself awake to drive it away. She sat up, hugging herself, rubbing her arms to smooth her prickling skin.

The jarring sound of the telephone brought her fully into the present. It was Alex on the line.

"Are you all right?" he asked. "Your voice sounds strained."

"Just tired."

"I shouldn't have disturbed you. You probably want to sleep."

"No—please. I really don't. I was just going to call room service and order some tea."

"Why not meet me in the café?"

"I can't. Derek went off somewhere and Susan's sleeping. I promised to stay around."

"Then why don't I join you?"

"All right. Give me a minute to dress."

"If you must," he said.

She laughed at the teasing tone and felt her coldness begin to fade.

"I'll call room service," he offered. "I'll give you ten minutes, okay?"

"Fine."

It took her less than that to change into a full-skirted green cotton dress. Room service and Alex arrived at the same time. Alex instructed the waiter to set the table on the balcony, then he signed the check and sent the man away with a large tip and a happy smile.

"Sandwiches, too," Kate noted as she sat down.

"I'm hungry. Aren't you?"

"I shouldn't be. It seemed as if the flight attendants on the plane were serving something every hour."

"Airline food doesn't stay with you."

"You're thinking of Chinese food."

"Whatever." He finished half the tray of sandwiches in no time. "You're not keeping up," he told Kate.

"I've had enough." She leaned back in the wicker chair and sipped her tea. "Tell me about that man we saw at the airport."

"That's the wrong topic for a beautiful June afternoon."

Kate persisted. "Is he your enemy?"

"Let's just say he opposes some of the things I believe in."

"You said he wants Steve Ngelindi's position on the President's Advisory Council. Do you think he'll get it?"

"Not if I can help it. But why are we talking about this?"

"Because it's important to you."

"Right now, what's important," he said, reaching across the table for her hand, "is that you're here . . . finally." He kept hold of her as he rose and came around; then he pulled her up into his arms.

His touch sent a trembling warmth through her. He kissed her, and his kiss blotted out her apprehension. Kate's mind drained of all thoughts except Alex, the touch and feel and smell of him.

"You can't imagine how much I've missed you," he whispered against her lips.

Kate pulled her head back. "Is that why you wrote such long letters?" she teased. She'd received only two brief notes from him since he'd left the States.

"I'm no good at writing, and long distance wooing's not my forte. But now that I've got you here..."

"Yes?"

"You'll see."

"When?" she asked provocatively.

They heard Susan's voice before she appeared in the doorway.

"Unfortunately not now," Alex said with a smile of resignation as Kate drew away.

"I thought no one was here," Susan complained. "Where's Daddy?"

Kate understood her niece's crankiness. Waking up alone in a strange place must have frightened her. "He had to go out for a little while, but he'll be back soon," she said reassuringly.

Alex took Susan's hand and led her to the table. "I'll bet you're hungry. How about some tea sandwiches?"

Susan brightened. "What kind?"

Alex pulled over another chair and sat her on it. "All kinds. You can have one of each."

Susan managed to eat three before giving up. Her good spirits had returned. "How come you call them 'tea sandwiches'? Sandwiches can't be made of tea," she said with a giggle.

"Because they're served with tea, that's why," Alex replied.

"I don't have any tea," Susan pointed out. "Can I have some of yours?"

"Sure."

Susan took a swallow from his cup, made a face and said, "Milk's better."

Alex reached for the small jug of milk on the tray. "No sooner said than done. I'll pour you a cup."

"Is the milk safe?" Kate asked.

"Sure," Alex said, handing Susan her milk. "Everything's pretty safe in hotels like this. It's out in the country that you have to be careful of what you eat and drink."

"Why?" Susan wanted to know.

"Because you've got American bacteria in your belly, and they have to get used to the Kenyan bacteria they're going to meet."

"What's bacteria?"

"Little microorganisms."

"What's micro... what you said?" Susan asked.

"See what you started," Kate said with a laugh.

At that moment Derek appeared. "You're just in time," Alex said hurriedly. "Your daughter's thirst for knowledge has her inquiring about bacteria and other microorganisms. Kate and I have to go. Your father will answer all your questions," he assured Susan. "See you later."

"Where are you off to?" Derek asked.

"We have a date," Alex said, propelling Kate toward the door.

When they were outside, Kate asked, "Whom do we have a date with?"

"Each other." He took her hand.

"Where are we going?"

"Not far." They walked down the corridor and around a corner. Alex paused by a door and took out a key.

"Alex Crane, are you trying to entice me into your room?"

He grinned. "Guilty. Do you mind?"

A spiral of warmth crept through her body.

"I need to be with you," Alex said.

She would be lying if she denied that she shared that need. Her smile gave Alex the assent he wanted.

Inside, the door locked behind them, Alex took her in his arms and buried his face in the silken gold of her hair. He kissed her and felt her melt against him. It had been so long…too long…for both of them. He ran his hands down her back, around her waist, over her hips, relishing the slender strength of her body. The thin material of her dress was smooth, but he craved the softness of her skin. Alex undid the front buttons, drew the dress away from her shoulders and let it drop. She trembled as he unclasped her bra and lowered his head to taste the throbbing fullness of her breasts. Then he removed her panties and lovingly surveyed her naked beauty.

"My turn now," Kate whispered.

"Feel free," he said, and rejoiced when she took the same liberty with him. But when she was finished and he had pulled her nude body against him, he brimmed with an urgency that could not be stemmed. Kate's fingers dug into his shoulders, her body arched to his, and the appeal in her eyes reflected her equally compelling need. He lifted her in his arms and carried her to the bed, where he lay down beside her.

Alex tried to prolong their lovemaking, to savor Kate's beauty and passion, but desire quickly rose in a frenzied spiral. Her soft moans indicated she was ready, and he held back, wanting to experience the force of her orgasm; then he allowed it to trigger his own.

Afterward he held her close, hoping she felt the same deep fulfillment. He hated the thought of her ever having been with another man. But, then, he'd not been celibate during the past years, either. Yet, holding Kate like this, their bodies still warm from lovemaking, he knew that no other woman could ever mean as much to him. Loving Kate was more than a physical act. She was a part of him, and their sexual union reflected and was powered by that mutual belonging.

The problem was that her love for him was linked to what she feared. Once that fear was resolved, however, Kate would change. She would feel free to love. He was determined to see that happen.

THAT NIGHT, the whole group went to the Carnivore, a popular restaurant just outside of town. People were waiting in line for a table, but the maître d' beckoned them forward and led them to a table on the patio. "This is fine, Simon," Alex told him.

"You must be a favored customer," Kate said when they'd sat down.

"Not really. Simon happens to be a friend. This isn't my kind of place."

"I love it," Melanie said. "Did you see that huge open pit? They grill every kind of meat imaginable. Last time I had impala."

A stream of waiters placed serving dishes of vegetables on a revolving platform in the center of the table. "I can't reach," Susan said. She was sitting between her father and Melanie.

Melanie took Susan's plate and swung the server around. "Know what they call this?" she asked the little girl.

"What?"

"A lazy Susan."

"How come?"

"It was probably invented by some smart girl named Susan to save herself the trouble of serving people."

Susan thought that over, then declared, "They should've called it a smart Susan."

"You've got a point," Melanie said, giving Susan a hug.

The waiters started bringing skewers of different kinds of meat. Alex and Kate both shunned the game meat.

"You don't eat game?" Melanie asked.

Alex answered for both of them. "We prefer not to make a meal of an animal that should roam freely."

"Don't cattle and sheep have the right to roam freely? You're being inconsistent."

"I know," Kate said, "but that's how we feel."

Melanie looked from one to the other, shrugged, then speared another piece of meat.

After dinner they relaxed with liqueurs and coffee, while Susan dug into a huge serving of ice cream. Kate suddenly realized that neither Melanie nor Alex had mentioned the sequel Melanie wanted to do.

"What's the status on another book?" She addressed the question to both of them. "Are you going to do it?"

"I'm afraid not," Alex said.

"I couldn't talk him into it. The man's got other things on his mind," Melanie said, giving Kate a meaningful look.

"I'm sorry," said Kate, not too truthfully.

"Don't be," Melanie told her. "I'll do another African book, but I'm considering a different focus. Derek's already given me a couple of ideas, maybe something on primitive art of the past and present. When we get back to Tanzania—"

"The two of you are going back?" Kate interrupted.

"For that seminar they're having," Derek explained. Kate remembered his having mentioned it earlier. "Melanie can take her pictures while I'm tied up with work and meetings. I'm getting valuable material for my doctoral dissertation. Really great stuff. There's enough research to keep scholars busy for a year."

"You don't have a year."

"I know. I'm only going back for a week."

"And Susan?"

"Alex and I have that all figured out," Derek announced. "It fits right in with your plans."

"Mine?" Kate frowned. "I wasn't aware I'd made any plans."

"You can't intend to spend your whole time here in Nairobi," Derek said reasonably.

"Why not?" Kate had not projected beyond her arrival and seeing Alex again.

"That's silly."

She stiffened, and her fingers tightened around her glass. "I don't think so." Here in the city she felt safe, insulated from what lay beyond.

"I thought you might like to see what your publicity efforts are going to help promote," Alex said. In a casual gesture, he covered her left hand, which had been resting on the table. "I've got a contingent of nineteen young people out on a summer safari. These are the first of many, I hope."

Kate remembered how important this Jambo Youth Safari project was to Alex.

"I'd planned to travel around with them this time, at least for a while, to see how things go, catch any problems that might come up," he continued.

"Don't let me interfere with your plans," Kate remarked coolly.

"You're part of those plans," Alex said with quiet insistence. "I thought you'd enjoy coming along."

Kate's fingers would have clenched had it not been for Alex's protective hand over them. "I don't think I can."

"Sure, you can. You won't have to rough it, unless you want to. Our camps are always near one of the game lodges, so you can stay there if you prefer."

"Some of them are positively luxurious," Melanie offered. "Tourist heavens. You hardly realize you're smack in the heart of a wildlife preserve."

"You'll be completely safe. We take care of our tourists," Alex told Kate.

So he was relegating her to that category. Well, that was all right with Kate. This could never be home again. She would be content to spend her three-week stay as a tourist. Perhaps it was the way she could safely confront her past. After all, she hadn't come to cower by herself in the city. She'd come to be with Alex, then to...

Kate couldn't complete the thought. *One hurdle at a time,* she told herself. "All right," she finally said. "I'm game."

Alex's smile was one of relief—and promise. "You won't be sorry."

The plan was that Susan and her father would spend a week at the seashore in Mombasa, and then Susan would join Alex and Kate for the second week. "When I get back, Suzie and I can spend some time with her grandmother," Derek said. "How does that sound to you, Suzie? First the beach, then camping with Alex and Kate."

Susan nodded furiously and, with a mouth full of ice cream, said something that sounded like "Good."

As they waited for Susan to finish, a slight man in a dark suit came over to their table. Kate recognized him as Bazeek's companion at the airport, the one who had hovered in the background. He had straight black hair and sharp, narrow eyes. Eurasian, Kate guessed. Alex introduced Harry Lunt, then stepped away for a few minutes' conversation with the man. When Alex returned, he looked angry.

"Bad news?" Derek asked.

"That man is bad news personified," Alex replied, then changed the subject.

Later that night, when they were alone in her room, Kate inquired about Lunt. "Another political enemy like Bazeek?"

"No. Bazeek's a bull, but he's up-front about what he wants. At least he has been until now. Lunt's a weasel. Their joining forces could be bad news, though. Lunt runs an import-export business, but his main trade's smuggling."

"What kind of smuggling?"

"Anything that pays well. Unfortunately rhino tusks are very lucrative. He's got a network of poachers who get him what he wants."

"I thought rhinos were protected as an endangered species."

"They are, but that doesn't mean a thing to Lunt, not with the tusks bringing top dollar in the Orient. With the whole species in danger of extinction, the government's trying to round up the rhinos and bring them to a protected habitat."

"So what's the problem?"

"Lunt. He heard about this being in the works. The bastard thought he could pump me for information. He probably wants to get as much as he can while it's still possible. He's got to be stopped."

"You're involved in so many crusades," Kate said.

He gave her a crooked smile. "Why make it sound like some sort of affliction?"

"If it exposes you to danger, that's what it is," she said.

He took her hands, but she resisted being drawn to him.

"Kate, danger's a part of being alive. You can't play it safe all the time."

"Why not?" she shot back, her question heartfelt.

"Because that would be like being half-alive, and that's not good enough for us."

She stopped resisting and let him pull her against him. In his arms, feeling the dynamic tension of his body, seeing his eyes kindle with desire, Kate felt her own passion flare. *Not good enough for us.* Alex used to know her mind as he did his own, and could speak for both of them. For a little while Kate would let herself believe this was still true.

They made love with an all-consuming passion that would not be sated. Awakening in the middle of the night, they came together again. Afterward Kate burrowed into his arms. "I wish we could hold back tomorrow...make this night last forever," she whispered.

"What? And miss all that's going to come?"

She smiled at his eagerness, then hid her face against his shoulder so he wouldn't see the apprehension in her eyes.

CHAPTER EIGHT

ALEX HATED TO WAKE HER. Seeing her like this, her silken hair strewn over the pillow, he felt an outpouring of love. After they'd made love last night, Kate had fallen into a deep sleep, her tiredness finally catching up with her. Customarily a light sleeper, anyway, Alex found himself awakening at intervals, as if to assure himself she was really there, curled up against him.

He knew that coming to Africa was a big step for Kate. She kept reminding him it was only for a visit, but if he could, Alex meant to make it more. In a way, it would be a step back to the past, to face whatever it was she feared; and then, even more important, a step forward toward their future together. If they were to have one. Alex wanted to believe they would, but first there were barriers that had to come down.

All these years he'd held Kate in his mind and in his heart. Not that he'd had any choice. He couldn't have torn her out of him without ripping the fabric of his being. He'd known other women, enjoyed their company and, at times, their sexual favors. Making love with Kate was so different, involving him totally, and on a deeper level than he'd ever thought possible.

As she lay there asleep, her sweet vulnerability aroused all his protective impulses. Yet he knew he couldn't shield her from the pain of experience. Kate had tried to protect herself, but in the process had stifled a vital part of her. He wasn't sure what these next weeks would bring. *One day at a time,* he told himself. *At least we're off to a good start.*

Alex kissed her softly on the mouth and smiled when she murmured his name without wakening. He looked at the bedside clock—seven o'clock. He was tempted, but decided it would be a crime to wake her from such a deep sleep. Slipping out of bed, he dressed quickly. He found some hotel stationery and wrote a note, which he placed on his pillow. At the door he turned for another look, and almost changed his mind. Then he sighed, congratulated himself on his self-control and closed the door quietly behind him.

STILL HALF-ASLEEP, Kate reached over, seeking Alex. She had slept soundly until just now, when vaguely erotic dreams had made her restless. But last night had been better than any dream. Her hand found only a crumpled pillow to caress. "Alex..." Disappointment shook her wide-awake. He'd gone. Then she read his note and smiled:

> Duty calls. I have a couple of things to take care of this morning. Meet me for lunch at the Thorn Tree at twelve.

She looked at the bedside clock—ten-thirty. She never slept this long, but it must have done her good, for she felt wonderful. She chose a cheerful outfit to reflect her mood, a white cotton skirt, bright yellow top and a matching scarf to tie back her hair.

She was about to go out, when there was a knock on the door. Alex? Had he changed his mind and come back early? She flung open the door, but it was Melanie who stood there.

"Good morning. How's the jet lag?" Melanie asked.

"Nonexistent. I feel great. Come on in."

Melanie sauntered in and looked around. "Nice room. It's larger than mine." She went over to the window. "Isn't it a glorious day? I hate it when it rains, don't you? Have you ever been here during the rainy season?" Noticing Kate's expression, she gave a little laugh. "But of course you have. You all used to live here—you, Alex, Derek and Elizabeth."

Kate thought she detected a wistful tone, but it was gone when Melanie asked, "Have you had breakfast yet? I thought we could go down together."

"I'm not big on breakfast," Kate replied. "Why don't you try Derek and Susan next door? They should be up by now."

"Up and out. I checked," Melanie said. "Derek's the kind that's awake at the crack of dawn. Yesterday he mentioned taking Susan to the university, to meet some of his old professors. They're probably long gone. Come on, join me. It's late enough so you can call it brunch."

Kate looked at her watch. "Not when I'm meeting Alex for lunch in an hour."

"Now that's another story." Melanie grinned. "I'm happy for you. For Alex, too." She paused, then continued, "Not that you don't know it already, but I sure read him wrong. Remember that conversation we had back in New York?"

Kate nodded.

"I said I thought Alex had finally gotten over you. Well, you should have seen him when he heard you were coming—the guy's nuts about you, Kate. He's yours if you want him, and if you don't you're a damn fool." Melanie managed a wry smile. "And when it comes to damn fools, I know whereof I speak."

"Problems?" Kate asked.

"Yeah."

"You and Derek?"

"You got it." Melanie gave a deep sigh. "I've never been in this kind of situation before. Usually a guy is interested or he's not. Either way I know where I stand. But not with Derek. I think he loves me, but there's a lot for us to work out, especially for him. Kate, I know you two are pretty tight. Has he talked to you about me?"

"No, but Derek's the kind who lets things stew in his mind for a long time."

"Tell me about it." Melanie sounded frustrated. "Sometimes, when we're together, everything's just great. Then suddenly he backs away again."

"It took Derek a long time to get over losing Elizabeth."

"Has he gotten over her? Sometimes I wonder."

Kate could understand Melanie's doubts. Derek had kept alive his memory of love as a substitute for the real thing. "What with work, graduate school and being a single parent, Derek hasn't had much time for himself these past few years," Kate said. "Susan always comes first." She gave Melanie a questioning look. "Maybe he's not sure you can accept Susan."

"Accept her? Are you kidding? I love that kid."

To Kate she looked defensive, as if expecting an argument, and also very vulnerable.

"Fooled you, didn't I?" Melanie asked. "Bet you never thought of me as the maternal type. Funny thing is, neither did I—but there it is."

Kate found herself believing Melanie. The realization of love came differently to people. She recalled how quickly Susan and Melanie had taken to each other from the very first. "Susan needs a mother," Kate said.

"The problem with Derek is that 'mother' means a reasonable facsimile of the one Susan had, and I don't fit the description. Wrong temperament and wrong heredity. But I'm working on it," Melanie said.

"Which? Temperament or heredity?"

"I can't do much about either. I'm not part Masai, and as for temperament—I am what I am. What I'm working on is changing Derek's narrow view. I can't be Elizabeth's replacement."

"Yet you said he loves you."

"I think he does. We're great together most of the time. We're even talking about doing a book on primitive African art. Maybe I can build that into a broader-based collaboration," she said with a grin. "I sure as hell am going to try."

"It might be a good idea if you went to Mombasa with Derek and Susan," Kate suggested.

"I'm way ahead of you," said Melanie. "I already invited myself along. Maybe Derek will get to like the idea of the three of us together."

"I hope things work out for you," Kate told her.

"For both of us," Melanie said.

KATE DECIDED AGAINST taking a taxi to the restaurant. When she left Melanie, it was still early enough, and the walk into town would give her a chance to think.

But her mind refused to function constructively. So many emotional threads were unraveling within their little group. Kate wondered how they'd be woven together. Melanie had once said something about Alex and Derek being hampered by baggage from the past. But that was true of all people, Kate thought, and Melanie was no exception.

For many reasons, Melanie had chosen a profession that provided independence and adventure. She had developed a forthright manner that verged on brazenness, using it to cut through red tape and get her job done. Making friends quickly was a natural talent, but her wandering life as a photojournalist had not been conducive to lasting relationships. If she felt differently now, Melanie would have her own problems reconciling the past with the present. She and Derek were an unlikely couple, Kate reflected, but maybe they would work things out. As for Alex and her...

Kate missed her turn and went down to Mama Ngina Street, then headed up Kimathi Avenue. She stopped to look at an assortment of gemstones in a store window, but was distracted by her own reflection—blond hair, yellow shirt, bright face—not like the murky muddle in her head. She made the reflection smile. Even better. The smile became real when she became aware of the owner who had come to the door of the shop. He wore a peculiar expression, and was obviously bemused by the young woman making faces at herself.

He began his sales pitch. "Won't you come..."

Kate glanced at her watch, a minute after twelve. Alex would be waiting. "Sorry, but I have to run. Another time," she promised, and hurried away. Inexplicably the incident lightened her mood.

When she got to the outdoor café, Kate searched the crowd for Alex. He was sitting at a table on the far side. He hadn't seen her yet. Kate paused to watch him for a moment.

Earlier she'd been contemplating the problem of reconciling the past with the present, but Alex didn't seem troubled by such thoughts. His sense of himself came from a fusion of both elements. He saw time as progression, without traumatic changes that altered his basic character. She couldn't argue with his vision of himself, but his vision of her—that was something else. It was rooted in the past, when they had loved each other with youthful abandon and had believed they would stay the same always. They had thought their world was beautiful, that they and those they loved would be safe and happy together forever. But *forever* didn't last.

Still, maybe they could recreate it for just a little while, Kate thought. Seeing Alex, his dark hair glinting in the sunlight, his face serene as he looked around, she believed it might be possible. She threaded her way over to him. With a welcoming smile, Alex rose, grabbed her hands and kissed her on the cheek. She sat down, and Alex pulled his chair close to hers. "Have you been waiting long?" she asked.

"About ten minutes."

They ordered cheese omelets and iced coffee. "You sneaked out this morning," Kate said.

"I didn't sneak. Besides, you were dead to the world."

"You should have wakened me."

"I didn't have the heart. Actually that's not quite true. I was tempted. My heart and body were allied in wanting to wake you, but my conscience said no to such selfishness. You needed to sleep."

"How very righteous of you!"

"Don't I deserve a reward?"

She had to laugh at his smiling appeal. "I'll see what I can do."

The waiter brought their lunch, and conversation took second place for a while. "That was good," Alex said, pushing back his empty plate. "I skipped breakfast this morning."

"Me, too. I hate to tell you what time I got up. Did you accomplish what you wanted to?"

"I did. Some loose ends to tie up before we leave. I also got in touch with a friend to see if Derek could borrow his villa in Mombasa. It's all set. He and Susan can have it for a week."

"Melanie's going with them."

"Fine. I figured she might. They'll love it. Plus it'll be good for the three of them to be off by themselves for a while. For us, too," he added.

"I thought we were joining your campers."

"We are, but we're not going to be locked into the group scene. I intend to see that we have a lot of private time." His voice held a seductive promise. "Starting tomorrow," he added.

Kate was startled. "Did you say tomorrow?"

"I did. We leave for Tsavo National Park in the morning."

"But that's too soon."

Alex frowned. "Too soon for what?"

"Too soon for me. I need time to get ready."

"What kind of readiness are we talking about? Clothes...a safari hat...a bush knife?"

"I don't appreciate your humor," she said stiffly.

"I'm sorry."

"Why can't we just stay here for a few more days?"

"Kate, listen to me. We can postpone leaving, but all that would do is give you a longer period in which to be apprehensive. What good would that accomplish?"

She realized he was right.

"One of the youth camps is in the Masai Mara," Alex continued, "right near where we lived. The compound's a ranger station now. A friend of mine, Jim McKendrick, is the senior game warden. He and his wife live in your old house, and I thought we'd stay with them and—" Her changed expression made him stop.

"Not the Mara," Kate said. A coldness clutched at her heart. "I couldn't go back there."

"Kate, there's nothing there to hurt you," he said gently. "Do you think I would let anything happen to you?"

Kate wasn't afraid for her physical safety. It was something else, intangible, hovering below her consciousness. She couldn't see it clearly herself, so how could she describe what she feared?

"I understand how you feel," Alex told her.

She shook her head. "You can't possibly." Her comment bothered him. "I'm not sure I understand myself sometimes." She forced a smile. "I don't see what's going to come out of this."

"That's what we're going to find out. That's what you came for, isn't it?"

"I came because of Susan."

"Your mother would have brought her."

"I also had some vacation to use up."

"All right. So let's make good use of it. Kate, why are we arguing? Do you think I'd force you into something you don't want? If you say so, the Masai Mara is out. Your father used to say you were the most willful girl on earth, and he was right."

"So why do you bother with me?"

He gave an exasperated laugh. "Because I can't help myself, damn it. I must be a sucker for willful women. Now are we through arguing or not?"

She had to smile at his frustration. "We're through."

"And we'll leave in the morning?"

She drew a deep breath. "We'll leave in the morning."

Alex gave a sigh of relief. "Thank God that's settled. Now we can enjoy the rest of the day."

"If you have other things to do..."

Alex interrupted. "I'm not leaving you alone for a minute. You might change your mind. For the rest of today, I want you to concentrate on our being together, nothing else."

But that night, Alex had his own troubling thoughts. He kept remembering Kate's remark that he couldn't possibly understand how she felt. Was there something different in her memory of the tragedy, something she'd never told him?

He recalled that in the aftermath of their fathers' accident, he'd tried to get Kate to express her grief. She'd kept it all inside from the very first, when he had found her and told her what had happened. His mind traveled back, seeking to remember.

It had been a strange day. Kate was upset that morning because Rusty, her pet donkey was still missing. Rusty often trotted along with them when Alex and Kate went cycling. The day before, Rusty had followed them to the glade, a fenced area with the crumbling remains of some abandoned workmen's shacks. It was one of the places Alex and Kate went to be alone. The afternoon had passed quickly as they'd talked and kissed and planned all the glorious things they would do together. The afternoon brightness had dimmed into evening when they started for home and realized that Rusty was gone. It was then they'd noticed that a portion of fence at the far end had been knocked over. Rusty had probably gotten out that way. Despite Kate's initial protests that she wanted to look for her pet, Alex had insisted they return home before it got dark.

In the morning Kate had wanted to go searching for Rusty, but her father had said the glade was now off-limits. He'd have to see about repairing the fence when he had time, but for now, it could be dangerous there. The two men then left for their routine inspection rounds. Kate had been disconsolate all morning until, just after lunch, Rusty wandered home by himself, badly scratched by thornbushes but none the worse for his adventure. Kate was relieved that her pet was all right and busied herself doctoring Rusty's wounds.

Kate wasn't around when Patrick Sloane had decided to go out after the two men and let Alex accompany him. No one was really alarmed yet. Vehicle breakdowns were common, and Patrick had gone on this same kind of mission before. But that day it wasn't the same. Sloane took the road the men would have traveled, even going beyond their usual route as far as the ranger station, but there was no sign of them. At the ranger station Sloane called the compound to report he hadn't found the men and was getting others to help search. Alex had known what fear that phone call must have aroused.

Sloane and Alex followed dirt tracks for another two hours before they got to the glade area. One of the search vehicles was there already, and a ranger came up and spoke to Sloane. Alex couldn't follow the native dialect, but he'd known something was wrong when Sloane made him stay in the van while he went to investigate. He returned and told Alex what had happened. Alex's father and Alastair Marlowe were dead. Their bodies had been taken to the clinic. Afterward Alex learned that Sloane had lied about that in order to spare Alex the grisly sight he'd just witnessed. They returned to the compound, where, from the anguished looks of the women, their news had been anticipated. But Kate wasn't anywhere around. Then Alex realized where he would find her—at Pambazuko.

Alex had struggled for the words to tell her, but it was as if she'd known what he wanted to say, and kept shaking her head in denial. There was such numb despair in her eyes, as if grief had permeated and frozen her being. He'd expected her to cry, but she never did, not then and not afterward. She had been untouchable, encased in the cold shock of what had happened.

There must indeed be something in her memory of that whole time that had made her grief more shattering than what any of them had experienced. But what? Alex was sorry that Kate had refused to go to the Mara. It was as though she feared something there. But that didn't make sense. Perhaps she would change her mind once they got out on safari. Somehow he felt it would be an important step for her—for both of them.

THE TWO GROUPS LEFT together early in the morning. Alex was loaning Derek his Land Rover, and he and Kate were being driven by Richo in the safari van.

Even Melanie, sleepy eyed but goodnatured, was on time for their 6:00 a.m. departure. "You made it," Alex teased.

"Hey, I'm a team player," she told him. "I sacrifice for the good of the group. I got up at the crack of dawn, with a little help from Derek, who acted as my alarm clock."

Derek's smile testified to his having enjoyed that particular duty.

"I was up before everybody else," Susan boasted.

Kate, who had slept very little, could have disputed her niece's claim. She'd known she wouldn't get much sleep and was glad they were leaving early. Prolonging her apprehension, as Alex had said, didn't make sense. She had decided to go with him on this... Kate didn't know what to call it. Pilgrimage to the past? Tourist safari? Romantic interlude? All of the above?

Kate wasn't sure what would come of the trip. She'd managed well in Nairobi the past couple of days, but the modern comforts of the capital didn't change the harsh reality of life but the modern comforts of the capital didn't change the harsh reality of life in the bush. They were as irreconcilable...as she and Alex were. But at least they would have this time together before they went their separate ways.

Susan was excited about leaving. "I put my bathing suit on top of my suitcase for when we get there," she exclaimed. "Can we go swimming today, Dad?"

"We'll see. It's a long trip. You may be too tired."

"I won't be." She was hopping around restlessly. "I wish Richo and Aunt Kate and Uncle Alex could come with us." The little girl was in a quandry—she was happy about going to the beach, disappointed they weren't all going, and wondered what she'd be missing by not riding in the safari van. She wanted to have it all.

"You'll be with them next week," Derek reminded her.

"And we're gonna sleep in a tent, right?" Susan asked Alex.

"Right," he assured her. "Now let's get going."

"No breakfast," Melanie asked.

"We'll stop on the way."

Derek opened the door of his vehicle. "Okay, move 'em out," he ordered.

Melanie grinned up at him. "This is Africa, not the Wild West. Stop making like a wagon master."

Kate was happy to see her brother so lighthearted. She hoped things would work out for him. They should, if he and Melanie loved each other. But then she remembered—love wasn't always enough....

Richo led the way, and soon they left the urban scene behind. For the first hour and a half, Kate gazed out of the window, aware in only a general way of what she was seeing. Alex sat next to her but made no attempt at small talk, for which she was grateful. She was sure he'd chosen the van as their conveyance so he could leave the driving to Richo. Alex wanted to be free to devote himself to her. But for the moment, she desired nothing from him. She had put her mind in limbo.

After a breakfast stop, Susan asked if she could ride with Richo for a while. Derek looked inquiringly at Alex. "Sure," Alex said. "We've got another two hours or more before we split up. The Tsavo Inn can be our next pit stop. Suzie can ride with us until then."

"With the top up?" Susan asked.

"Why not?" Richo raised the roof, Susan climbed in beside him and they were off. Having her with them was a welcome diversion for Kate. Susan kept up a running line of chatter and asked countless questions.

"What's those tufty things hanging from that tree?"

"Nests for the weaver birds."

"Why so many?"

"Because there are many birds."

"Oh." A moment later she pointed again. "That's a funny-looking tree."

"What does it remind you of?" Alex asked.

"I don't know," Susan answered.

"Look at the branches, the way they swing out, then curve upward. You know what a candelabra is?"

"Oh, yes." The comparison delighted her. "My friend Arnold's mother has one on her piano. Wait till I tell him there's trees like that."

Ahead of them, an elephant emerged from a clump of trees and was about to cross the road in front of them. Susan screamed, "There's an elephant, a real one." The sound of Susan's screeching and the squeal of Richo's tires as he braked caused the huge animal to stop and turn toward them. His ears flapped and his trunk flew up. Emitting a braying sound, the elephant advanced several steps, then stopped.

"He is giving us notice to stay back," Richo said in a quiet voice.

"What if we don't?" Susan asked. She sounded more excited than afraid.

"He might charge."

The elephant stood his ground for a few more seconds, then slowly turned and continued on his way.

"He was bluffing," Alex said softly, giving Kate's shoulder a squeeze.

He must have put his arm around her when he sensed her stiffening. Kate knew he was right. There was no danger. The elephant had been alone and was just warning them off. But that wasn't always the case. A charging elephant could overturn and trample a jeep and its occupants.

Kate shook off the dark memory and willed herself to relax and share Susan's pleasure.

When Susan spotted her first giraffe, she was so ecstatic she could hardly get the words out. "Oh...oh...look. It's a giraffe. No, it's two...no, there's four. Their necks are mixed up in the trees and I didn't see them at first."

Richo stopped the van, and then had to grab Susan who was ready to clamber out. "Not outside, little lady. You must never ever get out of the car."

Susan was contrite. "I know. Daddy told me. I forgot."

"This is their place, Suzie," Alex explained. "We're the visitors."

"I just wanted to see them from up close. Look, that one's eating leaves. What a long tongue he's got." Derek had pulled up beside them. "Daddy, do you see?" Susan yelled.."Oh, he's going away. Is he scared of us?"

"I doubt it," Alex said. "But as a general rule, it's better to be quiet when you stop and look at the animals."

They started off again. Susan was subdued for a while, but it didn't take long for her natural exuberance to surface. "What a funny-looking bird," she said, pointing. "He's running instead of flying."

"That one does very little flying," Richo told her. "It does its hunting on the ground."

"Birds don't hunt."

"Predator birds do."

"What's a pre . . . der bird?"

"A bird that hunts," Richo said with a laugh.

"What does he like to eat?"

"Lizards, small snakes, whatever he can get."

Susan thought about that, then said, "My daddy says that's the way nature is."

Kate remembered when she, too, had been able to accept her father's explanation of the natural order of life in the wild.

"Your dad's right," Alex remarked. "Each creature has its own method of survival."

"I don't like snakes much," Susan said, "but I hope the little lizards don't get caught."

As prearranged, they stopped at the Tsavo Inn, where Susan went back to her father and Melanie, and the two groups parted company. Derek took off first, while Alex was busy making a telephone call. Kate was in the van when Alex returned.

"We'll go into Tsavo by way of the Voi gate, then on to the lodge," he told Richo, who broke into a happy grin.

It did not take long to arrive at the town outside the gate. "Alex, if I stay here overnight, it would save you money," Richo hinted. "You could drive the rest of the way to the lodge."

Alex agreed and they dropped Richo off. Alex took the wheel, and Kate got in beside him. "Richo appears to have relatives all over the countryside," Kate observed as they drove off.

"Relatives—or special friends," Alex said.

She caught the implication. "Lady friends?"

"That's my guess." He grinned. "Richo said he couldn't afford more than one wife, but his diversions aren't that costly."

"You sound as though you approve."

"It's not my place to approve or not. The man spends a lot of time away from home. He has his own way of coping."

Kate decided not to delve further.

At the Voi Gate they had to stop for Alex to sign some kind of register. He got out of the van to confer with the two rangers. Kate couldn't hear, but Alex's expression told her it wasn't small talk. When he got back in, she asked, "Trouble?"

"No," he answered, and seemed to shake off his seriousness. "*Trouble*'s not in my vocabulary today." He gave her a warm smile. "I'm too happy."

Maybe it was catching. Kate felt herself relaxing. It was early afternoon now, and the Taita Hills to their right were bathed in sunlight, with indentations of dark violet color. She and Alex were quiet for a while, sharing, as they once had, the timeless magic of the land. On a rise, heads raised, graceful horns silhouetted against the sky, stood a motionless trio of impala. Then as if on cue, they bounded off. Kate felt a thrilling rush of admiration at the majestic strength of their movements.

"See, beyond them, that way," Alex said, pointing.

"Where?"

"Follow that line of thornbushes . . . way off . . . there's a herd of zebra."

"Oh, yes. I see them. Grazing as usual. No wonder they're such rounded creatures."

"It takes a lot of grass to make a decent meal. After a drought, they look—" He broke off. "But never mind.

There's been no drought this year, and they're healthy and plump and beautiful.''

"I gather you're in a 'think positive' mode."

"Anything wrong with that?"

"I can't think of a thing," Kate said, and for the moment meant it.

Before long, her eyes were once again adept at scanning the horizon and spotting the flash of color or movement that signaled an animal's presence. As children she and Alex used to compete, tallying the animals each spotted first. With no declaration that they were doing it, they played the old game again.

"Hartebeest," she called, and then, "Gazelles, two of them on the right."

"What kind?" Alex asked, challenging her memory.

Kate recognized the distinctive pattern on the rump. "Thomson's gazelles."

"Right you are."

A troop of baboons lurched across the road in front of them, and a gangly ostrich turned its back and waddled off at their approach. Kate marveled, as she had years ago, at the rich variety of animal life. She pointed to the right. "I'm not sure . . . just the antlers are sticking up." Alex pulled off onto a track through the high grass and stopped. The animal raised his head to reveal the graceful spiraling twists of his horns. "Kudu," Kate cried. The large antelope was at least five-foot high at the shoulder. The kudu raised his head, looked regally around, then sauntered off.

They continued their contest for a while until Alex said, "I concede. You haven't lost your touch. You win."

Kate was pleased. "Not by much."

He reached over to take her hand. "We were always close . . . well matched."

She smiled, acknowledging that he was right. Alex leaned closer, but then, over his shoulder, Kate saw a bronze flash in the dense thicket about a hundred yards off the track. Her heart stopped. She knew what it was. Hypnotically her eyes followed the movement of the animal behind the screen of bushes. She freed her hand from Alex's grasp and curled it into a tight fist. Alex swiveled around to see what was wrong. As the lioness emerged from the thicket, Kate shuddered and turned away, not wanting to look, fearing the sight of some recent bloody kill staining the animal's mouth. Alex took her in his arms. He said nothing, but the warmth of his touch was comforting.

Alex was trying to reintroduce her to the Eden of their childhood, but for Kate it was a tainted paradise.

CHAPTER NINE

THEY DIDN'T TALK about what had just happened. Alex got back on the road and continued on. He had anticipated there would be difficult moments for Kate. It would take time for her to feel secure here again. Drawing on her familiarity with Africa and her early joy in it were part of his plan. He could not, however, control every aspect of the environment. Nor did he want to. What use would it be to deny the brutal side of the natural order? He could protect Kate from physical danger, but not from the emotional impact of facing what she feared.

Perhaps ''fear'' wasn't the right word. As a girl, she'd acted as though the word had no meaning for her. Headstrong and confident, she'd been ready to face anything. He believed she still had that quality. Even now, Kate wasn't afraid for her safety. What colored her vision was the shadow their fathers' deaths had cast on every aspect of her former life. Her father had dedicated his career to this country and the preservation of its environment. In Kate's mind Alastair Marlowe's brutal death had been a betrayal, a betrayal she felt as her own. That's why she had turned her back on Kenya.

Alex was convinced that had she not left so soon afterward, Kate would have been able to work through her feelings, as he had. He hoped she'd be able to now. It wouldn't be easy. Her resistance was rooted in the tragedy that had frozen her emotional reaction. What had once been beautiful to her had become treacherous. Maybe this trip with him would change her. Kate was no longer a grief-struck girl, but a woman. It was time for her to tear away the shroud that darkened her past and closed him out of her future. If that didn't happen . . .

It was a possibility Alex didn't like to contemplate. Whether she meant to or not, if she rejected it all, Kate would be rejecting him, as well.

The last few miles to the Salt Lick Lodge were a bumpy drive. Kate and Alex gave up their game. In the heat of the afternoon, most of the animals had sought shade and a siesta. Dotting the road were red-earth termite hills—some as high as five feet—that resembled miniature castles. "That's the lodge up ahead," Alex said when he spotted the thatched roofs. Kate's initial reaction gratified him.

"It's like a little village," she exclaimed. The lodge was actually a group of hutlike structures, rondavels up in the air. "It's all on stilts."

Kate had to be aware of the reason—so that the animals could pass under—but Alex saw no need to mention it.

As soon as he parked, a smiling young man appeared to take their bags. Alex paused for a moment to talk to two men at the entrance who hailed him by name. "Armed guards?" Kate asked when he came back.

"Rangers. This is a reserve. The lodge is an accommodation for visitors, privately owned but subject to the regulations of the government."

They entered the cool dimness of the reception area, where the clerk's greeting made Kate smile. "Alex, baby, how goes it? What's new, my man?"

Alex introduced them, and Kate soon found out where the young man's jive talk came from. George had lived with an aunt in Manhattan for a number of years. He'd returned to Kenya only last year after getting an associate degree in hotel management. He was also a drummer. "I used to make some extra bread playing gigs with a couple of boys from Harlem—a little jazz, rap, bebop. Our trio did it all, man. Know what we called ourselves? The Freebies. Not that we didn't charge, but it made people think they were getting off cheap, if you catch my drift."

Kate nodded, then before the garrulous George could launch into another story she said, "Right now I'm ready to drift up to my room. We've been on the road since six this morning."

George immediately gave their keys to the man who'd taken their luggage, and Alex and Kate followed him upstairs. "You handled that very diplomatically," Alex told her.

"I did, didn't I? Did you notice my clever transition about drifting along to our room?"

"Very subtle. I commend you."

Upstairs, they came out on a walkway. The individual thatched towers were all connected by a network of wooden bridges. They followed their escort over several walkways until he stopped. The sign announced that this was Bura Lodge. "Bura's a river nearby," Alex explained. "Each section of the lodge has a different name." They climbed to the upper level, where their guide opened a door, making a gesture for Kate and Alex to enter first. He placed their luggage on the floor and left. Kate looked around. The room had a large double bed and a dresser. The headboard was fashioned of dried grasses in a colorful design, and a grassy fringe hung from the thatched ceiling, much like a valance.

"Is this all right?" Alex asked.

"Fine. I like the rustic look."

"This is the best part." He led her to the window, which overlooked a large watering hole about a hundred yards away. The sun was low now, and the still water absorbed its golden hue, except for where the trees bordering the far side cast their dark shadows.

"There's nothing moving," Kate said softly. "It's like a still life."

"It's early. That scene will change soon." He turned away. "You probably want to rest for a while."

"No. I'm too restless to rest."

He grinned. "That sounds illogical, but I know what you mean."

"Suppose I freshen up and let you buy me a drink."

"Sounds good to me."

"I won't be long," she said, and went into the bathroom. Kate scrubbed her face. Glancing at herself in the mirror, she was surprised at how different she appeared. She was used to seeing a sophisticated, polished look. Of course, she was casually dressed, windblown and without makeup. Or could it be more than that?

Kate brushed her hair, put on some lipstick and went out to Alex. "I'm ready for you," she said.

"I sure hope that's true," he said with a smile.

They made their way back to the public rooms. On the broad, open terrace, only a few tables were occupied. "The place is deserted," Kate said.

"It won't be for long." Alex looked at his watch. "In another half hour, the safari vans will head back from their afternoon game drives."

They chose a table where they had a good view of the watering hole. Kate noticed people at another table being served afternoon tea.

"I think that's what I'll have," Kate decided. When the waiter came, she ordered tea and crumpets.

"I thought I was buying you a drink."

"Tea is a drink. Besides, I'm feeling very British. How about you?"

"I'm feeling Kenyan. I'll stick to the local beer." Alex ordered a bottle and downed half the glass after the waiter poured it. Kate took a swallow of tea and almost burned herself.

"Better let it cool awhile," Alex cautioned. He pushed over his glass. "Here, try some of this. It'll wash the dust out of your throat."

Kate took a sip. "Mmm. It's good." She'd meant to take only one more swallow, but ended up emptying the glass. "You'd better order another. I didn't realize how thirsty I was."

He raised the bottle as a signal to the waiter, who quickly brought a replacement. Alex sampled her biscuit, which he washed down with the beer. "Crumpets and beer make a weird combination," Kate told him.

"Why? Who decides those things?" He was in a whimsical mood.

"Tradition."

"But people make traditions, so we can make our own. Right?"

"I used to think so once," she said. Alex wanted to believe that it was still possible, but Kate wondered if, after all this time, there was common ground enough for them ever to agree, except on things like beer and crumpets. Alex sensed her doubt, she knew, but he didn't argue. Instead his smile seemed to gather her in. At this moment she felt very close to him. She didn't want to spoil their time together by projecting too far into the future.

Alex had turned his head and was staring out at the watering hole. He looked back at her, then motioned slightly with his chin, directing her gaze to follow his. At first Kate thought she was seeing the same still life, except that the colors were subdued in the deepening dusk. Then she caught the movement. Huge shadows were noiselessly moving toward the watering hole—elephants, one after another, emerging from the covering of trees. Kate caught her breath at the eerie beauty of the scene, those huge beasts slowly appearing, each taking its place, as if by prearrangement, at the edge of the pond. Their reflections in the still water added to the magical aura. Then, coming from the other side, Kate spied the stealthy approach of another group. It was a herd of water buffalo. They waded in a few feet, but kept to their side. As her eyes adjusted to the shadows, Kate made out other animals interspersed, a topi and a gazelle, and the chunky ungainliness of a warthog. It was like witnessing a mythical pageant.

The elephants dipped their trunks in to drink, and several sprayed water over themselves. The pond's surface became a rippling pool; reflections lost their clarity and became shimmering apparitions.

"Do you think they see themselves in the water?" Kate wondered aloud.

"I don't think elephants care what they look like," Alex said with a soft chuckle.

There were sounds now, but they'd faded to no more than a liquid rustling by the time they reached the lodge. Kate felt something emanating from the peaceful beauty of the scene, something that touched her deep inside. Unconsciously she reached for Alex's hand.

She'd hardly been aware of the whispered conversations around them, but then a loud jarring voice intruded. "Who'd have thought such humongous critters would make so little noise. It's like they're walking tippytoed."

Alex turned and in an even voice told the man sitting behind them, "You would do well to emulate them, my friend."

"What?" The man scowled. He turned to his wife and in the same loud voice, asked, "What did that guy say?"

"I think he means for you to keep your voice down," she hissed, and pointed to a sign on the wall, which cautioned guests to do just that.

"Oh. Sorry," he apologized with a salute to Alex. Then sotto voce he said to his wife, "I didn't think it was going to be this tame. Elephants I can see in a zoo. I expected a little more action."

"If a lion comes, you'll see plenty of action," his wife said.

The relish in her voice disgusted Kate. "I hope they go home disappointed," Kate told Alex. "Why would anyone want to mar such a beautiful scene?"

"It's part of what they've been led to expect."

"So we provide the tourist with a taste of savagery?" she asked sarcastically.

"No." Alex frowned. "But it happens. Though I don't call it savagery that predatory animals stalk and kill in order to survive."

"And scavengers..."

"Scavengers follow their own programmed instincts."

"And lions do both."

"Yes."

"That's wrong, horribly wrong."

He shook his head. "Not the way I see it. We can't impose our moral order on the animal world. Their behavior is natural. Savagery is our interpretation, and horror our reaction. I wish we were as condemning of some human behavior. People *do* have a sense of morality, a sense of right and wrong, and the destruction of life and the environment is wrong. Hopefully we can still turn things around."

"You think you can recreate Paradise? Alex, you're an idealist. You want to change the world. That's a big arena to work in."

"Not the whole world, my love," he said with a wry smile. "Too big a job. I'm good, but not that good. I'm satisfied to concentrate on this country. Kenya's my arena. I'll leave the rest of the world to others."

"I guess that's the difference between us. Maybe it always was," Kate said thoughtfully.

"What?"

"My world was always narrower than yours, even when we were children—my home, the people I loved, the things I wanted to do. They were around me, tangible—I could hug them to me. The rest, what was outside, drew definition from what was close to me." She wasn't sure he understood.

"When we used to talk about what we wanted to do, we had the same plans," Alex said.

"Yes and no. I never thought about it then, but your motivation was always different. All I wanted was more of the happiness I had, with the added independence of adulthood. We would be together, we would have our animal orphanage, we would enjoy the things we both loved. I never had a global view of the future."

"At seventeen, I doubt that I did, either."

"Not as you do now, but it was there. My perspective was much narrower."

"Yet you were the one who left and traveled and changed."

"Did I really change? I wonder." Kate felt suddenly uncomfortable. "Let's talk about something else."

But the conversation lagged. Kate drank her tea, her attention directed inward.

Alex, too, was preoccupied, thinking about what Kate had said. She had done more than revive a memory; she'd been able to analyze what her state of mind had been and pointed out a difference in their way of thinking that had never occurred to him. Perhaps he'd been wrong...the way he'd considered them as two sides of the same coin.

Kate's world back then, so narrowly defined, had been shattered by the way their fathers had been killed. Alex had been able to see beyond that tragedy, but it had stained Kate's whole universe.

Alex realized Kate's world was still circumscribed, though on the surface it didn't appear limited. Kate was an independent woman with a successful career that offered high salary, travel and many social contacts. But boundaries weren't always geographical. Kate functioned in an environment she felt she could control, not like the one she had rejected. It offered advantages she'd convinced herself were necessary and more than adequate. But were they?

Alex had long felt that Kate was a vital part of him. He could exist without her—he had for thirteen years—but there was something essential missing from that existence, the richness of love and a shared life. Yet he couldn't move into her world because something in him would die if he left the work and the country he loved. Did he have the right to entice her back into his? She had implied that she'd embraced their youthful dreams not for an ideal, but out of personal devotion. Alex wanted to rekindle that devotion, but not to use it as a snare. He truly felt that Kate belonged here with him, but it was something she had to want for herself.

Kate broke into his reverie. "I think I'll go up to the room and shower the road dust off." She gestured toward the entrance, where people were coming in. "This place is going to get crowded."

"The vans are back from the game drives."

"So it appears." At the door, one of the rangers on duty was talking to a driver. The ranger beckoned Alex to join them.

"Go ahead," Kate told him. "I'll just go back and relax a while before dinner."

"Shall we have dinner early, about six?"

"All right."

But Alex never made it.

AT A QUARTER TO SEVEN, Kate decided to check the dining room in case Alex had gone straight there, but he wasn't around. She found George at the reception desk.

"You mean those dudes ain't back yet?" George said when she asked about Alex.

"What dudes? Back from where?"

"Alex went out with one of our rangers. But that was a couple of hours ago."

"Where did they go?"

He made a sweeping gesture. "Somewhere out there. Probably after something."

"What?"

"Who knows? Could be animal...could be human. Last week Hercules, that's the ranger, he had to waste a poacher when the damn fool pulled a knife on him." Kate blanched. "Hey, Miss Marlowe, there's no call for you to look like that. Ain't nobody gonna mess with those two. They'll be strolling back here anytime now. Don't you worry. Crane knows what he's about, and that Hercules, he's just like his name. He's strong as a water buffalo. His momma named him after some Greek hero. You ever heard of him?"

She nodded, her mind still troubled by Alex's absence.

George kept talking. "Hercules—it sounds strong, don't it? Not like George. Who ever heard of a hero named George?"

Kate guessed that George was trying to distract her from worrying. She appreciated his concern. "There was Saint George and the dragon," she pointed out.

"Say what?"

"There's a fable about a knight who killed a dragon."

"No kidding? And this guy was a George, was he?"

"If memory serves me."

"This I gotta hear." But just then a group of new arrivals claimed George's attention, and regretfully he went to serve them. Kate was glad to have made George happy, but relieved that she didn't have to relate the legendary Saint George's adventure, since all she could recall was the title.

Kate wandered back to the dining room. George was probably right; Alex would be back soon. After all, this was his territory and he could take care of himself. She shouldn't worry needlessly.

There was another woman waiting to be seated. "Alone, are you?" the woman asked.

"Yes. My friend seems to have been delayed."

"What say we share a table?" the woman asked cheerfully. "I'm alone, too, in a manner of speaking."

As it turned out, Margaret Carruthers was chaperoning a church youth group from Yorkshire. "I'm with them all day, but dinner's my time for privacy. Oh, not from you, my dear. From them. I'm in need of some adult conversation."

Margaret's definition of adult conversation meant herself as the main speaker, but Kate didn't mind. Exuding good nature and zeal, Margaret described her adventures with her brood. Kate was able to follow her enthusiastic descriptions by picking up the key words. "Marvelous country...such vistas...the herds...enthralling...an unforgettable experience for my little darlings."

Kate looked where Margaret was pointing. Her "little darlings" were a noisy group of a dozen teenagers. "This is an expensive trip for such young people."

"Isn't that the truth? To be sure, it's the parents who foot the bill."

Kate started to describe the program Alex was promoting. When she heard herself repeating his very words with the same enthusiasm, she smiled to herself. He'd brainwashed her.

Margaret was impressed. "A lovely idea. And scholarships for those who can't pay the whole tab, you say? I should so like to talk to your friend about it. Will he be along soon?"

"I don't know."

Alex got there just as they were ordering dessert. He was still in the same clothes he'd worn all day and looked tired. Kate felt an immediate relief, but as soon as her anxiety lifted, irritation took its place.

"Kate, I'm sorry," he said. "Something came up."

"Obviously."

"I didn't expect to be this long. I'm glad you found some company."

"Margaret Carruthers," the Englishwoman said, shooting her hand out for a hearty handshake. "Are you the fellow I've been hearing about, the one with the camping safaris?"

"I'm the fellow. Alex Crane. How are you?"

"Splendid. So happy to meet you. Do sit down, my boy. I've loads of questions."

With a sidelong glance at Kate, Alex said, "I'm glad someone is happy to see me." He gave Margaret a smile. "Let me wash the grime off my hands first. Have you ladies eaten yet? I see you have. Well, I'm famished. Kate, order for me.''

"Order what?'' she asked as he strode off.

"Whatever you had.''

"Such a handsome lad,'' Margaret said. "Are you two, uh, you know?''

"Not exactly.''

"Oh. Too bad.''

Alex returned quickly and, between bites of roast lamb and vegetables, explained where he'd gone. "The leopard population in the park is dwindling, and we've been tracking several animals with radio collars for a while now.''

"How does that help?'' Margaret asked.

"We get to observe their habits, and protect the animals if possible. Maybe we can do something about preserving the population before the situation gets really serious.''

Margaret nodded. "You mean like the rhinoceroses?''

"Exactly.''

"Oh, yes. I've read about the plight of those poor creatures. God made them ugly, but He gave them a place on this earth, so He must have known what He was doing,'' Margaret said. At Alex's smile of approval, she almost preened. "Leopards are much more beautiful.''

"But also in jeopardy. We can't afford to lose a single one. This afternoon, one of the drivers thought he spotted an animal we'd lost track of. The leopard looked wounded, and his radio collar was probably out of commission. I went out with a ranger to try to find him.''

"Did you locate the poor creature?''

The question came from Margaret. Kate didn't have to ask. Alex's expression revealed his discouragement.

"Not this time.''

Margaret got to ask her questions about Alex's project. She ended up volunteering to be his liaison in England, offering to head a committee to screen the British applicants. Through her contacts with schools and church groups, she could disseminate information about the Jambo project. "I'm sure I can get you lots of applicants from all over Britain," Margaret announced.

"I'm not sure I can handle many more campers," Alex told her. "Not without more funding. I'm counting on the book royalties to help expand the program, but I don't know how much will be coming in or when."

"You've done a book?" Margaret was again enthralled.

As Alex described *A Vanishing World*, the older woman hung on every word. Alex had a gift for arousing interest in his causes. His appeal, Kate decided, was both intellectual and personal. He talked about his book and environmental concerns and how they were connected to his youth safari program. His exposition was intelligent and soundly argued, but the force of his personal conviction was what swayed his listeners. Certainly it seemed so with Margaret.

"You must let me help, dear boy," Margaret insisted. "When it comes to raising money, I know all the tricks."

"Tricks, miracles, I can use all the help I can get," Alex said with a smile.

Kate injected a practical note. "What did you have in mind?" she asked Margaret.

Margaret described her connections with church groups throughout England. Kate's skepticism was justified. Margaret's fund-raising tactics were the kind that ladies' groups used to raise a few hundred dollars for a worthy cause. Her efforts could bring in enough to sponsor a few candidates for the program, but little more. Not that Kate thought to discourage such offers of help. The moral support from volunteers like Margaret had much more than monetary value. Kate could envision such enthusiastic staffers in countries all around the world. Sophisticated fund-raising, however, was something else.

It was becoming clear to Kate that Alex needed to look beyond his own resources and those available to him in Kenya. Margaret's proposals would yield little compared to what Kate knew could be raised through tapping large corporations and charitable trusts in North America. That was where her expertise would help.

Kate's first job after college had been as a fund-raiser for a national health organization. During her three years there, she had learned which prospects to contact, how to approach them, what to include in a grant proposal and the dozens of other details that comprised the ins and outs of raising money. That experience plus her publicity background at Blackwell's could be a tremendous asset to Alex.

Alex's vision had initiated this venture, and his idealism was its heart, but he needed someone to handle the practical aspects of fund-raising and managing organizational details. It could be a challenging and satisfying project. *Hold it,* Kate told herself. *Don't let yourself get caught up in Alex's life.*

After dinner, Margaret led the way to the lounge. The huge central fireplace with its cone-shaped stone chimney had a welcoming fire going. Margaret's group waved to her from a corner of the room. "You must let me introduce you," Margaret told Alex and Kate. "They'll be so interested to meet two people who actually live here."

Kate didn't bother to correct her. She and Alex joined the lively young teenagers, who were indeed interested and curious. They fired a barrage of questions at Alex. Some were serious, some silly, but he didn't seem to mind. Then one of the girls asked, "Was it difficult growing up here?"

Alex didn't answer. His eyes narrowed and he turned toward Kate. "What would you say? Was it difficult?"

Kate's eyes locked with his for what seemed like a long time, but must only have been seconds. "No," she said slowly, "it was quite wonderful . . . for a long time."

"Then why did you leave?" the same girl challenged.

"That's another story," Kate said, and was glad when Margaret changed the subject.

"I promised that we'd all go down for a look around in the bunker. Lights out at ten," she told her charges, "so best get to it now." They were already scrambling toward the stairway. "Won't you come along?" she asked Alex and Kate. The bunker was dug into the ground close to the watering hole and connected by a tunnel to the lodge. From it, the viewer was at eye level with the animals. "They'll no doubt want to know all about the animals they see," Margaret said, "and I'm afraid I'm no expert." She lowered her voice and added, "Please come. Having you with us will help, Alex. One mustn't make any noise in the bunker. They're more apt to mind the rules with you there."

"Sure we'll come," Alex said.

Kate demurred. "I think I'll beg off and turn in. It's been a long day." She said good-night and started off, but Alex caught up with her. "Go with them," she told him. "It's all right."

"I'll take you back first."

"I don't need an escort."

He didn't argue, just took her arm and walked with her. "You're not still angry with me, are you?" he asked.

"Because you disappeared? No, not really. I was worried, then relieved, then annoyed because you made me worry." She smiled at him. "All of which sounds very silly now."

"I should have told you where I was going. I'm not used to checking in with anybody."

It was an unfortunate choice of words. Kate stiffened. "I don't expect you are."

"I didn't mean that the way it sounded."

"There's nothing wrong with what you said, Alex." But Kate wasn't sure that was true. To change the subject, she asked, "What did you think of Margaret's ideas?"

"I'm not sure. What did you think?"

"She's great. You can use that kind of support, and a network of enthusiastic staffers like Margaret would be a tremendous asset, but her approach to fund-raising is very limited. You know what you need?"

"Tell me."

"Someone who can get the Jambo youth project the kind of publicity that leads to major funding grants, and a practical-minded assistant to manage everything for you."

"You're absolutely right," Alex agreed, "and I know just the person who can do both jobs."

"Oh, no, you don't," Kate said, shaking her head. "I wasn't applying for the position."

"Why not?"

"Alex, I have a job."

"Not like this one. Long hours, little money, a tyrant like me for a boss. It's a marvelous opportunity. Don't pass it up."

Kate laughed. "I'll have to think about it." On the surface the conversation was light, but with an underlying seriousness they both recognized.

At the door Alex said, "I won't be long."

"Don't rush on my account. I'm going right to bed."

He gave her a quizzical look. "Is that to punish me?"

"Of course not. I'm just tired."

"All right, then." He gave her a light kiss. "Sweet dreams," he said, and left.

Kate could not fall asleep. She felt restless, dissatisfied with Alex and with herself. Why had she come on this trip? To lure Alex away from his world? That seemed impossible. To join him in it? Equally impossible. She was tempted to help him make a success of the Jambo Youth Safaris, but it was his dream, not hers. Their lives had diverged so much since she had left Kenya.

Alex had said he wasn't used to checking in with anyone. Nor was she. He'd said he wanted her to share his life, but he didn't want her to monitor his activities. Yet she couldn't help being fearful for him. Nor could she understand his acceptance of danger as part of his existence. Not when there was an alternative.

Kate sat up in bed and turned on the light. Perhaps reading awhile might make her sleepy. She picked up the book on her bedside table, Isak Dinesen's *Out of Africa*. Harvey Blackwell had given it to her as a present when she left on her trip. Kate's father had been in the habit of reading aloud to the children, and this book had been one of his favorites. But after his death, Kate hadn't looked at a copy, and had avoided seeing the movie based on the book. She wasn't sure why she'd packed Harvey's present for this trip. To signal that she was ready to return? Kate stared at the unopened book, then tossed it on the table.

The room suddenly felt cold. She got out of bed and rummaged through her duffel bag for a sweater, which she put on over her nightgown. She drew back the drapes that covered the window and gazed out. The watering hole, lit at night so guests at the lodge could see the animals, was like a stage set. The scene was bathed in a soft glow like suffused moonlight. Silvery stars reached down from the sky's vast black canopy. Thornbushes, trees and rocks formed a frame for the picture. Nature was a skillful set designer, Kate thought.

It was very quiet now. A lone buffalo waded stolidly out of the water. A group of gazelles grazed nearby. A waterbuck came out of the darkness to drink, then stretched out on a grassy spot. Leaning against her window, Kate watched for a long time, soothed by the beauty and peacefulness of the scene. Suddenly the gazelles skittered and bounded off. Had they caught the scent of a predator? The waterbuck stood up, warily alert. Kate caught some movement in the shadows just beyond the lit area.

She heard a key in the lock and Alex appeared. "You're still up. Good," he said, and moved quickly into the room. "I'd have awakened you, anyway. I thought you'd want to see this. Were you watching?" He took her arm and propelled her back to the window. The waterbuck had backed up an incline, where he stood watching.

"Something scared the gazelles," Kate said, "but I don't see..."

Alex pointed. "There he is."

Out of the darkness on the right, a shadowy shape took form, moving in stealthy slow motion. The animal prowled the darker outskirts back and forth. The waterbuck retreated farther and then ran off.

Kate waited, feeling her pulse stilled in anticipation. Then the animal stepped forward and the lights picked up the leopard's tawny colors. Kate caught her breath. The sight sent a shooting thrill through her. Alex had been watching with his hand on her shoulder. His grip tightened, and she sensed his excitement. He, too, was reacting to the compelling force and beauty of the leopard. There was something deeply sensuous in their shared response. Both felt it. The leopard drank his fill and then, with the same majestic measured pace, disappeared into the black night.

Alex twisted her around to face him. The room was in darkness, but through the window came some light from outside, giving his face a golden patina and his eyes a liquid softness. "I can see something like that a thousand times, and each time, it's enchantment," he said softly.

He pulled her closer, and her hands flattened against his chest. He wore only a thin cotton shirt. "Aren't you cold?" she asked.

He gave a husky laugh. "Quite the contrary." He put his arms around her and caught handfuls of sweater in his fists. "Why're you wearing this?"

"I was cold before."

"I don't think you're going to need it now." He pulled her sweater over her head and tossed it away. "Or this," he said, and, lowering her straps from her shoulders, let her night-gown drop. He took both her hands and stepped back to look at her. A whirling warmth in her loins started to spread through her body. She felt bathed in moonlight, or was it just from the light and warmth of his eyes.

Alex released her, but only for the moment it took for him to strip off his clothes. Then he held out his arms and she entered the charmed circle of his embrace. When he kissed her, his mouth was a fiery command that released an answering need in Kate. There was about Alex a controlled power and heat that aroused her to a frenzy of desire. He lifted her, holding her nakedness against him, and brought her to the bed, where he laid her down. She immediately raised her arms to draw him over her. They made love with a consuming ferocity.

Nothing else existed as Kate gave herself up to the passion that engulfed them. She didn't close her eyes, but looked into the depths of his as he neared orgasm. He moved within her, holding back until he reached and fired the deep response he sought from her. His eyes were exultant as he felt her spiraling tension reach its apex and then explode beyond. He thrust into it, and their fulfillment fused into a single shattering culmination.

Afterward Kate slept in the shelter of his arms. She awoke in the morning, flushed with the remembered pleasure of love. But as she lay there, uneasy doubts crept to the surface of her mind. Kate burrowed closer to Alex's protective warmth, but the doubts were a barrier. Last night her surrender had been complete and joyous, but also fearful. She could argue that the surrender had been to her own desire, so there was no risk. But hers was not a generalized sexual need; her desire was specific to Alex and had no life apart from him. If she allowed herself to be absorbed into Alex's passion, she risked being absorbed into his life. Unless she could keep the two separate.

She was determined to try.

CHAPTER TEN

THEY WERE LATE leaving Salt Lick that morning. Alex's ranger friend, Hercules, joined them for breakfast. Kate was glad that Alex decided to let the rangers continue their search for the injured leopard without him. When Margaret Carruthers got back from her prebreakfast game drive, she collared Alex to ask more questions and to get the addresses she would need for their future correspondence. Her charges were busy attacking the breakfast buffet. The lavish assortment of food gave Kate an idea. She excused herself, then returned carrying a small basket.

"What's that?" Alex asked.

"Our picnic. One of the waiters provided the basket, and I raided the buffet table so we can have a picnic lunch later."

"Jolly good fun," Margaret said. "I don't suppose you'd care to have extra company—twelve blustery adolescents and their frazzled chaperon." She looked from Alex to Kate. "No, I thought not." As they left, she gave a cheery wave. "Have fun, dearies."

"We'll try," Kate said, meaning it.

In the reception area, George was helping another clerk check out a milling group of French tourists. When he noticed that Kate and Alex were on their way out, his face dropped. He came over. "You're leaving already? You just got here."

Alex was amused. "I'm touched, George, but I'm afraid we have to go."

"Where?"

"Amboseli."

George made a snorting sound. "Salt Lick's better. Like what's Amboseli got?"

"My campground, for one thing, and about twenty people there who are expecting us."

The other clerk called out something to George. "Okay, keep your pants on," George muttered. He said goodbye, shook hands, and as Kate walked off, called after her, "I never got to hear that story about the dragon killer."

"Next time, George," she called back. George flashed a hopeful smile.

"What was all that about a dragon killer?" Alex asked. Kate's explanation made him chuckle.

"If I could remember the whole story, I'd have taken the time to tell it," Kate said.

"Next time," Alex said, repeating what she'd told George.

Kate had used the words as an expression, not a promise. She would not be coming back here. But she didn't correct Alex and risk spoiling his happy mood.

"Come on," she ordered. "Let's get this show on the road."

"At your service, milady," he said, and planted a soft kiss on her lips. "Always."

They picked Richo up in the village. "Did you have a good time?" Alex asked him.

"Yes, sir," he replied with a wide grin that caused Alex to laugh. Richo didn't mind; he laughed, too. He took over the wheel and sang as he drove.

"He seems pretty happy today," Kate observed to Alex.

Alex grinned. "Richo's always happy when he gets to spend the night with a special friend."

"I see."

Alex took her hand. "I know just how he feels."

So did Kate. After a while she asked, "Do we have to go straight to Amboseli? I thought we could picnic at Mzima Springs."

"With the hippos? As I remember, you never liked them much."

"That's because they don't *do* much of anything. But the Springs is such a pretty area, and it's safe to get out of the car."

"Okay. Mzima Springs it is," Alex said.

When they arrived, Alex and Kate took a walk before having their picnic. They followed the trail down to the pools formed by the runoff from the Chyulu Hills. Kate pointed to the gray humps in the pool. "There they are, just like always," she said with a laugh. "Great big blobs floating in the water. If you didn't know better, you'd take them for rocks." Just then one lifted his head lazily, then submerged again. "What a funny-looking head on them. They haven't changed a bit."

"What did you expect?" Alex asked teasingly. "That they'd suddenly have become svelte and graceful?"

"No, but it would have been nice."

"Not for them. Beauty is in the eyes of the beholder. I'm sure hippos like how they look. Lady hippos are probably very enticing to the males."

"That better not be a preface to a lecture on the mating habits of the hippopotamus," Kate warned.

Alex put his arm around her and planted a teasing kiss on her mouth. "At the moment I find human mating habits much more tempting."

Kate pushed him away. "Not at this moment you don't." She grabbed his hand. "Come on."

"Where?"

"To finish our walk and work up an appetite."

"I already have an appetite."

"I know, but I'm talking about food." His laugh rang out. "Look," Kate said, pointing at the water. Three hippos had simultaneously come up for air. "They're checking us out." The heads dipped again. "What a short interest span," Kate said. "Well, you don't fascinate me, either," she called.

"I hope that remark was intended for them, not me," Alex said.

"Don't worry. You're much more interesting than any hippopotamus."

"Thanks—I think," he said with a grin.

They followed the trails for another half hour. The air was warm now, and fragrant with scents from the lush foliage all around. They chose a spot for their picnic, an embankment topped with a wide flat rock. Kate waited there while Alex went to get Richo and to fetch the basket. "Richo's busy socializing with some drivers he met in the parking lot," Alex reported when he returned. "He said he's not hungry."

"He probably thinks we want to be alone."

"I've always found Richo to be very astute."

"We're not really alone, you know."

"The hippos don't count."

"Don't you hear voices?" Other vans had been in the parking area. "There are people around."

Alex put down the basket and drew her into his arms. "Maybe the crocodiles will eat them." She started to laugh, but he sealed her lips with a lingering kiss. Finally they drew back from each other, but their eyes continued the embrace. The lush beauty around them permeated their beings.

Kate wanted time to stop, leaving her suspended forever in the sweet harmony of this moment. But the moment passed.

"Let's eat," she said. She spread out the repast. "Rolls, two kinds of cheese, ham and fruit. Plus this." She dipped into the basket and drew out a bottle. "Red wine, so it doesn't have to be cold." She took out a napkin and draped it over her arm. "Would monsieur care to read the label?"

"No. I'm sure it's perfect."

It was, or so it seemed to them. Even though they ate and drank lightly, everything had a special flavor. "There's plenty left for Richo when he gets hungry," Kate remarked as she packed up. They lingered for a few minutes longer, looking down the embankment at the shimmering pools, listening to the hum and trill of unseen birds in the vegetation. A large butterfly landed on a nearby bush, hovered, then flew off in a flash of yellow-, black-and-orange wings.

Softly Kate said, "Here it's easy to forget you're in Africa."

Alex's brow creased in a frown. "If you can love this beauty, why not accept its source?"

"Because that source generates other things I can't accept." Kate placed her fingers against his lips. "Please, Alex. I know what you're going to say. Don't. Don't spoil this moment."

His frown eased. He took her hand and turned it, pressing a kiss into her palm.

IN CONTRAST to Mzima Springs, the plains in Amboseli were sparse of vegetation. The wheels of the van sent dust clouds billowing from the dirt roads they now had to travel. Richo maneuvered a zigzag course to avoid the deepest ruts and jutting rocks. He had to stop when cattle blocked the road. The herdsmen were two Masai boys wearing the dark cloaks of the uninitiated. They would become warriors only after the ceremonial ordeal of circumcision. The older youth with them wore red and had long plaited hair dressed with ocher dye mixed with animal fat. More than his clothing, the lift of his head and the disdain in his expression showed him to be a warrior.

"Some things never change," Kate said with admiration. "The Masai are still the handsomest men I've ever seen. Even the old ones," she added, pointing to an elder who waited up ahead by the side of the road. The man was holding a large stick horizontally in back of his head. Though he stood on one foot, the other raised characteristically in a stork position, he was perfectly balanced.

"Remember that time—you must have been about ten—when we had a contest to see which one of us could stand that way the longest," Alex said.

"Elizabeth wouldn't play because she said only boys did it. Derek gave up first, then you, and I was the winner."

"Only because I had to sneeze and lost my balance," Alex insisted.

"You were mortified to have been bested by a mere girl."

He smiled. "It didn't take you long to lose your 'mere girl' status."

Kate wasn't sure when it had happened, when they had ceased being competitors and become inseparable companions. That had been such a carefree time.

Richo drove on. They waved to the young boys, who smiled and waved back.

"The grass is so sparse here. There's not much for the cattle to graze on," Kate said.

"I know. Amboseli's been trampled and overgrazed. This part's still a preserve, but the area we're going to was raised to national park status, which means more stringent regulations."

"Will that help?"

"It should, but it's a constant battle, Kate. The ecosystem's just too damn fragile to keep supporting increasing numbers of wildlife, cattle and people. We've got to turn things around." He gave a hopeful smile. "Maybe we can, now that young people are getting involved. There are successful reclamation projects that are the work of university students, and not just from this country. I think some of my campers are becoming interested enough to come back as volunteers."

"Where is your camp?"

"Not far. It's on a hill in the swamp area of Ol Tukai."

"The swamp?" She looked surprised.

"The rains are over. It's quite dry now. We were lucky to be able to take over the facilities of a commercial tenting safari camp that went out of business. Actually this camp is quite comfortable. We've even got separate male and female privies."

"Sounds like the height of luxury," she said dryly.

"You'll love it," Alex promised.

"We'll see."

They had to make a stop at the Amboseli Serena Lodge near the camp to pick up mail and supplies. While Alex and Richo were busy, Kate wandered down a corridor flanked with lush potted foliage. At the end was a spacious dining room overlooking a stream, with French doors open to the sunlit patio. The room was deserted except for an elderly couple taking pictures of black-faced monkeys scampering on the sloping lawn outside. Pitchers of iced tea stood on a side table. Kate poured a tall glass and sat at one of the tables.

Beguiled by the air of serenity, she relaxed. A duo of yellow weaverbirds flew inside and landed on one of the tables. If she'd had a crust of bread, she would have crumbled it up for them, as she used to do when she was a child. The birds played follow the leader for a while, darting around the tables, then flew away.

The older couple kept snapping pictures, until they ran out of film and left. The monkeys, unaware they'd lost two-thirds of their audience, kept up their entertainment. Kate watched lazily, enjoying their antics. She didn't hear Alex approach.

"Well, you look very much the memsahib," he said, smiling down at her. "Sitting here, sipping your cool drink, watching the monkeys put on a show for you."

Kate recalled how they used to make fun of newly arrived European ladies who played the role of the memsahib.

"It's a charming place," she said with a smile.

"Am I going to be able to entice you away?"

"What are you offering?"

"The more rustic charm of the Jambo camp, the chance to meet my pioneering group of young campers—and me."

Kate gazed up at him. A shaft of sunlight bronzed his face and electrified the glints in his dark eyes.

"An offer I can't resist," Kate murmured. She stood. He took her hand and they walked out together.

THE CAMP WAS in a scenic spot, with Mount Kilimanjaro looming in the distance. The top of the mountain was shrouded in fog. "Like the animals, Kilimanjaro sleeps now," Richo said as they neared their destination.

Kate smiled at the description. In African life, man was intricately linked to his surroundings. Ascribing human characteristics to nature seemed completely right.

The dust cloud raised by their van signaled their approach. When Richo pulled up, Alex got out and was immediately surrounded by a half-dozen young people. In colorfully accented English they vied for his attention.

"We've been waiting for you.... We saw a leopard yesterday.... Julio said he heard a lion close to camp last night.... When are we going to the Mara? Has the migration started? We've been helping the rangers track rhino.... Who's your friend?''

Laughingly Alex halted the question and comments. "Hold it. We'll have plenty of time to talk. This is Kate Marlowe from the United States."

"Have you come for a holiday?" a young woman asked Kate.

"You could say that."

"Kate used to live in Kenya," Alex explained.

"Oh!" The young woman was impressed. "So it is for you a welcome back home then?"

"Not exactly" was the only reply Kate could make. She didn't yet know just what this trip was going to mean.

A bell clanged. "Chow time," someone yelled, and they all headed for the outdoor dining area. Four folding tables were set up in a U. The students bringing out the platters of food paused to call a greeting. Kate found herself sitting between a tall, blond young Dutchman named Hans and a soft-spoken Japanese girl who introduced herself as Mitsu. Hans was studying veterinary medicine. Mitsu was an artist whose family lived in Tokyo. They were from completely different backgrounds, but from the looks these two exchanged, Kate surmised they'd managed to bridge cultural barriers.

Conversation during the meal was spirited and loud, with snatches of various languages. The young people yelled across to one another, table-hopped, teased and laughed. Their outfits could best be described as grimy casual, with jeans, khaki shorts and camp shirts predominating. Talking didn't interfere with their eating. They soon finished the platters of cold sliced meat, vegetable stew and fruit. Apparently a healthy appetite was something they had in common. But there was more than that, much more. While Alex was tied up with Ben Oloum, his resident manager at this facility, Kate got a chance to meet and talk with many of the others.

There were nineteen young people from various countries in Europe, Asia and North and South America. Kate couldn't keep track of all the names, but their unique personalities impressed her. The Mexican youth was the athlete, and the redhead from Ireland a real comedian. There was a beautiful Pakistani who would be going to medical school in the States next year, and her buddy was a willowy blonde with a Scarlett O'Hara accent. Each had his or her individual motive for having come. Some sounded frivolous. "Hey, it's a free vacation, mate."

Hans, somewhat older than the others, had been prompted by his interest in wild animals and planned to combine that interest with his veterinary studies.

But Kate guessed that whatever their original reasons for signing on, something was happening to these young people, something important. Alex agreed.

"Given such diversity, you wouldn't expect them to become such a cohesive group," Kate told Alex later as they walked to her tent.

"I know, but that's what happens here." Alex stopped in front of one of the smaller tents and put down the duffel bags he was carrying. "There's a group dynamic that comes into play much faster in this kind of setting." Alex looked around, his eyes narrowing to peer into the distance. Suddenly he smiled and pointed. "Look, the clouds have washed away from Kilimanjaro. You can see the snow on Uhuru Peak."

The vision filled Kate with a joyful awe.

"Sharing that kind of beauty is a powerful bond," Alex said.

Feeling at this moment very close to him, Kate knew Alex was right. "It's more than the visual beauty," she said after a while. "And more than the excitement of seeing the animals. These kids love the whole experience—getting to know each other and meeting people in the villages and markets. They're getting personal gratification—and something more."

"It's that something more that I want for them—and for us," Alex said.

"I think you're achieving what you want."

"Not entirely."

The message in his eyes had nothing to do with the others. It had to do with their being here together, reacting as they used to, to the natural beauty around them, and to each other. He kissed her, and it was all there—the memories, the joy in this moment and the longing for the future.

Hearing a barely suppressed giggle, Kate pulled away. "One thing about camping, there's not much privacy," she said.

He grinned. "I hope that's a complaint."

"It is."

"At least you have your own tent," he said, and led her inside.

It was a conventional safari tent with the bare essentials: sleeping cot, chair, two-drawer chest, wooden table and a lantern. On the table was a ceramic jug filled with wildflowers. Kate smiled with pleasure.

"What a nice touch," she said.

"We aim to please."

"You're doing pretty well."

"You might get used to all this luxury and never want to leave."

"You're trying to entice me."

"You'd better believe it. How am I doing?"

"Not bad at all," she had to admit.

"You know," he said with the hint of a smile, "this tent could accommodate two people."

"On one narrow bed?"

"It makes for closeness."

"More like symbiosis. Two people would have to be real friendly."

He grinned. "Exactly what I had in mind." He took her hands and started drawing her to him.

"What will people think?" she asked, but Kate realized that hers was a token resistance. What she and Alex thought was all that really mattered.

He pulled her closer. "If it concerns them at all, they'll assume that we want to be together," Alex said. "I think that's an accurate assumption. Don't you?"

He took her in his arms and found his answer in her yearning response to his kiss. Kate closed her eyes, letting herself be enveloped in the taste and smell and feel of him. He kissed her lingeringly, and her lips parted to invite the tender forays of his tongue. As she raised her arms to encircle his neck, her body arched into his. She felt him harden against her, and an aching need spiraled in her loins.

Alex's mouth trailed desire over her face, and his warm breath against her ear set her trembling. "Oh, yes," he whispered with seductive assurance, "that bed can accommodate two people, if need be." He kissed her again, his mouth now hotly demanding. "I think," he said against her lips, "the need is there—for both of us."

Kate couldn't deny it.

Later, their passion temporarily sated, Kate lay cuddled against him. "I've never made love in a tent before," she confessed.

"Like it?"

"Mmm."

"Do you know where I'd like to make love to you?" Alex asked. He tilted her chin so he could look into her eyes. "At Pambazuko, at our place."

Alex felt her shiver and she buried her head against his shoulder. "Don't spoil this, Alex," she said. "Please."

He wished he knew what she meant.

IN THE MORNING, Kate and Alex went along on the game drive. They rode in Richo's van with Hans, Mitsu and Casey, a flamboyant American who came from a circus family. "Your act must have something to do with animal training," Kate guessed.

"Nah. Of course, you're always around animals in the circus, but the Hallahans are acrobats and high flyers—have been for generations. My sister and I do a trapeze act."

"Casey can swing from the trees, like Tarzan," Mitsu said. "He showed us."

Casey grinned. "Damn near scared a couple of baboons out of their wits."

"How come you're here?" Kate asked. "Isn't summer prime time for the circus?"

"Gimpy leg," he said, patting his left thigh. "I ripped something when I took a bad landing on the net back in Salt Lake City. The doc benched me for six months. I was going nuts wondering what to do with myself, and then I met up with this guy here." He pointed to Alex.

"Casey showed up at a book signing Melanie and I did in Salt Lake City," Alex explained. "He told us how he loved the circus animals, and we convinced him he'd enjoy seeing them in their natural surroundings."

"You were right," Casey said. "All this—" he gestured extravagantly "—is totally awesome. I'm going to hate to leave."

"Oh, look," Mitsu cried. "A baby giraffe suckling its mother."

They all rose to get a better look from the open top. "That baby's probably only a few days old," Alex told them. "See how wobbly its legs are."

"I like to see the game when their day is getting started like this," Mitsu said. "You see them yawning, then grazing for breakfast, and playful, like they're shaking the sleep out of their bodies."

"There's a couple of wildebeests that don't look too playful," Casey said, pointing.

Ahead of them, two animals had squared off and appeared ready to charge each other. They scuffed their feet, bellowed a bit, advanced, then sidestepped away.

"Mitsu's right," Alex said. "They're just fooling around with a little game of chicken."

When the vehicle rumbled over some rocks, Kate sat down to avoid breathing in the cloud of dust. The three young people didn't seem to notice. They chattered away, pointing, taking pictures, handing around the binoculars they were sharing. After a while Alex joined her.

"You've got yourself a terrific bunch of kids," Kate told him.

"Their enthusiasm is great, but I think that's going to be the norm for all our groups."

"I hope so, for your sake. This means so much to you."

He was looking at her intently. "Why not for you, too, Kate? You could be part of this, you know. Doesn't it beat drumming up publicity for diet books and astrological predictions?"

Kate frowned. "Alex, you have your life and I have mine."

"That's where the trouble lies—that separateness. Why can't we do something together?"

"Because this is your dream."

"It could be yours."

Kate wasn't ready to admit that the idea appealed to her.

Suddenly Hans gave an excited yelp and pointed. "It's Bessie . . . and there's Bobo behind her."

They stood, and Kate caught a glimpse of a rhino horn, then a disappearing rump as the huge animal lumbered into a thicket. A small calf followed.

"The last time we saw her she was on the other side of the camp," Hans said with a mixture of awe and frustration.

"She keeps on giving us the slip," Casey added with a laugh. "That rhino lady's built like a truck and moves just as fast when she feels like it—which is whenever we think we've got her cornered. She just doesn't want to be caught."

"Who's trying to catch her?" Kate asked.

"We are. That is, the rangers are," Hans answered. "That little one—"

"We named him Bobo," Casey interrupted. "And Mama is Bessie."

"The calf can't take care of himself yet," Hans explained. "His mother is his only protection."

"But Bessie sometimes forgets her maternal duties," Mitsu said. "She leaves him on his own and goes wandering off."

"Three days ago a pride of lions spotted Bobo alone. He would have been a goner if the rangers hadn't been around," Casey said.

"Apparently this mother and calf have been targeted for transfer to a safer habitat in the Mara," Alex told Kate.

"The plan was to take them two days ago," said Hans. "The team was all ready. Dr. Kenga—he's the park service vet—was going to let me help him. Unfortunately Bessie had other plans and disappeared. It's the second time she's done that."

"She doesn't know we're trying to protect her and her baby," Mitsu said.

Kate noticed Mitsu's use of the proprietary "we." So did Alex.

"It sounds like saving Bessie and Bobo has become a camp project."

"We're only allowed to help track her," Mitsu explained. "In the capture just Hans can help."

"We'd better go back and tell Dr. Kenga and the others where his roving rhinos have gotten to," Alex suggested. "If his team is ready, he may want to try to take them."

Richo turned the van around.

At the ranger station, the senior game warden quickly mobilized his group and reviewed the strategy. Kenga, with Hans assisting, would subdue the mother by implanting a tranquilizing dart. While the drug was taking effect, the capture unit would move in on Bobo and crate him. Then Bessie would be loaded onto a separate truck. Kate objected when told that she, Mitsu and Casey had to return with Richo to the safari camp.

"But I want to be there. I want to help."

For a moment she thought she'd convinced Alex. He gave her an appreciative smile, and she guessed that he, too, was recalling a time when she always clamored to be in on any action.

But then he said, "Kate, the best way you can help is to get back to camp and send the other vehicles to us when they come in from the game drives. We'll need them to circle the area in case Bessie panics and tries to get away before she's fully sedated."

Reluctantly Kate agreed to return with the others. At the camp, one van was just pulling in. "We don't have to wait here," Kate decided, thinking quickly. They told Ben Oloum, the camp manager, where to send the others when they returned. Then, followed by the other van and its excited occupants, they started back. About two miles out of camp, Kate saw something moving in the distance. She focused her binoculars, but it was only an ostrich loping toward them. Then, beyond the ungainly bird, she saw another figure.

"Oh, no!" Serenely plodding across the plain was Bessie. But where was her calf? Then Kate spotted Bobo, half-hidden behind his mother, only his wobbling backside showing. "Damn! They're almost a mile away from where we left them," Kate said.

"Old Bessie's on the move again," Casey warned.

"She's heading for the large watering hole by Ol Tukai," said Richo. "But east of it is bushland. In there we will lose her."

Mitsu shook her head. "Hans will be so disappointed."

Kate's mind was racing. "Maybe not. Richo, tell the other driver to find Alex and lead them back here. We'll stay and track the rhino. If she makes for the bushland, maybe we can head her off."

"Yahoo!" Casey was delighted at the prospect.

"Simmer down," Kate cautioned him. "This isn't a Wild West rodeo." Inwardly, though, she felt the same excitement.

Richo left the track to follow Bessie, but stayed a distance to her rear. "Come on, get closer," Casey urged.

"It is not safe."

"She doesn't even know we're around," Casey said.

"Wrong," Kate told him. "She knows we're here. One thing we don't need is two tons of angry rhino charging us. Right, Richo?"

The driver gave her an approving smile. "Right."

They continued to follow the two animals, keeping a safe gap between them. Kate kept her binoculars trained on the mother rhino. Small oxpeckers dotted the thick hide. As they approached the watering hole, they saw a profusion of other birds—bustards, saddle-billed storks and cranes among them. Kate, drawing on the lore she thought she'd forgotten, named the different varieties for Mitsu and Casey, but all the while she kept a watchful eye on the rhino and calf. With water in view now, Bessie was picking up speed.

"If the team gets here soon, we'll be in good shape," Kate said as she sized up the area. "There's plenty of open space."

"She will not linger long," Richo predicted. "She'll head that way—" he pointed to the hilly bushland east of them "—to get out of the sun."

"The trucks will never be able to maneuver up there," Casey said.

Richo shrugged with fatalistic agreement.

"So we'll have to keep her here," Kate told them.

"How?"

"By delaying her getting to the water. We'll divert her."

"A big rhino like that will not be easy to divert," Richo said.

He was right. Richo picked up speed, circled around the rhinos and stopped about a hundred yards in front of them. Bessie halted, huffed warningly and veered to the left. "Gun it and block her," Kate cried.

Richo did, and Bessie backed off angrily.

"Is she going to charge us?" Mitsu sounded frightened.

"I don't think so." Kate's voice was tense. "Right now she just wants to get away from us. But if she gets riled enough..."

"Yes, yes," Richo said grimly, indicating that he'd be wary—and ready.

They had to repeat the blocking tactic several times. The last time, Kate saw that the rhino's frustration and anger had mounted dangerously.

"Hey, look." Casey was pointing to the road. "Reinforcements."

"Great." Kate felt relief as Richo sped off. The rhino stayed where she was, looking around suspiciously for a moment, then made a beeline for the watering hole.

Richo joined the other vehicles, and the capture operation got quickly underway. There were three safari vans with the ranger vehicles. Alex joined Kate in Richo's van and signaled to the other vans to follow and station themselves on the other side of the pond. From there Kate watched, completely absorbed in the unfolding spectacle. With three armed rangers as protective escort, Dr. Kenga and Hans, moving in crouched postures, approached on foot. Bessie, contentedly drinking and cooling herself, appeared oblivious. Bobo splashed nearby. The men stopped and waited...and waited. The time seemed interminable. Then Bessie, having drunk her fill, squatted to a resting position. Dr. Kenga inched closer, stood and raised his gun, taking careful, steady aim.

"It is important that he place his shot just right," Richo said in a low, tense voice, "or she'll get away."

"What's he shooting her with?" Kate asked.

Alex answered. "A dart propelled by a .22 caliber charge. It contains a powerful morphine derivative mixed with tranquilizer."

"Poor thing," Mitsu said.

"With that thick hide she probably won't feel a thing," Casey guessed.

"Little more than a sting," Alex said. "The drug is what puts her out, and there's an antidote to reverse the effects immediately if necessary. That's why a veterinarian is always part of the team, to monitor the animal's vital signs."

Just then the muffled report of the dart gun was heard. The dart hit its mark, and now protruded from the rhino's rump. Hans gave a triumphant thumbs-up salute to Dr. Kenga. Bessie reared up, bellowed and charged around. Kenga and Hans sped back to the safety of the truck.

"It's not working," Casey said.

Alex shook his head. "It's working. It needs about fifteen minutes to take effect."

After a while the huge rhino started to slow down. "Good...she's feeling it," Alex said. Bessie was veering dazedly.

Kate saw the second truck pulling close to Bobo, getting between him and his mother. He started running in the other direction.

"Atta boy, Bobo," Casey called. "Give 'em a run for their money."

Alex laughed. "He's got spunk. That's a healthy sign for his future survival. But you know this whole thing's for his benefit."

"Yeah, I know," Casey admitted, "but I always root for the underdog."

When Bobo was caught, it took three men to pen him in the specially built crate.

"How will they ever move Bessie?" Mitsu wondered aloud.

"They'll need an army for Big Mama," Casey said.

"No." Kate remembered how her father and Harold Crane had managed to transport large animals. "They have a system."

When Bessie finally succumbed, the rangers roped the barely conscious animal. Then Dr. Kenga and Hans moved in.

"Can we not go closer now?" Mitsu asked.

"Sure." Alex told Richo to drive to the other side. The other vans followed, but parked so they wouldn't be in the way of the working teams.

Hans covered the rhino's eyes with a cloth and plugged her ears with cotton.

"Why does he do that?" Mitsu asked.

"It helps calm her."

For the next ten minutes, there were other ministrations, which Alex explained. Kenga administered another shot, an antibiotic to protect against any possible infection from the dart. Then Hans helped him check Bessie's vital signs. Apparently everything was in order, so the road crew took over. They scooped several cubic yards of dirt to make a ditch next to the sleeping Bessie. Into the ditch went a twelve-foot long wooden sledge, padded with straw-stuffed burlap. It took all the men to maneuver the rhino onto the sledge. Then she was speedily winched into the open-topped crate on the truck.

Bobo's forlorn cries were pitiful. "The poor thing," Mitsu sympathized. "He wants his mama."

"They'll be reunited soon," Alex reassured her. "In a place where they'll be a lot safer."

Dr. Kenga and the rest of the capture team were gratified that they'd accomplished their mission, but nothing could match the jubilation of the young campers. They'd been part of the rescue effort. "It makes me feel good," Casey declared as they drove back to camp. "What a memory! Next year when I'm back home, I'll think of Bobo, fat and happy, prancing around here."

The thought of Bobo "prancing around" when he reached his full growth made Kate smile. But she understood Casey's feelings.

"I think they'd have gotten away from us if it hadn't been for you guys," Alex said. "That was quick thinking."

"Kate's thinking," Casey said. "She gets the credit. It was her idea to send the other van to pick you up while we stayed with old Bessie."

"And to divert her from reaching the watering hole," Richo said.

"Which got to be a bit hairy," Casey added.

Alex had been resting his arm on top of Kate's seat. He lowered it to give her a hug. "So you're the heroine," he said lightly, but the admiration in his eyes was undeniable. "Congratulations."

"It was nothing. All in a day's work."

Kate's offhand remark was a cover-up for her elation, which came from a deep personal satisfaction.

CHAPTER ELEVEN

AT THE END OF THE WEEK, Kate and Alex left for Lake Naivasha and their rendezvous with Derek, Susan and Melanie. It had been a good week. Kate was surprised at how close she felt to the group after such a short time. At first she'd been an onlooker, but soon she shared in their camaraderie. She was glad she and Alex would be rejoining the group with Susan.

"It's strange," she told Alex when they were on their way, "how ethnic differences don't seem to matter with that crowd."

"Not strange at all. Out here it's much easier to get in touch with what's important."

Kate peered out at the stark, majestic landscape. "There's so much beauty out there."

"That's only part of it. It's what's inside you that's vital—what you have to touch."

Kate knew what he meant. Something in her that had been buried for years was now reawakening. It was exhilarating, but there was also a fearful dimension to it, and Kate wondered where it would lead her.

"They're all excited about going to the Mara," Kate said, trying to keep the conversation from focusing on herself. "Hans wants to see how Bobo and his mother made out, and Casey's dying to take a hot-air-balloon ride."

"We could be with them if—"

"Don't . . . please. We have an agreement. When we pick Susan up, we'll camp with the group up north, but I'm still passing on the Mara."

If Alex was disappointed, he didn't show it. "You're the boss" was all he said.

After a brief stop in Nairobi, they continued north via the Uhuru Highway. The road climbed steadily and soon gave them a vista of the Ngong Hills. Leaving behind the pleasant suburbs, they came to the steep hillside farms of the Kikuyu people. At the junction beyond Limuru, Alex picked up A104. "I'm impressed," she remarked. "A really good road, for a change."

"The best in Kenya."

At first the road skirted the Rift escarpments. Alex slowed down often to point out the awesome views of the Great Rift Valley with its volcanic cones, some of them spewing jets of steam. On the second spur, Alex stopped the van so they could look into the crater at Mount Longonot.

The road then descended across the slope of the escarpment to the valley floor, and ahead of them was Lake Naivasha. Alex took the rough road that circled around the lake. When they were children, their parents had occasionally taken them to Naivasha for a holiday. Kate recognized the neighborhood of the bungalow they had stayed in. "But the lake looks smaller," she said with nostalgic regret. "And where's that little island we used to swim to?"

"These islands are made up of papyrus clumps, so they keep splitting and drifting and re-forming," Alex told her. "And you know the lake is never the same. It rises and spreads, or shrinks and falls—all according to the rains. This year the rains came late."

"Our bungalow was just around that bend, right?" she asked excitedly.

"Right."

"And Joy Adamson's house was down about a mile."

"Right."

"Remember how impressed I was that she'd lived there?" Kate asked. "I just loved *Born Free*."

"I remember that you swore you'd grow up to be just like Adamson."

"Kids have all kinds of dreams," she said with a wry smile.

"Dreams can become real—if you don't give up on them."

Kate made no comment.

Kama Sloane's cottage was on a hilltop overlooking the lake. Kate was looking forward to seeing her again. Elizabeth's mother had seemed such an exotic figure to Kate when they'd all lived together on the compound. Though Kama spoke English well and usually dressed in Western clothes, she became another person when she was getting ready to go back to visit her family. Kate loved to see her put on the rich colors of her native dress and adorn her neck and arms with brightly beaded necklaces and bracelets. She even seemed to carry herself differently when she was thus attired, with the proud dignity of Masai nobility.

"Kate..." Alex broke into her thoughts. "Do you remember...?" he started to ask.

"When the warriors would come to escort Kama back to her village?" Sensing that Alex's memory was exactly in tune with hers, Kate was able to complete his question. "They were so fierce looking. I kept trying to make them laugh, but they wouldn't. They ignored me."

"Only when you were making a pest of yourself. That stopped when you started to grow up."

"You must have told them when I reached puberty," Kate teased.

Alex laughed. "I didn't have to. That's when they started to look at you differently...appraisingly."

"Dad said he was offered ten cattle for me as a bride."

"And you felt insulted."

"Sure! I was worth at least twenty."

They laughed together. Kate realized this was the first time she'd been able to draw on a happy memory of her father and not have it tinged with the bitterness of his death.

Kama must have heard the van, because she was waiting outside. She wore a yellow blouse and denim skirt, similar to the outfit Kate had on. But her burnished mahogany skin, straight bearing and classic features announced her Masai blood. She forgot her usual reserve in her joy at seeing them. She hugged Kate and then held her at arm's length to look her over.

"You haven't changed at all," Kate said.

The older woman smiled. "You have. You left here a very sad little girl. You return a woman." She glanced at Alex. "A happy woman, I hope."

Kate didn't know what to say, but Kama didn't seem to expect a reply. She ushered them inside to an airy, shuttered sitting room, simply furnished with sofa and chairs of polished dark wood and cushioned with brightly hued native fabric. A sheepskin rug lay in front of the sofa under the low, oval table.

Kama excused herself for a moment and returned with a tray holding sandwiches and fruit and a large pitcher of juice.

"How did you know I was hungry?" Alex asked, helping himself.

"You're always hungry."

"And lunch was only two hours ago," Kate reminded him.

"My digestive system works quickly," Alex explained. "I have to keep up with it."

The women exchanged knowing smiles.

"Tell me about yourself," Kama said to Kate, but when Kate gave her a factual summary of her life in America, the woman held up her hand. "All that I know from Derek and your mother's letters."

"Oh, well . . . what did you want to know?"

"How are you really, what brought you back and how you think and feel inside, now that you are here."

"A tall order," Kate said, feeling uneasy at such questions.

"You're right," Kama said, backing off. "We will get to know each other again . . . all in good time." She turned her attention to Alex. "And you? You've neglected me."

"Not true. I stopped by here soon after I got back from America, but you were away. I heard your mother was ailing. How is—" Kama's grimace of pain gave him his answer. "Kama, I'm sorry."

Her chin went up, and her grimace became stoic acceptance. "It was her time. The tragedy is not death, but life that is empty or wasted. The old one had a full life."

"Your people will miss her," Alex said gently.

"Yes."

"They'll want someone to take her place. Did they pressure you to stay?"

"There are always the persuasions to stay. But I have become spoiled by European ways—and modern plumbing," she added with a wry laugh. "So I will go back and forth, dividing my time, as I have divided my life."

"That must be hard to do," Kate said.

"It was my choice when I married Patrick Sloane," Kama said simply.

"How is he?" Kate asked.

"He is well."

"You've heard from him?" Alex was surprised. He'd told Kate that when Sloane had learned of his daughter's death in America, he'd been desolate. For a while he drank heavily, but finally pulled himself together and found work as a guide, seeking assignments that took him away for long periods of time. It was as if Elizabeth's death had broken his connection to people. This last time he'd been gone for months, and Kama had no address for him.

"No, I haven't heard from him in a long time," Kama answered, "but he is well."

How could she know, Kate wondered. But, then, Kama's vision had always penetrated beyond what others could see.

"He will come soon," Kama said, and pointed to a large framed picture of a smiling Susan. "To see his daughter's child."

"You've written to him that Susan is here?" Kate asked.

"No."

"How can you be sure he'll come?"

"Certain things I know."

An image flashed across Kate's mind. Two days before Alastair Marlowe's death, Kama had gone away to her village, but that night she'd returned unexpectedly. Kate remembered the look on Kama's face when she'd entered the house. No one had to tell her what had occurred. She'd known.

The sound of a vehicle rumbling up the road sent Kama outside in a rush. "That must be Derek," Alex guessed. He and Kate followed.

It was Derek, with Susan and Melanie. Kate had wondered how Susan would react to her grandmother. She'd been a toddler the last time she'd visited Kenya. Susan hung back for a moment, watching as her father and Kama embraced. Then she approached, stood before her grandmother and bowed her head. Kate was surprised. It was the customary way a Masai child greeted her elders. Derek must have coached Susan. Kama smiled tenderly and, again as was the custom, placed her hand on Susan's head. But then Kama kneeled and opened her arms. Susan hesitated for just a second, then hugged her grandmother. Kate saw tears on the older woman's face and felt a sympathetic wetness in her own eyes.

Melanie stayed in the background until Derek called her over. "This is our friend, Melanie Pearson" was his introduction. "We're thinking of working on a book together. Melanie did the photographs for *A Vanishing World*."

Melanie had a deep, golden tan from her week at the beach and looked striking in an orange jumpsuit. But her smile was uneasy. Kate sensed that Derek was downplaying his relationship with Melanie. Perhaps he feared Kama wouldn't approve. He needn't have worried. When they all went inside, the conversation flowed. Kama, without being obvious, was taking pains to put Melanie at ease, and the young woman gradually relaxed. After some perceptive questions and silent observations, Kama seemed warmly accepting of her son-in-law's "friend." Now it was Derek who took on a nervous air. Kate wondered what had happened between Melanie and him at Mombasa.

At dinner that evening Susan held forth. She wanted to describe every detail of her wonderful stay at the beach. "I can hold my breath underwater and float on my back and Melanie taught me how to do the crawl . . . that's what they call it. It's swimming, but it really looks like a crawl 'cause this is how you have to move your arms."

Susan demonstrated, and Melanie had to be quick to rescue the glass the little girl almost knocked over. Susan was undaunted. "And then me and Melanie . . ." She began to relate another escapade, punctuated with many "me and

Melanie" phrases. Kama looked from the vibrant young woman to her eager granddaughter, and her warm smile embraced them both. "I wish I could have been with you," she said.

"It was fun," Susan said. "And when I go camping tomorrow with Aunt Kate and Uncle Alex, that'll be fun, too. *Ayah*, you can come if you want to."

"I wish I could, but we'll have to have our visit later on. Tomorrow I must leave, too. I go to the Mara for a very special ceremony."

"Is it a wedding?" the little girl asked.

"No, but just as happy. It's called *eunoto*, and is one of the four most important Masai rituals."

"Eunoto." Susan repeated the word, perfectly imitating her grandmother's pronunciation.

"Isn't that where Masai warriors graduate and become clan elders?" Melanie asked eagerly.

"'Graduate'?" Kama smiled. "Yes, that is one way of describing it. How do you know about *eunoto*?"

"I've done a lot of reading about Masai traditions." She glanced at Derek.

"Reading is good," Kama declared. "Seeing is even better." She looked thoughtful for a moment, then said, "Why don't you come—all of you?"

"What? Really?" Melanie asked.

Kate understood the surprise on Alex's face. Years ago they'd begged to witness one of the impressive Masai rituals, but it had never been possible.

"How can you manage that?" Derek asked. Outsiders seldom got to see these ceremonies.

Kama smiled. "I have much status now, Derek. In fact, at meetings I am permitted to sit with the elders. But in this *eunoto*, I take the part of a mother to one of the warriors."

She explained that her brother's son, Latana, was one of the men being elevated to the higher age-set. The mother of each warrior had a specific role in the complicated four-day ceremony, but her nephew's mother had erred sexually and would not be permitted to participate. Kama would be taking her place. "I go tomorrow for the preparations. The chief will choose the site, and there is much to be done. But the ceremony will begin at the end of the week. Masai people from all over will be coming. It will be something to see."

"Derek, do you think we can go?" Melanie asked eagerly.

"The symposium starts tomorrow, but I might be able to break away and then go back. Maybe we can catch at least the last day," Derek said. "It would be a shame to miss it."

"That's just what I was thinking." Alex directed his remark to Kate. "This may be our only chance."

"I'm afraid you're right," said Kama sadly. "The old traditions are dying."

"What do you say, Kate?" Alex asked.

"I don't think so." Kate's frown was an unspoken reminder to Alex about their agreement.

Kama gave Kate a questioning look, but said nothing.

After dinner the two men went for a walk. Kate and Melanie volunteered to clean up, leaving Kama to visit with her granddaughter. From the kitchen, the young women couldn't make out what was being said, but they heard the husky melody of Kama's voice and the eager curiosity in Susan's as she questioned her. Then there was only Kama's voice, and Kate wondered if Susan had fallen asleep. She went to the doorway to see. Kama was sitting on the sheepskin rug, her granddaughter opposite, their hands joined. The two were leaning toward each other, Susan with a rapt expression as she listened.

"And the legend is that Engai, the god of the world, had three children. To each he gave a gift. One received an arrow, to hunt for his food. The second was given a hoe, to cultivate the land. To the third he gave a stick. Can you guess what that was for?"

"Yes, yes," Susan replied. "My mother told me this story when I was little. The stick's for pushing the cows."

Kama laughed. "Yes, something like that. For herding cattle. That son's name was Natero Kop. He is the father of the Masai people. Traditionally the Masai live by their cattle. Only their children are more important. It is—or was—a simple life. The Masai live close to nature. They look to the heavens to send rain that will soak the earth and make the grass grow. With grass the cattle will thrive, and so will the Masai people. With no rain there is no grass—without grass, no cattle—and without cattle, no Masai." Her voice fell sadly. "That is what we used to believe."

"Do all Masai have cattle?" Susan asked.

"Those who live in the old way."

"Where's yours, *Ayah*?"

"Ah!" Kama gave a rueful laugh. "Here at Naivasha I do not live in the old way. I have no cattle."

"When I'm big, I'll buy you a hundred."

"Oh, thank you. But I fear that by the time you are grown, the old ways will be no more. Not yet, though. When I go to *eunoto* tomorrow, it will be as it has been from the beginning. It is a ceremony that happens only once about every fifteen years, sometimes longer. I myself have seen only one other. This may be the last."

"I wish I could see it."

"So do I. But I will tell you all about it when we have our long visit afterward."

"Tell me the story now, *Ayah*, about what's going to happen."

The more
you love romance . . .
the more
you'll love this offer

FREE!

Mail this heart today! (See inside)

Join us on a Harlequin Honeymoon
and we'll give you
4 free books
A free bracelet watch
And a free mystery gift

IT'S A
HARLEQUIN HONEYMOON—
A SWEETHEART
OF A FREE OFFER!
HERE'S WHAT YOU GET:

1. Four New Harlequin Superromance® Novels— FREE!

Take a Harlequin Honeymoon with your four exciting romances—yours FREE from Harlequin Reader Service®. Each of these hot-off-the-press novels brings you the passion and tenderness of today's greatest love stories . . . your free passports to bright new worlds of love and foreign adventure.

2. A Lovely Bracelet Watch—FREE!

You'll love your elegant bracelet watch—this classic LCD quartz watch is a perfect expression of your style and good taste—and it is yours FREE as an added thanks for giving our Reader Service a try.

3. An Exciting Mystery Bonus—FREE!

You'll be thrilled with this surprise gift. It is elegant as well as practical.

4. Money-Saving Home Delivery!

Join Harlequin Reader Service® and enjoy the convenience of previewing four new books every month delivered right to your home. Each book is yours for only $2.74*—21¢ less per book than the cover price. And there is *no* extra charge for postage and handling. Great savings plus total convenience add up to a sweetheart of a deal for you! If you're not completely satisfied, you may cancel at any time, for any reason, simply by sending us a note or shipping statement marked "cancel" or by returning any shipment to us at our cost.

5. Free Insiders' Newsletter

It's *heart to heart*®, the indispensible insiders' look at our most popular writers, upcoming books, even comments from readers and much more.

6. More Surprise Gifts

Because our home subscribers are our most valued readers, when you join the Harlequin Reader Service®, we'll be sending you additional free gifts from time to time—as a token of our appreciation.

START YOUR HARLEQUIN HONEYMOON TODAY—JUST
COMPLETE, DETACH AND MAIL YOUR FREE-OFFER CARD

START YOUR
HARLEQUIN HONEYMOON TODAY.
JUST COMPLETE, DETACH AND MAIL YOUR
FREE OFFER CARD.

If offer card is missing, write to: Harlequin Reader Service® 901 Fuhrmann Blvd
P.O. Box 1867 Buffalo NY 14269-1867

DETACH AND MAIL TODAY!

BUSINESS REPLY CARD

FIRST CLASS MAIL   PERMIT NO. 717   BUFFALO, NY

POSTAGE WILL BE PAID BY ADDRESSEE

HARLEQUIN READER SERVICE
901 FUHRMANN BLVD
PO BOX 1867
BUFFALO NY 14240-9952

NO POSTAGE
NECESSARY
IF MAILED
IN THE
UNITED STATES

"All right. Come here and sit close."

Susan scrambled over and sat between her grandmother's legs, leaning back as Kama held her around the waist. "It's a very special ceremony. It starts with the mothers of the most honored warriors building a *manyatta*."

"What's that?"

"It's like a village, a kraal, but when only warriors live there, it's called a *manyatta*. There are forty-nine houses in the *manyatta*, for the forty-nine noblest men. Each mother puts up the house for her son."

"Ladies make houses?"

Kama smiled. "Ladies do many things. These are simple huts made of grass and branches and mud. At the center they build the ceremonial house where all the food for feasting will be stored. There will be many, many people, some from far away. The warriors will come. Some will be sad."

"But why? You said it was a happy time."

"Because they have to give up their warrior life to become elders."

"Don't they want to?"

"Yes, because that is the way it must be. But they're also sad to leave the life of the *morani*, the guardians and protectors of their people. New youths are waiting to become warriors, so these must now take on the responsibilities of elderhood and marriage."

"Will there be a wedding, too?"

"Perhaps. Sometimes, after the ceremony, a bride is given to the leading warrior and there is a wedding."

"A wedding, too...." Susan was enthralled.

Kama continued with her story. Kate and Melanie went into the living room and quietly sat down to listen. Kate became distracted by her own thoughts. Susan and Kama sitting close that way, the child eager to hear about the traditions of her grandmother's people . . . Kate's emotions were stirred. Witnessing *eunoto*, especially seeing her own grandmother as a participant—that would be something Susan would always remember.

Alex and Derek returned and joined the group. One story seemed to lead to another, and Susan would have had her grandmother talking on and on, but tiredness finally took over. Kama took the sleepy child and put her to bed.

Kate stepped outside, and a moment later Alex joined her. They stood quietly. The moon cast a pale golden shaft across the dark water. "Alex," Kate said finally, "I've changed my mind."

"I thought you would."

She turned to face him. "How do you know what I mean? I haven't even told you what I've changed my mind about."

"About *eunoto* and going to the Mara."

"What made you think I'd change my mind?"

"Because I willed it . . . desperately," he said with a smile. "Maybe Kama sent out some persuasive thought waves, too. And Susan."

But Kate knew that her decision was not solely because of her niece. This country was reaching out to her. All the things she'd once loved were drawing her again. Perhaps it was time to face what she feared, the place that she associated with pain and unbearable hurt.

THE GROUP SPLIT UP the following day. For a moment during the leave-taking, Susan verged on tears, but Kama told her she would see her in a few days, and Derek promised to return for the ceremony. It was Melanie, however, who struck the right note by talking about all the fun Susan was going to have camping with Alex and Kate. Kate picked up the theme and told Susan about what a great time she'd had during the past week. When Susan heard about the rescue of Bessie and Bobo, she forgot her qualms. "Can we do that again?" she asked.

"You never can tell," Alex answered. "The rangers may need our help again. But there'll be plenty of other things to do. There's a place I know you'll love."

"Where?"

"The Mount Kenya Safari Club."

"You're going there? Now that's a place I adore," Melanie said. "Talk about living in the lap of luxury. Bill Holden knew what he was doing when he got into building that place. Suzie, you're in luck. There's horseback riding, and a big pool with a picture window on one side where you can see people swimming underwater."

"I can practice my swimming," Susan said.

"Right on." Melanie and Susan slapped palms. The affection between them was obvious.

"There's an animal orphanage there," Alex added, "where you can touch some of the baby animals. Even pick them up."

"Like the petting zoo back home?"

"Even better," Alex promised.

Susan was sold. The goodbyes ended on an up note.

"I didn't know a luxury resort was part of our itinerary," Kate told Alex when they were on their way.

"I just added it on," he admitted. "It's close to the campground, so why not? We'll take the whole group...let them see how the upper crust lives. And the Mount Kenya Safari Club's not your ordinary fancy resort. It's one of the most famous hotels in the world. It'll be an educational experience for them."

Alex had arranged to team up with the campers at Lake Nakuru, and from there the whole group would proceed to the tented cabins in Mount Kenya National Park. Alex stopped often so Susan, who'd become adept with her little camera under Melanie's tutelage, could take pictures of the animals. She was especially enthralled by the sight of a mother elephant leading her baby across a river. On the other side the mother stopped so the baby could nurse, and Susan snapped a picture.

"Wait'll I show Arnold my pictures," Susan said. "He went to Disneyland last year and kept bragging an' bragging."

"Well, you'll have a lot to brag about after this trip," Kate told her.

"Yeah."

"You'll get some good pictures of flamingos at Lake Nakuru," Alex said.

"Flamingos?" Susan wasn't impressed. "Arnold's grandmother's house in Florida has one on the lawn. He showed me a picture. It wasn't real."

"Well, the ones you see will be," Alex assured her. "A million of them . . . and all real."

Sure enough, the flamingos ringed the lake like a pink bracelet. Alex told Susan to hold her picture taking until they got closer. There would be a lot of other birds, too. Susan agreed. "Anyway, I like elephants better than birds," she said.

Alex scouted around and soon spotted his group. The four vans had parked at the edge of the lake and the young people had fanned out, trying to get close to the spectacle of thousands of birds in the water. Alex pulled up to where Richo and the other drivers were standing.

"*Jambo,* Susan," Richo cried. He lifted her and swung her around as she laughed with delight.

"How goes it?" Alex asked. "Any problems?"

"Just the usual," Richo said, and pointed.

An older driver was shaking his head. "I knew for sure he'd be one who would get wet." He was talking about Casey, whose right foot had sunk through the crust until he was calf deep in mud. The young man was laughing as he struggled to free himself. He'd just gotten his foot out, when his left foot cracked through, and then he laughed even harder. Hans and Mitsu were waiting for him, but he waved them on and returned to the embankment.

"Hi," he greeted them. Then to the drivers he said, "I know, I know...you told me to walk slowly and test each step before I put my weight on it. So I goofed."

There was a yell and more laughter from the lake bed as several others had the same misfortune. "See," Casey said. "More goofers. Walking on that stuff's not easy. And I've walked many a tightrope in my time."

Susan's eyes grew round. "You have? Really? Like the circus?"

"Really. In fact, *in* the circus. Sometimes with my little sister on my back. Hello. You must be Kate's niece."

"My name's Susan."

"Well, hi, Susan. Welcome aboard. I'm Casey. How'd you like to go out there with the others?"

Susan looked to Kate for permission.

"She's light enough, so she won't have a problem," Alex remarked.

"Especially if she's riding piggyback," Casey said, and knelt down. "Hop on."

When Kate smiled and nodded, Susan grabbed Casey around the neck, and he hoisted her up.

"You'll probably sink in again," Alex warned.

"Not to worry. I think I've got the hang of it now. Besides, I'm already mucked up, so who cares? Ready, Susan?"

"Ready."

"Off we go."

Kate and Alex followed them. Kate walked behind Alex. "I know your trick," Alex said. "If I fall through, you take another path."

"I'll lead if you like, but it makes more sense if the heavy one goes first."

He turned and confronted her. "Is that the role you've consigned me to—playing the heavy?"

"Only in weight, not character," she said, giving him a playful push. He caught her hands and stepped back, pulling her with him. They were both slightly off-balance and felt the crust below their feet begin to crack. Alex nimbly stepped to his right and Kate hopped over, also.

"Hey, that's a pretty neat dance step," Casey called to them, and they burst out laughing.

The laughter stayed with them all day.

SUSAN WAS AN IMMEDIATE HIT with all the campers. When they left Nakuru for Mount Kenya National Park, each van group vied to have her ride with them, but she remained loyal to Richo. She had also formed a special attachment to Casey, so the young acrobat, together with Kate, Alex, Hans and Mitsu, crowded into one van for the long drive. Susan became so adept at spotting game that Richo called her his assistant guide, and she giggled with pride and excitement.

At the camp Alex was concerned that all was not ready for their arrival. His manager had been called home for some personal emergency, and the preparations had been put on hold. Instead of being a problem, the group turned the situation into a party of sorts. There was no one leader. They just seemed to organize themselves. The tents were already there, but cots and bedding and chairs had to be brought from the storeroom and set up. Mitsu even had Susan helping.

Luckily provisions had been delivered before the manager had left, so the cook tent was well supplied. Casey and Kate decided on a menu of grilled lamb, vegetable stew and a salad, and the delighted cook found he had a half-dozen enthusiastic helpers to get everything done. They ate voraciously and everyone pitched in to clean up afterward. Then Alex built a campfire, and they all sat around. Someone—Kate didn't know who—started singing a German folk song. Another voice joined in, and when the group caught the melody, they hummed along. That started it. The next song was Spanish, then came another language and still another. The French "Frère Jacques" was one many knew the words to, and when Casey boomed out "The Bear Went over the Mountain," there was an appreciative laugh, and a crescendo of voices, Susan's included, joined in.

Afterward Kate was concerned that in Susan's overexcited state she wouldn't be able to sleep, but the little girl was out the minute her head touched the pillow in the tent she was sharing with her aunt. Kate heard her name called and quietly went outside.

"Everything okay?" Alex asked.

"Fine. She's fast asleep."

"Want to go for a walk?"

She did, but couldn't. "I don't think I should. Susan might wake up and get confused about being in a strange place."

"You know, you might consider letting Susan bunk with Mitsu and some of the other girls."

There was enough light for Kate to see the golden gleam in his eyes. "Are you sure your suggestion doesn't hide an ulterior motive?" she asked.

He put his arm around her. "Hey, Susan would enjoy their company—and I would certainly enjoy yours." His kiss emphasized his meaning.

Kate surrendered to the sweetness of the moment. "We'll see," she said when she drew away. "Good night."

"I'm right in the next tent, in case you need me."

"I'm sure we can get through the night just fine."

"I don't know if I can. So near—and yet so far."

"You'll survive," Kate said with a soft laugh. "Good night."

It took Kate a long time to finally fall asleep that night. Yet there was no restless tossing. As she lay on the narrow bed, she sighed with deep contentment. Tonight Alex was not lying next to her, but she felt very close to him. This journey with him was taking her back to a happy time they'd shared. She didn't want to think about what would happen when she confronted the place where that happiness had been destroyed. Not yet.

CHAPTER TWELVE

"HEY, MAN, this is unbelievable," Casey said, gazing around the reception area of the Mount Kenya Safari Club. "Are you sure they're gonna let us in?"

The other campers were similarly awed. Alex reassured them. "The manager's one of the supporters of Youth Safari. Plus he's an old friend. We're his guests. He's going to join us for lunch, then you've got the run of the place for the afternoon."

When they went into the elegant dining room, the young people joked about the contrast between their scruffy attire and the opulence around them. The maître d', with just the hint of a smile, escorted them to a more secluded section of the dining room and told them to help themselves to the buffet.

Casey returned with a plate laden with food. "Not to knock the chow we get on safari, but this is great. Any chance of taking a few doggy bags back with us?" Hans and Mitsu gave him disapproving looks. "No, huh? Okay, then, it's pig-out time. Stuff yourselves while you can."

Charles Mayfield, the manager, joined them. "So this is your launch group of Jambo campers," he said to Alex. "They look like a good bunch of kids."

"They are—with healthy appetites, too. I hope they leave something for your other guests."

"There's always more than enough."

Alex introduced Kate.

"This is a real treat for our kids. Thank you for having us," she said, then realized she sounded as proprietary about the group as Alex did—and indeed she felt that way. It was obvious Mayfield accepted her as Alex's associate, and perhaps more.

Rhetorically Mayfield asked, "You know how this guy of yours hooked me as a contributor? He said we had a common cause. We both love Kenya and want to give our visitors a happy experience, the only difference being that we cater to a different clientele."

"A logical argument," Kate said with a smile.

"You're prejudiced," Mayfield countered.

Kate didn't deny it.

When the young people were all back, Mayfield made a short welcoming speech. He told the group that if they wanted to use the pool they could freshen up and change in a hospitality suite, and invited them all to have a good time. There was a chorus of thank-yous, which Mayfield waved off. "I've got to get back to my office," he told Alex and Kate. "I'll see you later."

Susan, who had been sitting with Casey, ran up to her aunt as soon as she'd finished eating. "Can I go swimming now?" she asked.

"Not right after a heavy meal," Kate said.

"But I didn't eat nothing heavy."

"Oh, yeah?" Alex reached down and cupped his palm over her stomach. "That feels like a pretty heavy little belly to me. You plop that belly in the pool and you'll sink right to the bottom. How about we go to the animal orphanage first and then you can go swimming."

"Okay. C'mon Casey...Hans...c'mon Mitsu. We're gonna see the orphan animals."

They were all captivated by the place. Susan was ecstatic at actually being able to pet a lion cub. Hans was avid to learn how the animals were cared for. Mitsu fell in love with each one she touched, and Casey avowed how the playful animals were a miniature circus just doing what came naturally. "We used to talk about having a place like this one day," Alex reminded Kate.

"Not like this." Her gaze took in all the paying visitors from the resort. "Not that there's anything wrong with this," she added hastily. "It's a wonderful facility, and I'm sure there are advantages in being connected to a big resort, but..."

He completed her thought. "It's not what we had in mind."

"What we talked about was far more rustic, a habitat in the bush, with lots of space to care for injured and orphaned animals."

"Only until they could be returned to their own kind."

"Right." Kate laughed. "You were always afraid I'd get too attached and not want to let them go."

"Like with that baby elephant."

"I know better now."

He gave her a speculative look. "Then maybe we can go ahead with our plans."

"Alex," Kate said, shaking her head, "they were daydreams, not plans."

"That's how plans get started."

"You never give up, do you?"

"Nope," he said. Then someone he knew beckoned to him from an area marked Private–Employees Only, and he couldn't continue the conversation.

When the others were finally ready to leave for their swim, Alex was missing. "You go along," Kate told them. "I'll wait for Alex."

"You hafta come see me swim," Susan said.

"I will in just a while."

After they'd gone, Kate wandered around. There was a cheetah cub, as cute and playful as a kitten. She pictured the lithe, swift creature he would grow into. On their own, orphaned and injured animals had little chance to survive. One school of thought had it that such was nature's way, so why interfere. But Kate remembered her father's argument—since man had already interfered and put wild animals in greater jeopardy than ever before, he was obligated to save the ones he could.

Kate had just told Alex that their childhood notion about operating an animal shelter had been a daydream, but her thoughts right now contradicted that statement. Her mind had hit on an idea—the animal orphanage could be incorporated into Alex's youth program. Not just as an interesting attraction for a safari stop, but something in which the young people would be actively involved. The facility could be staffed by young professionals and interns on one- or two-year assignments. There would have to be a permanent manager, of course, but Kate could envision enthusiastic young people like Hans doing a residency.

The children who'd been playing with the cheetah cub departed, and the little fellow came up to sniff at Kate's shoes. She knelt and stroked him behind his ears. He closed his eyes contentedly. Kate picked him up. The cub nestled against her and promptly fell asleep.

"Want to keep him?"

It was Alex. She hadn't seen him approach. "Can I?"

"No." He took the cub and handed it to one of the attendants. "Where'd the others go?"

"For a swim."

"Sounds good to me."

On the walk back to the hotel, Kate told Alex about her idea. "What's the matter?" she asked when she'd finished. "No enthusiasm? Don't you approve?"

"Sure I approve. It's a great idea, Kate, but there's just no way I can tackle another project—not for a long time."

"Oh." Her disappointment showed. "That's too bad."

He seemed about to say something, then thought better of it and shrugged. Yet Kate could read his mind. He couldn't initiate the project she'd described, but if she really wanted to see it happen, she could take it on. Kate didn't volunteer.

THEY SPENT the whole afternoon at the pool. Alex rounded up the gang at six o'clock. "Time to go." They assembled outside where the vans were waiting.

"Hey, here comes Mr. Mayfield," Casey said. "Maybe he wants us to stay for dinner."

"I doubt that," the girl with the lilting Southern accent told him. "According to the posted rules, after sundown, 'proper attire' means skirts or dresses for the ladies and jackets and ties for the gentlemen. T-shirts and jeans don't qualify."

"You're kidding," Casey said. "A tie? Boy, this place is great, but no, thanks. Let's go home." He got into the van, then leaned out the window and waved. "Hey, Mr. Mayfield, thanks for the hospitality. We'll have to do it again sometime."

His brashness amused Mayfield, who smiled and waved back.

"Come to see us off?" Alex asked his friend.

"Yes and no. I wanted to say goodbye to your group, but why don't you and Miss Marlowe stay for dinner?"

"What's up?" Alex wanted to know.

Mayfield laughed. "What a suspicious nature. Actually there's someone here I thought you should meet. Josh Liebman, a Britisher who makes documentaries. I told him what you were doing, and he's interested."

"As a subject for a documentary?" Kate asked.

"Never can tell."

Kate immediately saw the marvelous possibilities. "That would be terrific." Then she looked at Alex's outfit and her own wrinkled poplin pants. "But I don't think we quite meet your dress code," she said with a helpless gesture.

"I can take care of that," Mayfield told them.

"Charley's got a special wardrobe he lends out when a guest isn't attired in suitable sartorial splendor," Alex said.

"Lucky for you I do," Mayfield told Alex. "I don't think you own a tie."

"Not true. I own several. But they're for the city, not a safari. Insisting on ties is pretentious."

"Our patrons like a little formal elegance in the evening. In fact, they expect it."

"Not this patron."

The verbal sparring was without rancor and apparently a habit with the two men. Alex turned to Kate. "What do you think? Should we stay?"

"Could be a good idea to meet with Mr. Liebman."

It was settled. Susan was happy at the prospect of bunking with Mitsu and "the girls." There was some teasing about Alex and Kate staying behind. "Want us to wait up for you?" Casey called as the vans drove off.

They didn't bother to answer.

MAYFIELD'S ASSISTANT, Janine, a stylish Frenchwoman, looked Kate over and said, "I have just the thing." She went to a room adjoining her office and returned with a dress on a hanger. "It's a size eight," she said. "It should fit. But I don't know about the shoes." She held up a pair of pink sandals. "These are the only ones that go with the dress. They're a seven."

Kate wore an eight. "I'll make do," she said. She took the dress, a pastel chiffon, very light and romantic looking. "Thank you. This is an unusual service you provide."

"An unofficial extra I thought of. And it costs almost nothing. Some of our guests are very wealthy, very temperamental women, the kind who wear something once, and then discard it. The clothes they deliberately leave behind..." Janine made a sound of Gallic disapproval. "You would not believe it."

"But this dress is gorgeous."

"Not on the one who bought it. It is youthful and she was not. On you it will be different. Go, put it on."

Janine loaned her a makeup kit. In the hospitality suite, Kate showered and changed. The dress was slightly big, but since it had no waistline and fell loosely from the shoulders, this didn't matter. A light, sheer ruffle formed the sleeve, circled the bodice and cascaded down the tiered hemline that came to just below her knee. When she returned to Janine's office, the Frenchwoman nodded approvingly.

"C'est magnifique" was her judgment.

Alex was to meet her in the lounge. When she walked in, his smile was admiring. "You look beautiful."

He wore a blue blazer, white shirt and striped tie. "Both of us in borrowed finery," she said with a soft laugh. "What imposters we are."

"No more so than others," Alex said, glancing around at the elegantly dressed crowd. "Everyone here is trying to make an impression."

"But I'll bet their shoes aren't a size too small."

Alex laughed. "Your shoes are tight and so's my collar. Think we'll make it through the night?"

Her laughter mingled with his. "We'll have to."

Mayfield and Josh Liebman joined them for dinner. Kate could see that the producer wasn't feeling well. "The African version of Montezuma's revenge," he explained. "I don't know what you call it here, but it's the same misery I had on location in the Yucatán last year."

"I can give you something that will help," Mayfield offered.

"Nothing I don't already have. I have tons of medication—preventive, purgative and palliative. The first didn't work, I don't need the second, but the third is beginning to do some good. I think the worst is over."

"Better eat lightly," Mayfield advised.

Liebman ordered a grilled chop and rice but barely touched it. He was much more interested in talking about his work. Kate liked him. His gruff geniality coupled with an acute intellect reminded her of her boss, but with an English accent. She was fascinated by his description of the film he'd just completed. It was about those first East German escapees who'd gone over the Berlin wall into West Berlin and what had happened to them in the intervening years. "It was interesting," he said, "but it's over. I'm ready for something different."

"Is Kenya your next setting?" Alex asked.

"I don't know. Maybe. That's what Mayfield here is suggesting. I came down for a short vacation before heading home, but I could be tempted to come back to do a film."

"About wildlife?"

"No. That's been done often enough. I'd want a new angle."

He'd given Kate the opening she wanted. "Maybe you've found it."

"Oh?"

"How about a focus that combines scenic beauty, wildlife, social issues and human interest?"

"Sounds like a winner," Liebman said.

Kate's voice quickened with eagerness. "It could be. And you could take advantage of the international aspect. Your documentaries are shown on the Continent and North America, aren't they?"

"Most of them, if I'm lucky. Mayfield's told me something about your youth safaris. I gather that's what we're talking about."

"It is." Kate knew better than to go into a long, dry description of the project. Instead she talked about the young people as individuals, Casey and Hans in particular, telling about their backgrounds and the experiences they were having. She related the story about the capture of the rhinos, Bessie and Bobo. She was actually suggesting pictorial segments Liebman's film could have. He looked intrigued.

"Could be you have something here," he said. "But it would take me months to set it up. Your group will be long gone."

"There will be other groups. This is an ongoing project, provided we get the funds we need to keep it afloat." Conscious of her repeated use of the pronoun "we," Kate glanced at Alex. His smile told her that he, too, was aware of it. "But this is really Alex's brainchild," she added hurriedly. "He should be the one to describe it."

"Not when you're doing such a good job," Alex said.

Liebman asked a few more questions, then announced he would confer with his associates when he got back to London, perhaps send a team down in a month or two to scout the possibilities. "Now you must excuse me," he said, getting up. "I don't think I can face that lavish dessert table. It was a pleasure meeting you. You'll be hearing from me."

"Wait. I'll walk out with you," Mayfield told him.

When they'd gone, Kate turned to Alex. "Wouldn't it be marvelous if he really followed through?"

"It would, and it would be your doing. But are you prepared to follow through, as well?"

"What do you mean?"

"Liebman might send a team down in a month or two. In a few weeks I'll be tied up in Nairobi."

She saw what he was driving at. "And I might have to be in New York." His smile bothered her. "Does that please you?"

"No. What pleases me is that you said 'might have to be' instead of 'will be' in New York."

"Did I?" New York and her work there seemed so far away, and the distance, which had nothing to do with geography, was becoming greater each day.

Alex's smile disappeared as he looked beyond Kate. She felt a hand touch the back of her chair and then Peter Bazeek was leaning over her shoulder, an unctuous smile on his broad face.

"What a delightful and unexpected surprise to see you here," he said. "You've finished dinner? May I join you for coffee?" Without waiting, he took Mayfield's chair and snapped his fingers to summon the waiter, ordering coffee for them all. He even poured when the waiter brought the porcelain server. It was obvious, Kate thought, that the man liked to be in charge.

"Are you here for business or pleasure?" Bazeek asked Alex. "But with such a beautiful companion, how can it not be pleasurable?"

"On that we agree," Alex said. He'd decided to endure the man's intrusion to satisfy his curiosity about what Bazeek was up to. "How was your conference in London?" he asked.

"Like all such conferences. Meaningless speeches." The man made a dismissive gesture with his heavy hands. "As you know, it is behind the scenes that the wheels turn and decisions are made. Public forums are for show."

"So why do you attend?" Kate asked.

"For the contacts, my dear, the contacts."

"Is that why you're here?" Alex asked. "More contacts?"

Bazeek's laugh reminded Kate of the fat man in *The Maltese Falcon*.

"One never knows," he said. "I came for a few days of relaxation and had the good fortune to run into you. Just when I wanted to talk to you."

"What about?" Alex asked.

"The future."

"Yours?"

"Perhaps yours, as well. When the president returns, he will be choosing Steven Ngelindi's successor."

Alex waited.

"I wanted to tell you I've decided to offer my services in that capacity."

"I thought you might." Alex's face was composed, but his eyes became wary.

"There are others who are interested," Bazeek said. "Whom do you intend to support?"

"Someone with Steve Ngelindi's ideals."

"Outdated ideals. Isn't it time for a change?"

"Depends what you mean by 'change.'"

"Progress?"

Alex shook his head. "Not the way you define it."

"Progress is inevitable, and you would do well to support it. Those in the way could get trampled."

Kate recognized the threat, which the man's toothy smile made only more ominous. But her main reaction was one of anger.

Bazeek mentioned two developmental projects he'd apparently long lobbied for.

"I thought those projects died when the sponsoring company went broke," Alex said.

"Arista Construction is solvent again," Bazeek assured him, "and quite ready to start as soon as we get approval. I cannot comprehend why you're not in favor. Our country needs to modernize."

"Not at the expense of the environment."

"Always the environment." Bazeek snorted impatiently. "There are other factors to consider."

"Such as your company's profits?"

"It is not my company."

"But it's run by your relatives."

Bazeek laughed again. "My grandfather and father both had many wives, so I have many relatives. I have a small share in Arista Construction, but I don't own the company. Actually, Alex, a small investment on your part could bring you substantial returns."

"Not interested, thank you." Alex leaned forward. "Though I confess I'm curious about where their new-found solvency is coming from. It wouldn't by chance be from Afro-Asian Trade Limited, would it?"

"What a clever guess."

"Not very clever," Alex said. "Harry Lunt's one of the few who can provide that kind of capital. Don't you care how he gets his money?"

"It is not my affair." The pudgy man's attention was drawn across the room. "Ah, there's Harry now."

"Another coincidence?"

"No. We traveled from Nairobi together. Shall I ask him to join us?"

"I'd rather you didn't."

Bazeek's smile was chilling. "As you wish. I regret that you cannot see things differently." He turned to Kate. "Miss Marlowe, you must forgive us for all this business talk. Such things must bore you."

"On the contrary. What's happening here in Kenya concerns me deeply."

"How nice of you to say so, but a vacation is for pleasure."

Kate was annoyed that Bazeek had dismissed her statement as nothing more than a social pleasantry. It was much, much more.

"You mustn't let Alex dwell on politics while you're here," Bazeek continued. "If I were he, I would forget all else except the pleasure of being with such a lovely companion." He pushed away his cup and got up. "Good night, then. Perhaps, Miss Marlowe, we will meet again before you leave."

Alex watched as Bazeek headed for the table where Lunt was seated.

"Why the worried look?" Kate asked.

"Those two are an unholy alliance."

"But you've suspected a connection all along."

"Bazeek's not hiding it now. That bothers me. He's too confident that things will go his way."

"He can't be that sure. He wouldn't be courting your support if he were."

"I hope you're right. I wish he hadn't come over."

"You're going to have to deal with him."

"I know, but that battle is for another time. Let's forget all that now." He reached across the table and took her hand. "There's one thing Bazeek said that I agree with."

"What?"

"That I should forget everything except—how did he put it—'the pleasure of being with such a lovely companion.'" The pressure of his fingers sent a tingling warmth through her.

"Do you think you can?"

"When you smile at me like that, you make it damn easy." He stood and pulled her up from her chair. "Come on. Let's have an after-dinner drink on the terrace."

They sipped Grand Marnier and, in the waning evening light, watched the exotic birds strolling on the sloping lawn. A peacock landed on the terrace and strutted around, but withdrew haughtily when someone offered it a piece of bread. "What do peacocks eat?" Kate wondered out loud.

"Caviar and truffles," Alex said, making her laugh.

"Let's take a walk around the grounds before we leave," Kate suggested when they'd finished their drink. Outside, Alex immediately loosened his tie and Kate took off her borrowed sandals. They followed a path around the orchid garden, then over to a pond where geese honked a welcome and a family of ducks nestled by the shore. Mount Kenya was still visible, but the mist hovering above the peak would soon descend to cloak it for the night. Dusk deepened, and they started back toward the hotel, now glittering with lights. "From here it looks like a fairyland," Kate said.

Mayfield met them in the lobby. "Well, you two certainly scored with Liebman. He's really interested."

"Kate's the one who sold him," Alex said.

Mayfield nodded. "You're lucky you've got her."

"Tell me about it," Alex said, smiling down at her.

"Thanks for the compliment, but we'd never have met Liebman if it hadn't been for you," Kate told Mayfield.

"Kate's right. Thanks for everything, Charley," Alex said. "Not just the introduction to Liebman, but the whole day. The kids had a ball and so did we—except for this damn tie.''

"Speaking of which, it's time to return our borrowed finery.''

"You're leaving?'' Mayfield asked. "It's early. Even Cinderella had until midnight. I have an idea. Why don't you stay for a few days, as my guests? You don't have to follow a strict timetable, do you?''

"We couldn't,'' Alex replied.

"Let the lady speak for herself, old boy,'' Mayfield told him.

"Of course.'' The hint of a frown crossed Alex's face, but in a second it was gone. His words to Kate were pleasant, betraying no disapproval. "If you want to stay, I can take Susan to the Mara. No problem.''

Her response was immediate. "I wouldn't think of it.'' It wasn't just Susan. Without Alex, this luxurious place had no attraction. There was also something else, something pulling her to the plains of the Mara, a fearful magnetism she couldn't understand—or ignore.

That night Kate slept very little. Susan was sharing Mitsu's tent, so she was alone. She tried to focus on what had happened that day. With the exception of Bazeek's intrusion, things had gone so well—Mayfield's hospitality, the pleasure of the visit, her ideas about the animal orphanage, the successful meeting with Liebman....

But tomorrow she and Alex and Susan would leave for the Mara.

Kate couldn't conjure up a picture of what was making her uneasy. When she tried, the image dissipated into shadows. But shadows had no substance. Why, then, did they feel so oppressive? Her chest constricted. She got out of bed, put on a cotton robe and stepped outside, welcoming the chill air, breathing it deeply. The night was clear, the tents starkly outlined in the bright moonlight. There was a rustle, then a figure emerged from a nearby tent and came toward her.

"You couldn't sleep, either?" she asked softly.

"No," Alex answered. He looked down at her. "You're apprehensive about tomorrow, aren't you?"

Of course he knew. He always knew. Some people had remarkable sensitivity to the feelings of others, but Alex's understanding went deeper than that. He lowered his head to kiss her, and his lips were tender and undemanding.

"Do you want me to stay with you?" he asked.

"I want you to hold me," she whispered. "Just to hold me all night long."

"That will be my pleasure." He put his arm around her and they went into her tent.

In the reassurance of Alex's embrace, Kate finally fell asleep, but when she awoke in the morning, he wasn't there. She realized he'd left for propriety's sake, but it came to her suddenly that she could not use Alex as a shield against what she had to face.

CHAPTER THIRTEEN

"IT HASN'T CHANGED MUCH, has it?" Elsie McKendrick asked as she led the way inside. The compound where Kate and Alex had lived was now a ranger station, and Kate's house was the home of Jim McKendrick, the senior game warden, and his young wife. Not waiting for a reply, Elsie chattered on in her cheerful Scottish brogue. "Not that it couldn't do with a bit of updating. Especially the kitchen and bath. The plumbing's apt to get troublesome, and even a wee storm puts out the electricity. Was it that way when you lived here?"

"Yes, it was," Kate said. She only half listened as Elsie continued talking. It felt so strange to be back in this house. Even some of the old furniture was in place—that rocker, the grandfather clock on the far wall and the Oriental rug, its burgundy color faded and the worn spot in the center medallion much enlarged. There was a different couch and armchair, but positioned in front of the fireplace where the old ones had been.

Elsie led her to her room, the one she'd had as a child. Kate paused in the doorway. "My God. It's exactly the same."

"Is it? The senior warden before Jim wasn't married, so the extra bedrooms didn't get much use. I guess he left them just as they were. When Jim and I have children, I'll probably turn one of them into a nursery." She went to the large window and opened the shutters. "For now, though, this room is yours again. Is there anything I can get for you?"

"No . . . no thank you. I'm fine."

"Then I'll leave you be for a while. You'll be wantin' some time for a bit of nostalgia." Elsie closed the door quietly as she left.

Nostalgia? Was that the name of this strange feeling? Kate looked around. She remembered how she had cleaned this room just before she'd left, giving it this uncharacteristic neatness. It was as though she'd walked out just yesterday, not thirteen years ago. She gave a slight laugh. There was nothing here to be afraid of. Memories only. She sat on the bed and smiled as she slid toward the sagging middle. Alex had once teased her that a hippo must have slept on her mattress.

"Still sags, doesn't it?"

She leaped up.

"Hey, I didn't mean to startle you." Alex grinned at her from the window. "Remember how I used to climb in?" He put one leg over the sill and swung into the room.

"Until your mother made you stop."

"When my voice changed," he remembered with a laugh. "She didn't trust me in your bedroom once my male hormones were all charged up."

"She needn't have worried."

"That was then." He came closer and put his hands on her shoulders. "This is now."

He started to pull her to him, when they heard Susan calling. A second later the little girl appeared at the open window, her face flushed with excitement. "Look," she cried. She was cradling something in her arms.

Kate broke away and went over to the window. "What've you got there?"

"It's a baby goat. His mother won't give him milk, and Mr. McKendrick brought him up here for Mrs. McKendrick to take care of. She said he could be my special pet. I've got to go feed him now." And she raced off.

Kate gazed after her. "I hope she doesn't get too attached to him. Next she'll be wanting to take him back home with her. Remember how I was with—" She stopped.

"With Rusty," Alex said. "Yes, I remember."

Kate felt a stab of apprehension. That memory was too close to the event that had ended her happiness here.

They went outside. On the veranda, Susan was perched on a wicker stool, happily feeding the little goat from a baby bottle. She looked up. "See how hungry he is. I'm naming him Arnold. He didn't have a name, so Mrs. McKendrick said I could. I'm going to take a picture of him to show my friend Arnold when I get home."

"Do you think he'll like having a goat named after him?" Kate asked.

The question surprised Susan. "Why shouldn't he?"

Alex smiled and said, "I'm sure he'll recognize the honor."

"Yeah," Susan agreed.

It was hard to pry Susan from her new pet to come inside for dinner. First she made sure he was settled in the storage room, in a box Elsie had padded with an old blanket. After the meal Alex and Kate took Susan for a walk around the compound and showed her where her mother's house, now demolished after a fire, had stood. Susan pointed. "That must be the tree."

Kate didn't understand her meaning. "It's just an acacia."

"Mama used to tell me stories about when she was little…how she and Daddy played and what they did. She said there was this tree near her house, where they used to sit and read. I think that's the one.''

"I'm sure it is." Kate knelt and hugged her niece. "Well, tomorrow you and I can come here and sit under this tree and read together. Would you like that?"

Susan nodded. "Can I bring Arnold?"

"If you like."

As they walked back, they passed some children playing in front of the rangers' quarters. One little girl, about Susan's age, detached herself from the group and followed them. She was barefoot and wore a simple shift along with elaborately beaded neck bands and bracelets. Susan kept looking back. She finally halted, turned around and smiled. The child accepted the invitation and ran up to her. They looked each other over curiously. "My name is Susan."

The other girl pointed to herself. "Nekaritini."

"That's a pretty name. I'm seven. How old are you?" When the native child shook her head, Susan held up seven fingers.

Nekaritini grinned and held up eight.

"Oh, you're eight . . . but I'm as tall as you," Susan said, and put her shoulder against the bare brown shoulder of the other girl to prove it.

They walked together after that, behind Kate and Alex, but close enough so that Kate could catch snatches of their conversation, if the jumbled mixture of Masai, English and Swahili, interspersed with giggles, could be called a conversation. They were communicating, as children always manage to do. When they got to the McKendrick house, Susan went to the storage room and carried Arnold out in his box. If Susan had sought to impress her new friend, she was disappointed. Nekaritini just shrugged. She was much more interested in the cookies and milk Elsie McKendrick offered.

"She didn't like Arnold," Susan said after the girl had gone.

"I don't think that's it," Alex said. "The Masai have a real respect for animals, and they don't make household pets out of them. Especially not goats."

"What do they do . . . ?"

Alex must have guessed what her question would be and skillfully changed the subject to avoid telling her that goats and sheep were usually raised to be eaten.

Kate was occupied with Susan all that evening. The child was thrilled to be in the house Kate and Derek had grown up in. There were endless questions and exclamations.

"Did my daddy take his bath in this tub? . . . Wait'll he sees me sleeping in his very own bed from when he was little. . . . But where's he gonna sleep? . . . When's he coming, Auntie Kate? . . . Is that the same lamp he had? . . . I bet Melanie will just love Arnold . . ." Her mind darted from subject to subject.

It took a long time for her to quiet down. Kate sat with her until Susan finally fell asleep, then joined Alex and the McKendricks on the veranda. The men were talking shop. "We've got seventeen rhinos in that section by the river. That includes the mother and calf from Amboseli."

"The ones we saw taken?" Kate asked. "Bessie and Bobo?"

McKendrick smiled. "They didn't give their names."

He was a rangy man, about forty, Kate guessed, his forehead permanently creased with worry lines. But he had a quiet humor. Kate liked him.

Alex described Kate's involvement in capturing the rhinos. "That's why her special interest in that particular pair."

"Quite so," McKendrick said. "Well, I think they'll be fine here . . . if we can keep the predators away from them."

"Lions?" Alex asked.

"People."

"Trouble with poachers?"

"Alex, we always have trouble with poachers. You know that. Even without the extra lure of so many rhinos in one area. I wish I had more men to put on patrol there."

"Is that *eunoto* celebration going to be a problem?" his wife asked.

"I hope not. The Masai are not poachers. But I'm not at full strength right now. I'd feel better with more men."

"If you're shorthanded, I'm available," Alex told him.

"Thanks, Alex. I figured you would be."

"Maybe I can help, too," Kate offered.

Elsie McKendrick laughed. "No offense, Kate, but my husband thinks women are frail creatures who need protection."

"In the bush, city-bred European ladies like yourself are indeed frail creatures," Jim countered. "Kate is different. She grew up here and can handle herself."

"Now there's a vote of confidence, Kate," Elsie said, then turned to her husband. "And just how long do I have to live here before I get the same from you, Jim McKendrick?" she demanded.

"Check with me in ten years," he replied.

"If I last that long."

Despite their teasing, Kate could see the affection and understanding between them. Soon they excused themselves and went inside.

"Want to walk?" Alex asked Kate.

"I don't think so."

He was disappointed. She knew what he had in mind. That night in Washington when they'd first met after so many years, he'd talked about being with her at Pambazuko.

"Perhaps tomorrow." She shivered. "It's cold tonight."

He drew her up from her chair and put his arms around her. "I can keep you warm."

"I know you can, but not tonight, Alex." She reached up to kiss him lightly, resisting the urge to invite his passion and submerge herself in it. "Tomorrow's going to be a busy day. I think I'll turn in early."

"Want company?"

She drew back. "Shame on you. What would the Mc-Kendricks think?"

"I hope they'd approve. But I can always climb in the window after everyone's asleep."

"You wouldn't."

"I would if you wanted me to." Suddenly serious, he said, "Kate, perhaps you shouldn't be alone tonight. I know how you hated the thought of coming here to the Mara, stirring up old fears...."

"I'm all right, Alex. As for stirring up old fears, I'll have to deal with them...myself."

He looked at her searchingly for a long time. "I'm here for you."

"Yes, I know."

Kate kissed him good-night and went to her room. She tried to find reassurance in what he'd said, that he was here for her. There was, however, another presence hovering just out of reach, a fourteen-year-old girl who had lived here happily until something happened that had made her flee in terror. Kate knew that before she left the Mara, she would have to rediscover that girl.

IN THE MORNING, they ate breakfast on the veranda. The compound was on a hill, with a sweeping view of the plains around it and of a Masai village to the east. Elsie said that for days there had been much coming and going around the village, but this morning the activity was centered north of the village, much closer to the river. "That's probably the site the Masai chief chose for *eunoto*," Alex said.

"I wonder if Kama had anything to do with it," Kate said. "She knew this is where we'd be staying."

"I wouldn't be at all surprised," Alex said. "Kama has a special stature with her people. Sometimes women attend meetings of the elders to voice a concern, but they have to stand while speaking. Kama has been allowed to sit among them."

After breakfast Jim asked Alex to join him on his morning rounds. When they left, Elsie and Kate lingered over a second cup of coffee. Nekaritini showed up with her older sister and another girl. They thought it very funny to see Susan holding Arnold in her lap and feeding him from a bottle. Elsie gave them some hot cereal, over which they heaped spoonfuls of cinnamon sugar. "They tolerate the porridge for the sake of the sugar," Elsie said. "Sweets are not in their normal diet, and they love them."

When they were done, Susan was still busy with Arnold, so the girls started a game in front of the house. They had a long stick, which two of them held. The other had to jump over it, and the stick was raised higher and higher. "I know that game—High Water, Low Water," Susan said. "Only we play it with a jump rope at school." The little goat had finished and was falling asleep, so Susan put him back in his box and ran out to join them.

"They call it *engilaut* here," she yelled back to the adults on the veranda.

Susan proved herself as adept as the others at clearing the stick without touching it. The two older girls soon tired of the play and wandered off. Susan and Nekaritini came back to the veranda.

"We can't play with just two," Susan complained. "We have nothing to do."

"Well, I've got to go to the market," Elsie said, getting up. "Who'd like to come along?"

"Me," Susan cried, and held up her hand. "And her," she said, lifting Nekaritini's hand.

"I think I'll pass," Kate said. "I'm feeling lazy."

That was not quite true; she wasn't sure how to define her feelings at this moment. When she was alone, Kate let her mind travel back, remembering when she'd first come to the compound. She'd been even younger than Susan. She'd loved everything about it—the wild beauty and the freedom. Perhaps, idolizing her father as she had, she'd absorbed his enthusiasm. And then there was Alex, who was part and parcel of all she loved, and who became part of herself. Or so it had seemed.

Kate made no effort to dwell on any one thing. Her thoughts drifted, but never went beyond the day before her father had died. There was no conscious resistance. On the contrary, she felt that everything happening to her since her return to Kenya was in some way a preparation for what had to come. Something had been locked away that had to be brought to light—and here was where it would happen.

When Elsie returned, she was alone. "I let Susan off at Nekaritini's house. She wanted to visit for a little while. It's just down the road, and I know the mother. Do you mind?"

"No. I'm glad she's got some company—besides Arnold, that is."

Elsie laughed. "It's a wonder how the child loves that little goat. We passed by the glade where we keep all the livestock for the compound. It's just down the road...you know where..."

Kate felt a tightness in her chest. "Yes." Her voice was barely above a whisper. "I know."

Elsie, who had no idea that the glade was where Kate's father had died, went blithely on. "And I let the children out to see the animals. There are all kinds—donkeys, cows, chickens, sheep and goats. They're not as exciting as the wild animals, but they're a lot more approachable.'' Elsie laughed. ''Susan wanted to know which goat was Arnold's mother. Well, not knowing one from another, I just picked out a female. Susan said the goat looked nice enough and why wouldn't she want such a cute little kid—you'll pardon the pun—like Arnold? I told her I didn't know, but that we might try getting them together again. She's such a bright little girl.'' Elsie became serious. ''Is it hard for her in the States, being of mixed blood?''

That elusive dark picture slipped away from Kate again, and she focused on Elsie's question. ''Not at all. She's a happy child. Susan and my brother live in a very cosmopolitan community with all kinds of ethnic groups and cultures. Derek wants Susan to be proud of her African heritage.''

''As she should be,'' Elsie said. ''The Masai are a grand and beautiful people.''

In a throaty voice someone asked, ''Is that my cue to announce myself?''

''Kama.'' Kate rose to greet her. ''I didn't hear you drive up.''

''I walked. In addition to being grand and beautiful, being nomads, we Masai are great walkers. Only, I have become soft,'' she said, indicating the canvas shoes she was wearing. ''I can no longer go barefoot on these rocky paths. How are you, Mrs. McKendrick?''

The two women knew each other and exchanged pleasantries for a few minutes. ''Where is my granddaughter?'' Kama asked.

''Playing with one of the children,'' Elsie replied. ''She'll be along soon.'' Elsie went inside to get them some iced tea.

"Thank you for bringing Susan," Kama said to Kate. "You have given me much happiness, and I know it is hard for you." The woman's dark eyes held compassion, and something more—a penetrating understanding Kate had never come across in another person.

"What is it you know, Kama?"

Kama waited before answering. "You will find the one you seek."

"I'm not looking for anyone."

"Then someone seeks you."

That's all she would say.

Elsie came back with the tea. "My goodness," she exclaimed. "That's quite a sight, isn't it?" On the plain below them, hundreds of people had already converged on the ceremonial site, and newcomers could be seen coming from all directions. "There must be a thousand people."

"There will be more," Kama said. "They will come from far, from all the parts of Masailand. Some have walked for days."

"Couldn't they take the *matatu*?" asked Elsie, referring to the crowded, rickety buses that clanked and bumped their way over the rutted roads.

Kama smiled and shrugged. "If they did, their soreness would be elsewhere, not in their feet. But it is also the tradition to walk together as a group. This will be the largest ceremony for many years. Perhaps the last. That is the reason so many come."

"Why does the government discourage these traditions?" Elsie asked. "Jim explained it, but I still don't understand. If there's no political impact..."

"It is because the government in Nairobi fears that tribal loyalty is dangerous to unity. If tradition weakens, national feeling will replace it. That is the theory."

"Is that wrong?"

"Yes. At what price, patriotism? Too much is lost—pride in self, then family, then tribe, then country. Destroy one and all will suffer."

"There has to be a middle ground," Kate suggested.

"Then young people like you will have to find it," Kama told her.

Kate knew Alex felt a part of this struggle in Kenya, a struggle to improve living standards without sacrificing old traditions, to find a balance between progress and preservation, commercialism and conservation. And Kate, who'd never had much interest in politics, found herself becoming concerned.

Kama got up. "I should go back now. There is much to be done."

"You haven't seen Susan."

"I shall see her in the morning. Will Derek and Melanie be here?"

"I don't know. I haven't heard from them yet."

"I'll come for you early. Be ready."

Just then Susan came running up. She was glad to see her grandmother, but Kate could tell something was troubling her.

"Tell me about *eunoto*, *Ayah*," she asked Kama. "Tell me what they do and about all the things they eat."

"Eat?" Kama smiled. "The feasting is not the important part." She ruffled Susan's dark hair. "But I will tell you about it all when I see you in the morning. Kate, feed this child. She must be hungry to be thinking about food."

Kama said goodbye and went on her way.

"Are you hungry?" Kate asked her niece.

"No, no," Susan cried. "Where's Arnold?"

The vehemence of her question surprised the two women. "Why, he's probably where you left him," Elsie said. Susan sped off and returned with the baby goat.

"Susan, come here," Kate called.

The little girl came over and rested the box holding Arnold on her aunt's lap.

"Is something wrong?" Kate asked.

Susan petted Arnold's furry body, and when she looked up, her eyes were filled with tears. "Nekaritini's sister and that other girl...they said...they said..." She swallowed. "That there's gonna be this big feast at the ceremony where everybody eats a lot...they cook lambs and goats over these big fires outside...and they said that Arnold..." The tears started to fall and her words came out chokingly. "They said that Arnold was going to get cooked, too."

"That's not true," Kate cried. She put the box down and stooped to gather Susan into her arms.

"Those girls were just being mean and nasty, and they'll hear from me about it," Elsie said angrily.

"What if they come looking for goats to cook?" Susan asked between sobs.

"They won't get Arnold," Kate told her.

Susan wasn't consoled. "Maybe—*hic*—" Her tears had brought on the hiccups. "Maybe we can—*hic*—hide him. Or—or we can take him down to the glade—*hic*." She turned to Elsie. "And give him to his mother. When she sees how nice Arnold is, she'll take care of him and protect him, won't she—*hic*? He'll be safe there."

Susan had an exaggerated belief in the protective power of maternal love, but Kate didn't disillusion her. "Darling, he's safe right here," Kate told her. "No one's going to take Arnold away. I promise you."

"That's right, love," Elsie murmured. "Arnold will be perfectly all right."

Susan's tears gradually subsided. Melanie's arrival about an hour later was a welcome diversion. Of course, she got an immediate introduction to Susan's pet and, when she heard the child's concern, added her reassurances that Arnold was safe where he was. Kate asked about her brother. Melanie told her Derek would be coming in a day or two…she wasn't sure. Kate thought that strange, but didn't comment.

When the men returned, Elsie suggested a picnic lunch. Alex and Jim carried the table from the veranda to a stand of acacias behind the house. Susan helped the women assemble a cold meal of sliced meat, salad, hard-boiled eggs and cheese. Kate could see how happy Susan was to have Melanie there. Over lunch they all traded stories about what they'd been doing. Melanie was enthusiastic in her description of the Tanzanian cave art discoveries, but when Alex asked about the book she and Derek might be doing, she hedged and said nothing had been decided. Her account of her trip from Nairobi on a decrepit *matatu* laden with people and livestock had them all laughing.

The mention of animals was enough to make Susan drag Melanie off to see Arnold again. Elsie and Kate had finished clearing up and were in the kitchen, when Melanie reappeared. "Arnold was taking a siesta, so I suggested it might be a good idea if Susan did the same," Melanie said. "She's taking a nap in her room."

"I'm glad you got her to rest," Kate said. "She's kind of overwhelmed by all that's happening."

"Aren't we all!" Melanie exclaimed, but her strained expression gave her reply an ominous undertone.

Kate was glad when Elsie left on an errand. Jim had taken Alex off to show him some new computer tracking equipment, so the two women were alone. They sat at the round kitchen table. "This is the same table we had," Kate said, running her fingers under the rim. "Derek and I once carved our initials on the underside. Boy, did we hear about it!"

"Please, Kate, no more reminiscences," Melanie said.

"Okay." She paused, then asked, "Something happened between you and Derek, didn't it?"

"Like what?"

"Whatever put that sadness in your eyes."

"Is it that obvious?"

"Compared to the way you were before, it is. And how come you took the bus instead of waiting to come with Derek? Are you running away from him?"

"No. I split because I figured a temporary separation might be good for both of us. At least, I hope it's only temporary."

"What happened? When you left for Mombasa, you, Derek and Susan were ready for a great time."

"And that's how it was at first. We had a marvelous time. As though we were on the way to becoming a family. But in the middle of the week we bumped into a married couple, Natundi and Ellen. They're old friends of Derek's. Do you know them?"

"No, but I think Derek's mentioned them. Is this the Nat he was in college with?"

"Right. Apparently Derek and Elizabeth and those two were real tight when they were students in Nairobi. All they talked about was the good old days." Melanie smiled bitterly. "One reminiscence after the other."

"And you felt excluded."

"Damn right."

"Melanie, I'm sure it wasn't intentional."

"Does it matter? That's what happened, intentional or not. The message was that I didn't belong. That's the message Derek was getting, too."

"Maybe you're making too much of this."

"Wait," Melanie said. "I haven't finished. For the rest of the week, we were constantly with Nat and Ellen. The one time I brought it up, Derek got angry...asked why I couldn't accept his friends. He didn't like it when I suggested it was the other way around. If it hadn't been for Susan, I'd have been miserable. That is one great kid."

"She's crazy about you, too. Derek must see that."

"I'm not sure what he sees. Something else happened, Kate. The night before we left, Nat and Ellen took the three of us out to dinner. Our waiter said something to Ellen about ordering for her daughter. Ellen is black, so he just assumed that Ellen was Susan's mother."

"Come on, Melanie. That's understandable," Kate said. "Did you feel hurt that he didn't take you for Susan's mother?"

"No! Hell, I know that's not likely."

"Then you shouldn't have let such a minor incident upset you."

"It wouldn't have if Derek had treated it as a minor incident. But he didn't. He started brooding. I could see it. When we dropped Susan off with you at Naivasha, couldn't you tell he was different?"

Kate remembered Derek's awkwardness in introducing Melanie to Kama. "He's confused by his own feelings."

"Well, he sure as hell is confusing me. Kate, I love him, but he keeps backing off."

"If you love each other, it'll work out."

"Such a pretty platitude," Melanie said sarcastically, yet with an undertone of regret. "But we both know it doesn't work that way. Love isn't a static condition. You've got to act on it, do something with it, make it a part of living. Otherwise it's hollow, and hollow things crumble."

Melanie's observations surprised Kate. The breezy photographer had an emotional sensitivity that wasn't always apparent. Kate was also aware that what Melanie had said applied to her own relationship with Alex. Kate hadn't tried to label what she and Alex had together. There were so many parts to it—nostalgia, remnants of youthful adoration, the sensual passion of maturity, plus mutual affection and respect. And love?

What Kate felt was certainly more powerful than anything she had known, but, as Melanie had said, love had meaning only if you made it part of your life. But her life and Alex's were irreconcilable. Or so she had once thought. Now she wasn't so sure.

"You're right," she told Melanie. "I shouldn't be offering platitudes as consolation. For what it's worth, though," she added with a smile, "I'm rooting for you. And so's Susan."

"Thanks. I appreciate that. But the crucial vote comes from Derek. He's got some time alone to think things through." She gave Kate an approximation of her usual jaunty grin. "Maybe he misses me already and he'll be different when he gets here. I'm going to think positive. Right?"

"Sure," Kate agreed, glad to see Melanie perk up.

"Enough about me. How're you and Alex doing? Are you making out? Oops, didn't mean that like it sounded."

Kate laughed, but Melanie's directness unsettled her. "We're okay."

"Then things are working out for you?"

"We've had a good time. It's been a good vacation."

"Vacation? Is that all?"

"What did you expect?"

"I could ask *you* that." Noticing Kate's uneasiness, Melanie backed off, saying, "But I won't, because I don't think you want to answer."

Melanie was right. Kate didn't want to answer. Her original expectations in coming to Kenya had been so vague, masking her deeper needs. The reality she was experiencing was changing how she felt about this country, about her work back in the States, about Alex . . . And about herself? There was something still to come, something meant for her alone. Here—in the Mara.

BEFORE DINNER, Susan reminded Kate she'd promised to read her a story under the special acacia tree where her parents used to sit, but she was perfectly amenable to Kate's suggestion that Melanie do it instead.

"I know why you suggested that," Alex told Kate. "You know how much I want to be alone with you."

"Do you? And here I thought Jim McKendrick had replaced me in your affections," she teased. "You've spent more time with him than with me."

Alex laughed. "Is that a complaint? I sure hope so. Come on." He took her arm and pulled.

"Where to?"

"You know where to."

As they walked, Alex kept hold of her arm, as if he expected her to break away. He remembered how she'd often raced him to their meeting place on Pambazuko, and he'd deliberately let her go ahead for the joy of watching her lithe figure, feet hardly touching the ground, fly ahead of him. But not the last time. From the heaviness of her tread, Alex knew she was remembering that particular day.

She'd come alone, but he'd known where to find her. Alex had been out with Patrick Sloane all afternoon, searching for Alastair Marlowe and his own father. The later it got, the more his apprehension grew, but at least he was doing something. He'd known what agony it must be for those awaiting news back at the compound. Especially Kate.

When Patrick had come back from the glade and told him his father and Marlowe were both dead, Alex had felt a crushing grief. Then his thoughts had gone to Kate. She adored her father. Alex wanted to be with her when she heard the news, to hold her, ease her pain if he could. When she wasn't at the compound, he'd known where to find her.

Alex remembered how he'd run all the way to Pambazuko, and his sense of relief and dread when he saw her sitting on that stone up ahead. He'd stopped for a moment, but she seemed not to see him. Then, wiping the perspiration from his face and composing himself, he joined her. Haltingly he told her the terrible news. Her reaction had been more dreadful than tears—that cold and isolated withdrawal he hadn't been able to cut into. He'd taken her in his arms...her flesh had felt so cold. She couldn't say how long she'd been sitting there, seemingly unaware of where she was.

"You were so far away from me that day," Alex said softly. "That's when you really left me, not later when your mother took you away." They came to the stone, and he stopped and turned to face her. "Do you remember, Kate?"

"Why do you want me to?"

"I don't know. I thought if you came here again, you could look back with a different perspective." He put his arms around her. "That you would remember and cry and this time let me comfort you."

"I have no right to tears."

"Why?"

"You can't understand." She gripped his arms. "Alex, I don't want that memory. It's ashen. Today...today is what counts."

She pulled his head close, and her kiss was like a flare that sought to burn away the past. Alex held her tight. She was offering her passion, but he felt something was missing, something without which their love could not survive.

THAT NIGHT, after dinner, Elsie McKendrick felt the uneasiness of her guests. Melanie was distracted by some inner concern. Kate and Alex sat close, talked and sometimes touched, but their intimacy felt strained. The little girl needed constant reassurance about Arnold's safety and insisted that the baby goat sleep in her room that night.

When Elsie and her husband were in bed, she told him, "Something's in the air, Jim. I can feel it."

"Good or bad?" he asked.

"I wish I knew."

CHAPTER FOURTEEN

KATE WAS THE FIRST ONE UP the next morning. She brewed some strong coffee and took a cup out to the veranda. The first rays of the sun were coming up over Pambazuko. She watched the countryside slowly come alive. Already there was activity down in the ceremonial village, but the sounds were muted by the distance. Clusters of animals headed toward the river, which, as it absorbed the sunlight, looked like a golden ribbon. Kate let her mind wander, allowing her senses to make her a part of the scene. Everywhere she gazed there was beauty, and she was at its center.

Minutes passed; how many she didn't know. Alex was the first to join her. She was sitting on the wooden steps, and he sat down next to her. He said good morning and brushed her lips with a kiss. His manner was subdued, and Kate guessed he had spent a troubled night. As he leaned back on his elbows and gazed around, she sensed his reaction was like hers.

"Beautiful, isn't it?" he said, letting out a deep sigh.

"Yes."

They were quiet for a while. But suddenly his mood changed. He turned to confront her. "How can you think of leaving?" he asked harshly.

He'd shattered her serenity. Why did he have to bring that up now? She didn't want to answer.

"You ran away once," he said. "Don't do it again." He grabbed her hands. "Kate, this is where you belong. Here—with me."

There was such appeal in his eyes. "Sometimes I believe that," she said. She shook her head and looked away. "But then..."

"Then what?"

Kate pulled her hands away. "All this can be so deceiving." Her gesture took in the surrounding landscape. "There's not just beauty and peace here." Her voice tightened. "There's darkness and violence and blood." She stopped short.

"Yes, but why dwell on it? There's nothing you can't handle."

"I'm not so sure."

"You're doing it now."

"No. No, I'm not." It was a strange denial, Kate thought, and she wasn't sure why she'd made it. Alex apparently felt she'd already proven something in her time here. That was partially true—but there had to be more.

"Hey, you two, how about coming in for breakfast?" Elsie called from the kitchen.

The rest of the household was up now, and Alex and Kate's conversation ended.

TRUE TO HER WORD, Kama arrived early. Susan's eyes widened with awe and pleasure to see her grandmother in native dress, regal in a saffron robe, layers of beaded necklaces around her throat. Her wrists and ankles were similarly adorned, and colorful hoop earrings hung from her earlobes.

"*Ayah*, you look beautiful," Susan said. She hugged her grandmother, then ran her fingers almost reverently over the necklaces.

Kama took off one of the smaller ones and slipped it over Susan's head. It was too big, but Susan didn't care. She turned to face the others. "How does it look?"

She was wearing jeans and a T-shirt Melanie had brought her from Tanzania. The shirt was red and stamped with a picture of a tree lion.

"Perfect," Kate said.

"We will exchange it for something your size when we get to the village," Kama told her.

"But I want to keep this one because it's yours."

Kama's eyes filled with love, and she hugged Susan tightly, as if to clasp this moment close.

When they got to the ceremonial village, Kama held on to Susan's hand as they threaded through the crowds. Kate, Alex and Melanie followed. People made way for Kama, who was treated with great deference. She led them to a group of men assembled in front of the central hut. "Those are the leading elders from all the communities," Alex said in a low voice. Seated in the center was an older man. He held a whisk made from a wildebeest's tail, with which he brushed away the buzzing flies.

"He is the *laibon*," Kama told the group.

"That means he's the chief, doesn't it?" Susan asked.

"Yes. The leader."

The *laibon* saw Kama. He motioned her forward imperiously. Still holding her granddaughter's hand, Kama approached. Susan bowed her head. When the old man placed his palm against her hair, Susan looked up and gave him a big smile. He smiled back benignly. Then he turned and spoke to Kama, who replied briefly.

"What did he say to you?" Melanie asked curiously when Kama and Susan rejoined them.

"That it would be a blessing if the child and I stayed on to live in his village." Kama shrugged. "I told him it could not be. Her life is elsewhere, and mine—'' Kama gave a wry smile ''—mine is half elsewhere.''

Kama said a few words to a woman, who disappeared and returned with a handful of beaded ornaments. These were sized for a child. Susan gasped with delight when Kama slipped two bracelets on her wrist and put a beaded choker around her neck. ''Melanie, look. Now I'm Masai,'' she said.

Melanie's smile was strained. She was probably wondering what Derek would be thinking if he were here.

People began to converge on one area. Susan couldn't see through the crowd, so Alex lifted her onto his shoulders. Some Masai children laughed, but most looked envious of her high perch. *''Ilmeek,''* a woman muttered as they passed, but another woman hushed her and pointed to Kama.

''What is *ilmeek*?'' Melanie asked.

Alex knew. ''It means foreigner. Without Kama we wouldn't be accepted here.''

The crowd let them through. In an open space in front of them, the warriors were assembling. They were an imposing sight. ''God,'' Melanie said, ''I wish I had my camera.'' Kama had told her to leave it behind, but had promised she would try to get permission for Melanie to take photographs tomorrow or the day after.

''They're in complete war gear,'' Alex noted.

''It is their last opportunity,'' Kama said.

Alex let Susan climb down from his shoulders. Her eyes sparkled with excitement as she took her grandmother's hand again.

This was the first time Kate had seen Masai warriors in such numbers and in full regalia. ''Those headdresses are magnificent.''

''They're made of black ostrich feathers,'' Alex said.

"But some are furry and orange," Susan pointed out.

"Those are lion manes," her grandmother told her. "The warriors do not hunt for sport. It is forbidden by law. But the killing of a predator beast cannot be faulted."

Each warrior held a shield made of elaborately patterned buffalo hide. Their spears all had black ebony inserted into the shaft. "To show their senior status," Kama explained. "The spears of junior warriors have light wood."

"How come there's feathers on those spears?" asked Susan, referring to the crowns of black feathers attached to the tips by a string of beads.

"It means peace," her grandmother explained. "To show that the spear is not meant for war presently."

The warriors stood proudly, all tall, ramrod straight and muscular. Their hair was braided into long plaits and dyed with reddish ocher mixed with animal fat. Beaded ornaments adorned their ears, necks, arms, waists and ankles. One of them took a step forward, catching Kama's eye. With a smile she acknowledged the young man, who then lifted his spear in solemn greeting.

"That one," Kama said, "is my nephew Latana. He is your mother's cousin, Susan."

"He is?" It was obviously a thrilling discovery for the little girl. "Wow!"

"The one in front of him wearing the headdress of the lion mane, he is the *alaunoni*, whom the warriors have chosen as their leader."

A group of a dozen men had formed a semicircle in front of the others. A chorus of chanting started, and these men began to dance. Kate had seen Masai and Samburu dancers a number of times, and had found their jumping somewhat monotonous. This time, however, there was something grand in their movements. They didn't leap forward, but from a standing position shot straight up into the air. Each took a turn; sometimes two or three men jumped together. The simplicity and strength of the dance were, Kate realized, symbolic of the Masai way of life.

Susan's head bobbed up and down as she watched. "I bet if they had a trampoline," she said, "they could reach the sky."

When the dancers finished, the *alaunoni* stepped forward. This signaled the warriors to form lines behind him. They started to chant as he led them out of the village. A tinkling accompaniment came from the metal bells some men had strapped to their thighs.

"Where are they going?" Susan asked.

"To a private place by the river. Tomorrow they will come back for *eunoto*."

"*Ayah*, is tomorrow when everybody celebrates and eats a lot?"

"Tomorrow and until the ceremony is over," Kama said.

Kate noticed that Susan looked apprehensive. She still feared her pet would be made part of the feast.

Kama had arranged for them all to have a midday meal with her brother's family, but Susan wouldn't eat. A half-dozen children came and watched from a distance. Alex called them over and gave each a pencil from the supply he had in his shirt pocket.

Kama approved. "They ask always for candy or chewing gum, but the pencil is a better gift."

The Masai children looked Susan over curiously. Nekaritini was walking by, when she saw them and ran over. She pushed past the others and put her arm around Susan. She preened a bit as she spoke, apparently introducing her friend and enjoying the added status that knowing Susan gave her. The children started to leave, and Nekaritini reached for Susan's hand to take her along.

"Aunt Kate, can I go?"

Kate hesitated.

"Let her," Kama advised. "She will be safe. There are always many eyes to watch over the children."

"All right," Kate said, and the girls ran to catch up with the others. The child needed to get her mind off worrying about her pet goat.

Kama guided Kate and Alex and Melanie around the ceremonial village. The pageantry there was not as dramatic as the assemblage of warriors, but each scene contributed to the interesting panorama. Women chatted together as they worked on finishing the huts they were building. Others were cooking or preparing honeybeer for the ceremony. A young woman approached and greeted Kama. Like the others, her head was shaved, and heavy ornaments had elongated the large holes in her ears. She carried a baby in a pouch slung around her neck. Kate's blond hair intrigued her, and she came up to her. Suddenly she took the swaddled baby and thrust it at Kate.

"Take it," Kama told Kate. "It is a compliment. Also, she is *endingi*, the least favored wife. She thinks it will be a good sign if the golden-haired woman favors her boy child."

Kate took the baby. She held the infant in front of her and bobbed him up and down. He responded with a gurgling grin. She brought him close, cradling him for a moment, amazed at how good he felt. She hadn't held a baby since Susan was little. She sensed Alex's eyes on her, and suddenly self-conscious, she returned the infant to his mother. The woman said something, then took a metal bracelet she was wearing and put it around Kate's wrist. Kate knew not to decline. "Thank you," she said. Kama nodded her approval. It was the right thing to do.

Sounds of laughter drew them toward a large group of youths. Their shaved heads and dark tunics indicated they were uncircumcised, not yet warriors. They had been practicing the jumping dance. Some were already adept. They talked and laughed among themselves. Teenage girls in colorful finery formed an appreciative audience.

"Now there's a happy gathering," Melanie said.

"This ceremony is important to them," Alex said. "Now they'll be able to move up."

"Oh, that's right," Melanie said. "The age-set tradition. They can't become warriors until the present ones become initiated into elderhood."

"That is the way it must be," said Kama solemnly. "They have waited long, and now they will pressure the *laibon* to set a time for the initiation of the new warriors. Each age set has its trials, which one must pass before moving up. That is Masai tradition."

"Not only Masai," Alex said. "It's common to all people, but the Masai have wisely made it a ritual."

"Why 'wisely'?" Kate asked him.

"Because it makes a person think about what has gone before and what will come, and he or she makes a conscious decision to do what is necessary to move ahead."

Kama agreed. "Just so."

As they walked on, Kate pondered what Alex had said.

When it was time to leave, they located Susan. She was with Nekaritini and three other girls, and had rolled her jeans up above her knees. The girls had all painted their legs with red ocher paste and were intent on drawing patterns with their fingers while the paste was still wet on their skin. The wavy lines in the designs were similar, but Susan was working on her own innovation—a happy face on each knee. She giggled when she saw her grandmother and the others.

"It's just like finger painting," she said, "only you get to do it on yourself."

Melanie went closer to examine. "That is neat," she proclaimed. "I'll have to take a picture of you."

"Yeah."

"When we get back. I don't have my camera here." She took Susan's hand. "Come on."

"But I'm not dry yet."

Kate had to laugh. They gave Susan a few minutes for her decorative legs to dry before they started back. Kama said she would stop by the following afternoon. "Will Derek be here?" she asked Melanie.

"I hope so."

"Can we go to the glade on the way back?" Susan asked. "Arnold's mama goat lives there."

"It's the long way around," Alex said. He was watchful, waiting for a reaction from Kate.

"I don't think we should." Kate made her objection sound casual. "I told Elsie we'd be back in time for tea." To ease Susan's disappointment, she added, "You can introduce Melanie to Arnold's mother some other time."

"Maybe we should bring Arnold with us when we visit his mother," Susan said.

Melanie agreed. "Sure, why not."

IN THE MORNING Richo arrived from the safari camp to confer with Alex. First Susan monopolized him to tell him about all the exciting happenings, foremost of which was her acquisition of Arnold, who was now skittering around a small enclosure next to the house. Then Nekaritini came by, and Susan ran off to play. Alex and Richo went into the study to talk; Elsie was in the kitchen, and Melanie had gone back to her room. Kate watched as Susan and Nekaritini improvised a game of jacks using a collection of small, round stones. After a while Nekaritini's elder sister came along. She was holding the long stick used in yesterday's game and was urging the younger girls to play with her. Nekaritini apparently refused. Her sister became angry and kicked at the stones the girls were playing with.

"Hey, quit that," Susan yelled.

There were more words, and the older girl taunted Susan. She pointed to Arnold's enclosure and pretended to eat, bringing her hands to her mouth. Susan got up and kicked the remaining stones away. "I don't want to play anymore," she said to her friend, and ran back to Kate. Nekaritini left with her sister.

"Don't pay attention to her teasing," Kate told Susan.

"But why does she do it?"

"To bother you."

"But they do take sheep and goats to eat. I saw them."

"They won't take Arnold. Besides, he's too little to make much of a meal," Kate said, trying to ease Susan's concern.

It was the wrong approach. The child scrunched up her face doubtfully.

"Susan, I promise you, Arnold will be safe." She gave the little girl a hug. "Come on. What say you and I find a story book and go sit under that acacia and read together? Just as your mother and father used to when they were small. Didn't we say we were going to do that?"

Susan let herself be cajoled. First she put the little goat in his box and took him to the storeroom. Then she got the book of folklore Melanie had given her and she and Kate went to sit under the tree. Kate read aloud, and was relieved that Susan seemed relaxed and attentive.

After about a half hour Susan said, "I think I better go feed Arnold now."

"I'm sure he's all right."

"But he'll be hungry."

Kate looked at her watch. "I guess it is almost lunchtime."

They walked back together. In the kitchen Elsie gave Susan a bottle for Arnold. "Why don't you bring him in here and keep us company while we prepare lunch?" Kate suggested as Susan started out.

"Okay."

While they were getting lunch ready, Kate and Elsie got into a discussion about the women's movement in Kenya. Melanie, who had slept in, joined them. Suddenly Kate realized that twenty minutes had gone by and Susan hadn't returned. "I'd better go see what's up," she told the others.

Susan wasn't in the storeroom. Neither was Arnold. Kate looked in Susan's room, but it was empty. She felt a stab of apprehension. Susan was nowhere in the house. Kate went outside, but saw no one. "Susan! Susan, where are you?"

Elsie and Melanie came out. "She's not around," Kate told them.

"She probably went for a walk," Melanie said, but without much conviction.

"She knows she's not to go off by herself," said Kate, her apprehension sharpening.

Elsie had a thought. "Maybe Nekaritini invited her to play over at her house."

"She wouldn't go without asking."

"We let her play there the other day," Elsie reasoned. "She may have assumed it was all right. I'll go see."

"I'll come with you," Melanie said.

Kate let them go, even though it didn't seem likely that Susan would be there.

Especially not with Arnold.

With chilling certainty Kate knew that Susan would never take her pet to that house, not to where the girl who'd taunted her earlier lived. If anything, Susan would hide her pet from the danger the girl kept prophesying. There was, however, a place Susan could take Arnold to for safekeeping.

Kate started to walk down the dirt road away from the compound. Without conscious deliberation, almost with a sense of inevitability, she headed for the glade. She walked quickly, then broke into a run. The sun was high now, and Kate felt its heat on her face.

There was a fearful familiarity in all this—the path to the glade...racing there, anxious...her heart pounding. She rounded the sharp curve in the road. The glade was below her. Slashes of memory streaked through Kate's brain, cutting open the scars that had kept them from her consciousness. A scene of such horror appeared in her mind that she closed her eyes to bring down again the black curtain that had shielded her all these years.

Kate stumbled, stopped and opened her eyes. She saw the small figure up ahead and called out. Susan turned around, the little goat cradled in her arms. Kate ran up to her, knelt and hugged her tightly.

Susan struggled free. "Aunt Kate, are you mad at me?" Without waiting for an answer, she started to defend herself. "I know I'm not supposed to go off alone...and everyone keeps sayin' and sayin' that Arnold's safe...but suppose someone comes to take him when I'm not there... and he's so little, they'd catch him easy even if he ran." She paused for a breath. "But in the glade, he can hide with all the other animals...and his mama's big, and she'll take care of him."

Kate couldn't scold her. Susan's anxiety reminded her of her own anguish years before, at this very place, when she'd feared for her own pet. She and Alex had been in the glade, oblivious to anything but each other. When they'd started to leave, Rusty was missing. It was getting dark, so they couldn't search for him that night. But then the next day their fathers had forbidden them to come to the glade. And then . . .

Other memories started to break through.

Kate hugged her niece to her, seeking to keep back the past.

"You're squeezing Arnold," Susan said, and broke away. She looked over Kate's shoulder. "There's Melanie and Mrs. McKendrick."

When Susan wasn't with Nekaritini, Elsie had guessed where she'd gone. "You must never go off by yourself like this, young lady," she said sternly.

"I know, but—"

"No buts." Susan's forlorn expression made Elsie pause. In a softer tone she asked, "Will you feel better if we keep Arnold in the house from now on? When you're not around, I'll watch him. That's a promise. Now come on, lovey. Let's go home. Want me to carry him?"

Susan must have felt reassured, because she surrendered Arnold and took Melanie's hand.

"Coming?" Melanie asked Kate.

"Not yet," Kate said. Her voice sounded strange to her. "I'll be along in a while."

Melanie gave her a searching glance, but didn't argue. Kate watched them leave, tempted, for a moment, to join them and avoid what lay ahead. But she couldn't avoid it . . . not any longer. She didn't want to.

When they were out of sight, Kate turned and continued toward the glade, walking slowly now. Her mind slipped into the past, to that time when, alone, she had raced to this place, not telling anyone where she was going. No one had known, not even Alex. For thirteen years she'd erased it from her consciousness, as if it had never been. But it *had* happened. . . .

EVERYONE AT THE COMPOUND was so upset that afternoon after Patrick Sloane called up from the ranger station to report there was no sign of the missing men. A major search effort would be launched, and he and Alex would check out some of the side roads on the way home. They'd be back in two or three hours. Kate couldn't stand the fearful worry on her mother's face. Alex's mother had been determinedly cheerful, but her optimism was fading. Kate felt stifled in the house and went outside, but the air was still oppressive. Why couldn't they find her father and Harold Crane? Why? Why?

Something started building in Kate's mind, a fearful notion. Alex and Patrick Sloane had checked out the stops on the men's usual itinerary, but there was one place they hadn't gone. Why should they have? No one knew about Kate's secret appeal to her father that morning.

She had begged to be allowed to look for her pet donkey, but the adults had been adamant about the glade being dangerous and off-limits with the fence down. Kate had followed her father out and added something to her good-bye kiss, a whispered plea that no one else had heard. "Please, Daddy, please see if you can find Rusty. You can take a little detour. It could be he went back to the glade. Please."

Her father could never resist that kind of appeal. "All right, princess," he'd said with an indulgent smile. "I guess we can scout around a bit on the way back. Though I've got a hunch that the little critter's going to make it home on his own." Kate had thanked him, hugged him hard and kissed him again.

Her father's hunch had been right. Rusty made it back. In the joy of having her pet return, Kate had forgotten about her secret appeal and her father's promise. She'd been so busy looking after Rusty, so sure that Alex and Patrick Sloane would find the two men and they'd all soon return with some story about the usual kind of car trouble. Only it wasn't working out that way.

Suddenly the memory of the promise she'd exacted from her father assaulted her. Without telling anyone, Kate left the house. She started for the glade, breaking into a run, certain that's where her father would be, hoping that he and Alex's father would be all right.

But if they were this close, why wouldn't they have walked home?

If they'd met harm, it was her fault...her fault...her fault.

The questions and accusations bounced painfully in her head as she ran.

She got to the glade and slowed to a walk. First she saw that the area of downed fence was much enlarged, probably trampled over by animals. The afternoon sun slanted into her eyes, causing her to see through flashing sunspots. There was something over there. Slowly she approached, and the scene of horror flashed in blinking segments—the overturned jeep, the bodies nearby, mangled, bloody, beyond recognition. But she did recognize them. Deep inside her a scream exploded: DADDY....

But no sound broke the awful stillness.

She stood there numbly, thinking, *Oh, no. Oh, no. Please, God, no-o-o-o!*

This couldn't be happening. It wasn't real. She had *not* begged her father to come out here. She had *not* asked him to come to his death. No! No!

Kate backed away. She turned her face to look directly into the sun, willing it to blind her, to blacken the picture of horror into nothingness. She looked back at the horror. Sunspots scorched her eyes and blanched the scene. She stared and stared until the shapes faded and blended and there was nothing there except grass and sky and sun. Nothing. She saw nothing.

Somehow she made her way to Pambazuko. She sat there, sometimes with eyes closed, sometimes staring into the sun, protecting the blindness that shut out the horror, welcoming the numbing coldness under which she could bury it. And then Alex came.

"KATE."

It was Alex. Kate shuddered, opened her eyes and came back to the present. She was kneeling near the entrance to the glade, but there was no scene of horror in front of her, just domestic animals in penned enclosures. Yet that other scene had been real, and she could finally acknowledge its having happened.

Alex knelt beside her. "Melanie told me where you were. She said something was wrong—" The look on her face made him stop.

"Alex . . ." She reached out, and he took her in his arms. Now, finally, Kate was able to let her tears flow—tears that the adolescent, guilt-ridden girl had been unable to shed. Her tears were of grief and loss, the loss of loved ones and the loss of a part of herself, which she'd buried here. Alex held her until her tears subsided. Then, tremulously at first, Kate told Alex what had happened to her here those many years ago.

"My God!" he said. "Kate, why didn't you tell me? When I found you at Pambazuko, why didn't you tell me what you'd seen?"

"I couldn't. I blocked it out. It never happened."

He took her face between his hands; there was tenderness and love in his eyes and in his touch. Finally he understood why she'd run away. No one had shared her horror; no one could share her grief.

They sat and talked for a long time. When they started back for the house, Kate turned to look at the glade. "How ordinary it appears," she said. Sounds came to her, the bleating of the domestic animals, the swishing of birds in flight. Kate looked beyond the glade—to the meandering river, to the far-off hills, which the lowering sun cast in dark violet hues, and to the plain below where the Masai people were celebrating an ancient rite of passage of their men. She had opened her eyes to the past, and thus could open her heart to the beauty and life around her in the present, to Alex and to herself.

In the distance billows of dust showed a vehicle coming their way. "I'll bet that's Derek," Alex said.

It was. He arrived at the house a few minutes after they got there. Kate was so glad to see him. Someday she would tell her brother all that had happened, but not yet.

Derek lifted his daughter up, swung her around, then hugged her close while she planted sticky kisses on his face. Melanie came out and she and Derek just looked at each other. Then Melanie resolutely approached, put her hands on his shoulders and kissed him. "Hi, stranger. I missed you."

Derek hesitated, then admitted reluctantly, "I...I missed you, too."

Dinner was a subdued affair. Jim McKendrick excused himself early. There was a rumor afloat that poachers were slipping past the Tanzanian border guards, and Jim wanted to check around. He quickly accepted Alex's offer to go along.

Susan was overtired. On principle she rejected Melanie's suggestion of an early bedtime, but finally acquiesced and let Melanie lead her off. "Will you read me a story, Daddy?" she asked.

"Sure."

"First a bath," Melanie told Susan. To Derek, she said, "I'll call you when she's in bed."

Derek and Kate went outside, where Derek lit a cigarette. Kate was surprised. "I thought you quit years ago."

"I did." He took a deep drag. "Someone offered me a cigarette the other day, and without thinking, I took it."

"Don't tell me that's the same cigarette," she said lightly.

"So I bought a pack. Don't bug me, Kate. I've had a lot on my mind lately."

"Like Melanie?"

"Yeah. Like Melanie. Has she said anything to you?"

"A little. Derek, that girl loves you. And for a while there, I thought you felt the same."

He stubbed out his cigarette. "It's not that easy."

"Love never is."

"Lately I keep thinking about Elizabeth."

"I can understand that. But don't you think that Elizabeth would want you to be happy?"

"There's Susan, too."

"Melanie's great with Susan. I'm sure Elizabeth would approve."

"Would she? I don't know. My choosing a woman like Melanie to replace her...it would be like a rejection and betrayal."

"No way," Kate argued. "In the first place, Elizabeth can never be replaced. You had so much together, and your love produced a wonderful child. But what's wrong with finding a partner to share your life now?"

"Nothing, I suppose. But Elizabeth was Masai, half black," he said.

"So?"

"Suppose Susan thinks I'm rejecting that part of her mother's heritage and trying to deny it in her."

"She won't think that because it just isn't true," Kate told him. "Derek, you're creating barriers where none need to exist. Don't you think it's ironic that you had no such compunctions when you and Elizabeth wanted to get married?"

"We always knew we'd be together."

"And the racial thing wasn't important?"

"It was important. We knew there could be problems, but loving each other was more important."

"It still is. Aren't you rejecting Melanie solely because she's white?" The accusation got to him. "Being with the person you love is still more important than anything else. That hasn't changed. Do you love Melanie?"

"I've tried not to let myself."

Kate touched her brother's cheek. "Go for it, Derek," she told him. "Let it happen."

He took out another cigarette, started to light it, then blew out the match and tossed the cigarette aside. "Thanks, Kate" was all he said before he went back inside.

Kate realized she could give herself the same advice. She'd been afraid to give in to her love for Alex. Years ago, in her need to escape her unbearable guilt, she'd blamed this land for her father's tragic death. But the guilt and blame had both been misdirected and had caused Kate to reject everything about the life that Alex loved. During these weeks together, he'd tried to revive the happiness they'd known as children. Today she'd confronted the harshness and brutality of the land that sometimes thrust through. Alex was able to accept both as part of his life.

Kate hadn't wanted to. Could she do so now?

America's Favorite Author

Janet DAILEY

SWEET PROMISE

One kiss—a sweet promise
of a hunger long denied

83210-$3.25

SWEET PROMISE

*E*rica was starved for love. Daughter of a Texas
millionaire who had time only for business, she'd
thought up a desperate scheme to get her father's
attention.

Unfortunately her plan backfired and she found herself
seriously involved with Rafael de la Torres, a man she
believed to be a worthless fortune hunter.

That had been a year ago; the affair had almost ruined
her life. Now she was in love with a wonderful man.
But she wasn't free to marry him. First of all she must
find Rafael . . . !

CHAPTER FIFTEEN

SOMETHING HAD HAPPENED between Melanie and Derek. The two of them had disappeared after breakfast. They were gone over an hour, and came back holding hands and smiling. Melanie, in response to Kate's questioning glance, nodded and gave her a happy grin.

Alex caught the interchange. "What's all that about?" he asked Kate. They were sitting side by side on the front steps.

"I think they've come to some kind of understanding."

"Good for them. Maybe I can get some pointers from Derek," Alex said.

Kate leaned over and planted a kiss on his mouth. "You're doing just fine on your own."

There was satisfaction, and a little surprise, in his expression. "And just what does that mean?"

"I'm not sure yet." Kate turned away. "Oh, look." She stood up. "There's a procession leaving the warriors' private place by the river."

Alex got up, but his eyes were still on her. "Are you changing the subject?"

"Yes. Alex, I need some time. Do you mind?"

"Sure I mind, but I've waited over thirteen years already. I guess I can manage a while longer."

"Good." She called over to Melanie and Derek. "Where's Susan?"

"In the kitchen with Elsie. What's up?"

"We ought to get going if we don't want to miss the action."

"Should I take my camera?" Melanie asked.

"Put it in a shoulder bag," Alex advised. "Then if Kama says it's okay, you'll be ready."

They took the jeep partway down, but had to leave it and walk the last half mile.

Kama was waiting. She greeted Derek affectionately, then turned to Melanie. "Your camera?" she asked.

Melanie patted her bag. "In here."

"You don't have to hide it."

"I can take pictures?"

"As many as you like. The *laibon* gives permission, and in return asks that you send him a set of your prints."

"Terrific," Melanie said. "Sure I'll send him a set. But does he know I'm a professional photographer, that these aren't just for personal use? I may want to work them into an article for the *Geographic*, that kind of thing."

"He knows. I told him he can trust your judgment, and that you would do nothing to dishonor our ways."

"Thank you."

Derek caught the smile the two women exchanged, with its implications of personal trust, and Kate could see he was gratified.

"Now let us see the return of the warriors," Kama said. "Then I will have to leave you."

The procession had arrived outside the main entrance of the village. "They look different," Susan said, clutching her father's hand tightly. "What's that white stuff on them? They're scary."

"No, child," her grandmother said. "There is nothing to fear. That's a chalk paste prepared by the elders for the ceremony. The warriors paint their bodies to show they are ready to change roles, just as they have changed their appearance."

The young men started singing as they filed through the gate. It was a long and solemn parade. Inside, they formed a semicircle around the central clearing, where the *laibon* was seated. He addressed them. It didn't matter that Kate couldn't understand the words. She understood the solemnity and grandeur of the occasion, as well as the underlying emotions—happiness, pride and some regret.

"I must go now," Kama said when the warriors started to disperse. "I have a duty to perform."

Melanie apparently knew what that duty was. "May I come with you?" she asked.

"Not yet. First I must be alone with my brother's son. Today I act as Latana's mother. After a half hour, then you may all come."

After she'd left, Melanie told them what she'd read about this part of the ceremony. "Now is when the mother of each warrior shaves off his long hair. I guess it's kind of personal, and Latana may not want us to watch."

They sat with the entourage of the *laibon* while they waited. The old man signaled to Susan to come to him. "Go ahead," her father told her, and she ran over. He motioned for her to sit on the stool next to him. The *laibon* spoke to her, and Susan said something in reply. They were an interesting picture, the regal Masai chief and the bouncy little girl, dressed in jeans and a red shirt but with Kama's beaded circlet around her neck. She was obviously enjoying herself and turned and waved to her father and the others.

"I've got to take a shot of that," Melanie said. She stepped forward, holding out her camera. When there was no objection, she crouched and focused on her subjects. The chief leaned forward and placed his hand on Susan's head, then looked toward the camera and smiled.

"He's posing," Derek whispered. "Son of a gun."

The camera clicked several times. Melanie straightened, made a slight bow to the chief and came back.

"Now Susan will have a picture to remind her of the day she sat with a Masai chieftain," Melanie said with satisfaction. She turned to Derek. "This is so special for her. Probably more than she realizes right now."

"It's special for all of us," Derek said.

Susan came running back to them. "What did the *laibon* say to you?" her father asked.

"He said he likes me. He wants me to stay longer, but I told him I have to go back to school soon. He's kinda nice. I think he said that he knew my mother. Did he know her, Daddy?"

"He may have," Derek replied. "I'm not sure."

Kate was pleased to see that the mention of Elizabeth didn't turn Derek to brooding this time. Melanie's smile showed that she, too, had noticed. "I think we can go to Kama now," Melanie said.

Kama and Latana were outside the hut Kama had built. Alex cautioned Susan and the others to stand quietly back so as not to intrude. Latana's head had been shaved, and he gazed solemnly at the long plaits of hair on the ground. Kama spoke softly to him. Words of solace, Kate guessed, for what he was leaving behind, and words of encouragement for the life he was about to enter. Kama dipped her hands into a bowl and rubbed the reddish paste over Latana's head, smoothing it gently to cover his scalp.

When it was over and they were following the young men into the central clearing, Susan was full of questions. "Was that the same red stuff I had on my legs yesterday?"

"Yes."

"But why did *Ayah* cut Latana's hair off? The others, too. They're all baldy now."

"It's to show that they're elders."

Susan fingered her own pigtails possessively. "Can't they just tell people what they are?"

Kate had to smile. "That's not the way it's done."

The next occurrence was much more to Susan's liking. The leader of the newly initiated elders was presented with the girl chosen as his wife. There was a jubilant cry to salute the young couple. "Is there going to be a wedding?" Susan asked excitedly.

"Not just this minute," Melanie told her. "Probably in a couple of days."

"I think Melanie knows more about what's going on here than the rest of us," Alex said.

"Comes from being a photographer. Research is part of the job. Of course," Melanie added with a smiling glance at Derek and Susan, "I have to admit to a special personal interest here."

None of this interested Susan. "Can we stay for the wedding?" was what she wanted to know.

"We'll see," Derek replied.

The young men were given milk to drink, and this was followed by a communal meat-eating ritual. When the chief and senior elders rose to bless the group, the whole assemblage of over a thousand people did likewise and responded to the blessings in unison. Derek had lifted his daughter up so she could see, and Susan was joining the cries. Excited and happy, held by her father, surrounded by her grandmother's people, Susan was in tune with both.

Kate was proud of her niece. Alex, too, moved easily in both worlds, Kate thought. He was accepted and respected by black Kenyans, including the unique Masai, as well as by white settlers and visitors to Kenya. But, then, he had a knack for feeling comfortable with all kinds of people.

The day's events ended with the warriors, their voices raised in song, leaving the village and then reentering through the main gate, as befitted their new status. The sun was low now, and the air cool. As the men filed out, the hundred voices faded, became a distant chorus, then surged as they returned. On either side of the palm-decorated entrance stood a senior elder who anointed each man as he passed. The day's ceremonies were now over.

Kate sensed that Alex felt what she did, both awe and empathy.

They found Kama and said good-night, then started back to where they'd parked the jeep. Derek carried Susan, who was half-asleep.

"Why don't we walk up?" Kate said. "It's a beautiful night."

"Susan's bushed. Besides, we can't leave the jeep here," Derek said.

"Derek, she doesn't mean us," Melanie told him.

"Oh. Right." Derek grinned. "We'll see you two later, then."

Kate and Alex left the dirt road to take a narrow path. He put his arm around her. Without thinking, she matched her steps to his, her body picking up his rhythm. "What a day!" Alex said after a while.

"Hmm. It was a wonderful experience."

"Kama's right, you know. We may never get another chance to see it again."

"It was quite a spectacle."

"More than that. Historically these traditions have been the basis for a cohesive way of life for the Masai. I hate to see that change. They're such a proud people."

Kate glanced up, noting the strength of his profile. "I can see how you'd identify with the Masai."

"I do. The differences aren't as important as what we have in common. This is our country." He gazed around him. "We belong here." He tightened his arm on her shoulder.

"I know what you're thinking," Kate said.

"That you belong here, too." He pivoted her around to face him. "Kate, you've changed. You're not the same person who got off that plane in Nairobi."

Kate couldn't deny it. "I was so determined to be a tourist. I thought I hated Kenya, but I didn't reckon with..." She paused, seeking the right word. "With this feeling I have that there's a vital connection between me, this place and the people."

"Like what you felt as a child?"

"Even deeper."

"Perhaps because you've connected with a part of yourself that you'd been denying. When you first came, I wanted desperately for you to remember how it used to be with us. The future can be even better."

She knew what he meant. Kate felt free, able to engage in life as a total person, not with part of herself buried in the past.

Alex rejoiced to see her acknowledge her change of heart. He longed for her to take the next step, but controlled his urge to seize this moment and press her for a commitment, a promise to stay and to marry him. Earlier that day she'd asked for more time and he'd agreed. He understood what she'd gone through and fully appreciated the trauma of these past days. But it had been a catharsis that would enable Kate to move ahead, to choose the life she wanted. Loving her as he did, now more than ever before, he felt that they belonged together. But he couldn't let his need overpower her freedom of choice.

Alex bent his head and covered her mouth with his. His kiss bespoke his loneliness without her, his pent-up passion, his pride in her, his promise of happiness—his love. Her lips received the message warmly.

THERE WAS A LAZINESS about the house the following morning, a reaction to the dramatic events of the preceding days. Susan played with Nekaritini, and the older sister wasn't around to bother them. Jim McKendrick had gone to work, but the other adults sat on the veranda. Nostalgia ruled their conversation as Derek, Kate and Alex remembered how life had been when they were growing up here. Derek contributed his share of reminiscences, often in answer to a question from Melanie. It was obvious Melanie no longer felt excluded. Derek's attitude was different. In offering her his memories, he was asking her to understand his feelings and letting her become part of his life.

Elsie loved hearing all their stories. "I've had my doubts about raising children here," she admitted. "But it sounds as though you all had a wonderful time. Too bad it had to end as it did. Oh . . . Kate, I'm sorry. I didn't mean to bring that up."

"That's all right." The sorrow Kate felt was familiar. It would always be there. But gone was the shrinking horror of the past thirteen years, a horror made more terrible because its source had been hidden. That black curtain was lifted now. "What happened doesn't negate all the good times we had."

Alex smiled at her. Derek, too, sensed something climactic in her words. "Glad you came?" Derek asked.

"Oh, yes."

THAT AFTERNOON Melanie and Derek took Susan to a native market to buy some gifts for her friends back home. Elsie went with them. Alex and Kate declined the invitation to go along.

"Looks like we'll have the afternoon to ourselves," Alex said when they were alone.

"Is that an evil gleam I see in your eye?"

"Am I that obvious?" he asked with a laugh. He took her in his arms. "So be it. Kate, I haven't made love to you in ages."

"That's an exaggeration."

"Well, it seems like ages," he said, pulling her to him. He caressed her back, then pressed her closer, rubbing his cheek against her hair. "You feel so good," he whispered, "so silky and warm."

His voice, his touch, his scent, tapped a vein of passion deep within her. It *had* been a long time, she thought, raising her lips for his kiss. His mouth was gentle at first, but caught fire at the urgency of her response. Kate had never thought of herself as a sensual woman, and nothing before had prepared her for the onslaught of desire Alex aroused in her. The attraction was always there, just beneath the surface, easily activated by a look, a word, a casual touch from him. And when he unleashed his passion, as he was doing now, she was caught in a wave of longing that drowned out all else.

His tongue probed and tasted and met the fiery thrust of hers. He kissed her eyes, her cheeks, her ear. He ran his hands over her, molded her hips and pressed them against

him. When he undid the top buttons of her shirt and lowered his head to the soft hollow between her breasts, Kate
pressed her cheek against his dark hair. Her legs felt weak,
but at the same time a throbbing ache originating deep in
her loins strengthened its demand.

Alex raised his head. "Kate, I don't want to stop," he
said.

Kate smiled tremulously. "Who said anything about
stopping?" She took his hand and led him into her bedroom.

Alex undressed her, his movements deliberate, prolonging the anticipation. He helped her to remove his clothes,
then held her again as they stood, their nakedness adding a
delicious sensuousness to their embrace. Kate clutched his
shoulders, then circled her hands around his neck, rising on
tiptoe, pressing against the length of him. She felt his growing desire, and her kiss told him she was ready to meet it.
Alex eased her back on the bed and sat beside her. His eyes
ran a caressing course over her nude body, a course that his
tantalizing fingers soon followed.

Kate gazed up at him. "I used to imagine us like this, you
know," she said softly. "Years ago when I lay in bed and
couldn't sleep for thinking what it would be like when you
made love to me. Sometimes I hated you for not wanting
to."

"Not wanting to?" The words came out like a groan. "I
was in an agony of wanting. It took every ounce of
willpower I had to wait."

"That was long ago."

As Alex bent to kiss her, Kate reached for him, drawing
him over her, gasping as his body crushed hers. All those
immature longings she'd once had—they were nothing

compared to the reality of the overriding passion that now gripped her.

He kissed her face and throat, then brought the searing magic of his lips to her breasts. He meant to prolong her pleasure, but Kate felt a writhing urgency deep inside. "Alex, don't wait," she whispered. "Please."

He raised up on his elbows and saw in her eyes confirmation of what he'd heard. He entered her slowly. As he sank into her, Kate curled her legs around him. She felt an inner involuntary tightening as Alex started to move within her. Kate geared her movements, her body rhythms to his, but as he thrust deeper, the tightness started to dissolve in melting waves, then build again. She resisted, then suddenly her resistance broke.

Alex sensed the change and exulted in it. He matched her ardor and absorbed her frenzy into his passion. Kate arched against him, feeling herself coiling in an upward spiral, tightening, tightening, until the ultimate was reached—and the coil unraveled, scattering its remnants. Kate called Alex's name, then felt the shattering tumult of her orgasm intensify as he plunged to his own climax.

For a long time they stayed entwined, letting the passion ebb from their bodies. Then Alex eased onto his side, propping himself up on an elbow to gaze at her. "To think of all the years we lost," he said after a while. "Actually, I'd rather think of all the years to come. Or am I getting ahead of myself again?"

"You're getting ahead of yourself," Kate said.

Alex was the one who heard the vehicle stop outside. "Dammit!"

"What's the matter?" Kate asked.

"I think they're back."

"Already?"

Alex looked out the window. His expression changed. "No. It's Richo." In a second he was up and getting into his clothes. "Something must be wrong."

Kate didn't linger in bed when he'd gone. She dressed and joined the two men, who were talking in the living room. "Is there a problem?" she asked.

"Yes," Alex replied. "One of the campers is sick. Ingrid. She's the little Swedish girl."

"Is it serious?"

"Hans thinks it could be her appendix," Richo explained. "I called the Flying Doctor Service in Nairobi, and they will come to take her to the hospital there."

"I'd better go with her," Alex said.

"Do you have to?" Kate immediately withdrew her question. "Strike that. Of course you do."

He came over and took her hands. "I should be back tomorrow. Will you be all right?" he asked, a concerned look on his face.

"Sure. There's nothing going to happen here. I'll be fine."

Alex kissed her goodbye and left.

The house was suddenly very quiet and very empty. Even after the others returned Kate felt lonely. She missed Alex.

Jim McKendrick returned home later than usual that afternoon. Kate and Elsie were alone in the house. Susan had taken her father and Melanie down to the glade. McKendrick asked for Alex and was disappointed to learn that he'd left. Then a call came that left him grim faced.

"What's wrong, Jim?" Elsie asked.

"I think there's going to be trouble."

"What kind of trouble?"

Kate came over to hear his response.

"Poachers." He spit out the word. "It's because of the rhinos. They're the draw. With the ones shipped here from other areas, we've got a bigger concentration than anywhere else."

"But that was the plan, to have a rhino sanctuary," Kate said. Alex had pointed the place out to her, a natural enclosure, bordered by rivers and trees and a fence of thornbushes at the narrow entrance. "They're supposed to be safer here. I saw that you had two guards posted by the entrance."

"Well, they're not there now," McKendrick said grimly. "That call I just got—it was from the Mara Sopa Lodge. One of the tour guides there just got back from a game drive. Mahmoud said there were no rangers on duty around the rhino preserve."

"Maybe they just took a break," Elsie said. "You know, a short call behind the bushes. Something like that."

"No. Mahmoud scouted around. No ranger vehicle. No guards."

"What do you think happened?"

"Someone told them to disappear. Either paid them or scared them off."

"Can't you replace them?" Kate asked.

"That's just the trouble. I'm shorthanded. I've got men on leave and more than the usual number who are sick. God, I wish Alex were here!"

"What do you think's going to happen?" Kate asked.

"A raid. Not from a lone poacher. A big operation. There's a fortune in rhino tusks and hooves in that one place. And I've got only one armed man available."

"But you can call for help from other preserves," Elsie said.

"I already have, but I can't count on them getting here in time. The poachers will probably come at night. Even if I got the replacements—not knowing the terrain, they'd be handicapped in the dark."

"I've an idea," Kate said. "Kama Sloane's brother, Lomali, is a guard at the Mara Sopa Lodge. He carries a gun, and he's down in the Masai village here."

"Do you think he'd want to help?"

"We can ask."

"I guess it's worth a try."

"I'll go with you," Kate said. "I've met the man."

They were on their way out, when Derek and the others returned. On hearing what was up, Derek immediately volunteered to go with them.

"I'd feel better knowing you were here with them," McKendrick said, indicating Susan and the women. Derek agreed to stay.

When they were out of earshot, Kate asked, "You don't expect trouble here, do you?"

"No. Derek means well, but someone not experienced at this game would be in the way."

"I hope that doesn't include me," Kate told him.

He gave her a curious look. "It doesn't," he said.

The compliment gratified her.

At the Masai village, they found Kama and her brother, Lomali, and another man. Kate gasped with surprise. It was Patrick Sloane, much aged and completely gray, but with the same stiff, upright bearing. "How wonderful to see you," Kate cried. The usually undemonstrative Englishman gave her a hug. Kate remembered how taciturn he'd always been, except with Elizabeth. In that respect he hadn't changed. In explanation of his return Sloane said only, "It was time."

"But what trouble brings you here?" Kama asked Kate.

Kate let McKendrick explain. Sloane immediately offered his services, as did Lomali.

"We can handle them," Sloane said. "Poachers are usually a sorry lot."

"Not these, I'm afraid," said McKendrick. "I think Harry Lunt may be engineering this raid. He'll have brought in a tough crew."

"This Lunt," said Lomali, his gaze hardening, "I have seen him at the Mara Sopa. He is there now."

"That's what I figured," McKendrick said. "I've got one guard available. We'll pick him up on the way. With the four of us, maybe we can scare them away."

"Four?" Lomali repeated. "Why not twenty-four?"

Kate and the two other men didn't understand, but Kama nodded and smiled with approval. "Latana and his troop of warriors," she explained. "Officially they are now elders, but how they would welcome one last opportunity to act together as *morani*."

"Especially against the man Lunt," Lomali added. "His name is known among us as one who contracts for animals from poachers."

Lomali's disgust was obvious. The Masai, Kate knew, thought it reprehensible to kill animals for profit.

As predicted, Latana and the warriors from his *manyatta* were eager to be part of the operation.

"You stay with Kama," Patrick Sloane told Kate.

"No way."

"All right. We'll drop you off at the compound," he said.

"You don't understand. I'm going with you."

Patrick Sloane frowned and looked ready to argue. Kama put a restraining hand on his arm.

"Patrick, as a girl, this one did not take to being ordered about. Do you expect her to accept it now?"

Sloane grunted, then turned to the senior warden. "You're in charge here. It's your call."

McKendrick hesitated for only a second. "I think Kate can handle herself. Come on, then. Let's get started."

Kate flashed him a grateful smile.

CHAPTER SIXTEEN

KATE DIDN'T TRY to rationalize why she'd insisted on coming. It had something to do with responding to the challenges that living here entailed. She would analyze her motives later, however; right now there was a job to do.

Sloane rode with the other ranger, whom they'd picked up at his office. Kate was in the vehicle with McKendrick and Lomali. The Masai followed on foot, but arrived at the rhino preserve soon after the others. Their reputation for speed and stamina was well deserved.

McKendrick's original plan was to put on a show of force and scare away the intruders.

"We've got help now," Kate said. "Why not take them?"

Sloane frowned. He might not be reconciled to her being there, but when he spoke, it was to support her suggestion. "She's right. They'll try again if you don't."

"It's worth a shot," McKendrick agreed.

They hid the two vehicles behind a dense copse of bushes and stationed themselves just within the narrow entrance to the sanctuary. Dusk deepened into blackness. The young Masai occasionally talked among themselves in low voices. Kate sensed their excitement, and the tension of waiting.

Suddenly Lomali issued a warning sound. "Zssss..." Moments later, the others, too, heard the vehicles approaching. Her eyes now accustomed to the darkness, Kate made out two pickup trucks, and a Land Rover that followed at a distance.

"The men next to the driver in each truck," McKendrick whispered. "Those two are the ones who are armed."

"There's a third," Sloane said. "In the back of the second truck with the rest of them. Those three bastards—they're the hunters."

"What about the others?" Kate asked.

"Butchers," McKendrick said with distaste. "They get to cut what's valuable from the animals that are killed and leave the rest for the scavengers."

Kate shared his revulsion. "I meant the men in the Land Rover. I think there are two of them."

"I don't know," McKendrick said. "The driver's staying too far back. Could be Lunt's man, making sure his boss doesn't get cheated."

Or Lunt himself, Kate thought.

McKendrick directed his guard and Sloane to go back to the vehicles. "When the trucks stop," he told them, "I'll yell out 'now,' and you get those jeeps out in the open and aim your lights right at the poachers. Then take cover and be ready for—" he paused "—for whatever the hell comes after that. Got it?"

"Wait," Kate said. "Let me take one of the jeeps. Keep Patrick with you. He'll be more use to you here."

"Are you daft, girl?" Patrick whispered angrily. "You stay here out of the way."

"I'll be more out of the way taking cover behind the jeep. Those guys won't be able to see beyond the headlights."

"She's got a point," McKendrick said. "If there's any shooting, I'll need you here, Sloane. All right," he told Kate. "But you jump out of there the minute you get those lights on. Hear?"

"Don't worry."

Lomali crouched and slipped into the darkness to alert the warriors. Kate and the guard moved stealthily away to where the vehicles were parked. She motioned to the guard, showing him the direction she would take when they pulled out, so they wouldn't get in each other's way. He signaled that he understood. Kate settled into the driver's seat, put the key in the ignition and waited.

Minutes passed. Kate felt the same excitement and tension she'd sensed in the warriors. An exhilaration, too, despite the element of danger. She could have avoided this, could have stayed behind and played it safe. Alex faced risks constantly, and she hadn't understood why he would choose such a life. But risks were a part of life. Her father had known and accepted that. Kate finally realized that she could, also.

It seemed that the trucks were coming at a snail's pace. She noticed that the third vehicle had stopped farther back. The trucks had their lights off, so there was a shrouded eeriness to their lumbering approach. They came to a halt, and the men started to leap off. Kate took hold of the key, tense, every sense alert. She peered through the darkness to where McKendrick was hidden. He stood up, and she heard him yell "Okay—now!"

Kate started the engine and pulled out. In seconds the two vehicles were in position, their glaring bright lights illuminating the scene. Kate jumped out and crouched behind the jeep.

"Halt!" McKendrick shouted. He fired a warning shot into the air. "Put down your weapons."

The poachers started to scatter, but found themselves surrounded by the Masai warriors. Kate hadn't even heard anyone give them an order, but they'd moved swiftly through the darkness, fanning out around the poachers and beginning to close in. Sloane and the other ranger, guns drawn, had joined McKendrick, but it was the advancing Masai who put the poachers in a frenzy.

In a panic, the driver from the first truck drew his gun and fired wildly, hitting an advancing Masai in the shoulder. A fearful cry rang out, and he found himself the target of four angry warriors coming at him with raised spears.

"No. No."

The man dropped his gun. Terrified, he backed away. Other warriors blocked his escape. His companions, frozen with fear, offered no help. The man reached down to tear out a clump of grass with each hand, then extended his arms, holding the grass out in a recognized gesture of surrender and a plea for mercy. The wounded Masai advanced alone. Spear raised, he stopped before the trembling poacher. Then, with a controlled movement, the warrior pierced the poacher's shoulder. A cry of approval went up from the other Masai. It was not a severe wound, but was accepted as fitting retribution.

Kate felt the tension drain from her body. The worst was over. She looked toward the crest of the hill to where the third vehicle had parked. It was gone.

McKendrick questioned the wounded man. He was still so frightened about being left to the mercy of the Masai that he revealed everything, giving McKendrick exactly the information he wanted. His confession implicated Harry Lunt, and identified him as the one behind this raid, as well as other such incidents in the past. Lunt had been in the Land Rover, and the captured poacher was bitter about Lunt's having disappeared when he saw the trouble start.

"I think we've got the bastard this time," McKendrick said with satisfaction. "If we can nail him on this, we can close down his whole operation. There will be a lot of fall-out from this arrest.''

One such fallout, Kate realized, would impact on Lunt's providing financial backing for Peter Bazeek's commercial developments. The projects that Alex opposed could never be approved once criminal charges were brought against Harry Lunt. Bazeek would no longer be able to shrug off the accusations against his friend Lunt as mere rumors. Alex would be elated when he heard.

ALEX HAD A DIFFERENT REACTION, at least initially, when he got back late that night. Ingrid had undergone an emergency appendectomy, but had come through it fine. When he'd heard that the doctor's service had a helicopter returning to the Mara, Alex had hitched a ride. He'd been surprised to find the whole household assembled and talking excitedly. When he heard the story, Alex was appalled that Kate had been exposed to such danger. He turned to McKendrick. "How could you let her talk you into going along?''

McKendrick shrugged. "She's got a mind of her own, this lady of yours, Alex. You weren't around, so she offered to help. Did a damn good job, too.''

Alex shook his head. To Kate he said, "You had no business being there.''

"Hold on," she said. "You have no business telling me what I have no business doing.''

"What?" He started to laugh. She was right. Hadn't he wanted her to make her own choices?

"You heard what I said." But Kate, too, started to laugh.

"Doesn't this have a familiar ring!" Derek said. "You two always used to argue like crazy, then laugh, kiss and make up.''

"I'm ready to get on to the third part of that," Alex told Kate.

She shook her head. "Uh-uh. Not until I get the commendation I think I deserve."

"You're right." He took her by the shoulders and, with the air of a French commandant, kissed her on one cheek, then the other. "Bravo." Dropping his pose, he added, "I mean that sincerely."

"Now that's more like it," she said.

He liked her pride in herself, even though the thought that she'd been in danger had scared the hell out of him at first. Kate had changed, and it was all her own doing.

Choosing to relive the experience she had repressed for so long had been a supreme test of courage. She could finally expunge the guilt she'd buried deep within her for so many years. Now, free from a hatred of this country and the nameless fears it had stirred, Kate could make choices and cope with danger. Her actions tonight proved that.

There was, however, something still to be decided. Would Kate stay and make her life in Kenya with him?

FOR MOST OF THE NEXT DAY, McKendrick, Sloane and Alex were occupied with the business of the poachers' arrests, taking statements and getting corroborating confessions from some of the others in custody. Derek and Melanie started planning the kind of book they might do on African folk art, then got sidetracked with the idea of a magazine article about Masai tribal life. Susan had been begging to go back to the village. Though the main ceremonies of *eunoto* were over, Susan kept hoping she would get to see a wedding.

Kate made Susan very happy when she said, "Why don't we go? Melanie, you might be able to take some interesting photographs."

"That's a thought," Melanie replied. "Who knows when I'll get another chance like this?"

There was no wedding, but Susan found the children she had played with, and happily joined their games. The village was buzzing with the story of the Masai warriors' involvement in capturing the poachers. The wounded Masai was the hero of the occasion, but all the young men who had participated were being honored. "Latana, he is very proud," Kama told them. "Now comes a time of responsibility. The duty of the elders is to marry, to see to their families, to advise on village law. The honor of being warriors will fall to the next group. But last night they were warriors again."

Kama took them around and was their entrée into some of the houses. Melanie snapped picture after picture, and Derek jotted down notes as Kama translated the answers to the questions he asked. Kate was content to be a bystander and take it all in. She had a strange and deep feeling of serenity today.

Patrick Sloane arrived, and when Susan spotted him, she ran over. Their meeting the night before had been brief, but Sloane had been an instant hit with his young granddaughter. He opened his arms and swooped her up.

"I thought she might be shy with him," Derek said to Kama. "She can't really remember him. She was so young when she last saw him."

"She remembers that he loves her. That is memory enough."

"He's so different around her," Kate commented. "His whole face lights up."

"It was that way with Elizabeth," Kama said, her voice tinged with sadness. "Elizabeth could always make him smile. Perhaps now that he sees her in his granddaughter, he will be happy again."

"Do you think he'll stay this time?" Melanie asked curiously.

With a fatalistic shrug, Kama said, "No. He will go—and then he will come again. That is the way it is."

"You don't mind?"

"He is the man I chose." She repeated, "That is the way it is."

The answer didn't satisfy Melanie, but Kate understood.

LATE THAT NIGHT, the whole group sat outside the McKendrick house, looking down the hill at the flickering fires in the ceremonial village. In the morning, the assembled tribes would head back to their homes.

"Well, *eunoto* is over," Melanie said regretfully.

"The ceremony, yes," Kama said. "The change that happens inside each man—that takes longer." Kate felt Kama's eyes on her. After a long pause, Kama continued. "My people make a formal ceremony, but there can be different rituals for *eunoto*, internal ones, that individuals experience. And afterward they move into a new age-set. A maturity like the Masai elderhood."

Kama's glance swept over the others. She smiled at Derek and at her granddaughter, sleepily resting against Melanie. Kate was glad Kama had given them her blessing. Derek had told his sister that everything was going to be all right, and Kate, borrowing some of Kama's sixth sense, saw joy in their future as a family.

With a sense of deep contentment, Kate breathed deeply, drawing inside herself the beauty and clarity around her. She recognized that Kama's words applied to her. Her whole experience in Kenya could be likened to a ritual, each step of which had brought her closer to a recognition of the past and finally to this acceptance and trust in herself. It was a precious feeling, one she didn't want to lose.

Kama and Patrick Sloane said good-night, and soon the others followed. Kate and Alex lingered. After a while Alex took Kate's hand. "Come on," he said. She didn't have to ask where they were going. As they neared Pambazuko, Kate let go of his hand and started to run. Not from any sense of urgency, but just for the sheer joy of it. Alex quickly caught up with her. They reached the top of the hill and stopped, then found a rock to sit on. Kate looked around her. She was breathing hard, and her heart swelled inside her chest.

"It's ours again, isn't it?"

"It's ours." Alex put his arm around her.

Kate leaned against him, relishing the warmth of his body. Here, in this place, she felt so close to Alex. But soon they would have to leave. They would return to the camp, and then to Nairobi, and then . . . Kate remembered the date on her return ticket and what awaited her back in the States. She shivered.

"What is it?" he asked at once.

"I was just thinking."

"What about?"

"Going home."

Alex tilted her face up to him. "Kate, you *are* home."

He was right. The prospect of returning to her former life filled her with dread. She had feared the savagery here, but sophisticated forms of savagery were just as deadly. She had survived, even prospered in that life. Her success had fed her ego—and withered her heart. Here, with Alex, her heart had expanded again.

Alex cupped her face in his hands. "I love you. Even over those long years when you were lost to me, there was never anyone else. I knew that we'd be together again. I think you must have known it, too."

His eyes were magnets, drawing from her the only response possible. During all the years they were apart, the boy she once loved had remained in her heart. But the man he'd become now filled her being.

"I love you, Alex," she said. Her voice reflected her wonder and conviction and soaring joy. "I love you, and I want to stay here with you."

Alex dropped his hands to her shoulders and drew in a sharp breath. His smile was both triumphant and tender. Then, in the distance, they heard a lion roar, and Kate stiffened.

Alex held her close. "That sound frightens you, doesn't it?"

"It always will," she told him.

"Kate, I can't change that."

She gazed deep into his eyes. "I know. It's all right." She could accept the wildness because it coexisted with beauty and grace and majesty. There was a harmony in the natural order, where land and people and wildlife could flourish. Their love had been born in this place, and here it would live and grow.

She rested contentedly in his arms. After a while she stirred. "Remember that partner you said you needed?"

He nodded, and his mouth curved with pleasure as he guessed what she was thinking.

The prospect of using her skills and experience working with Alex was exciting. There was much she could do to gain outside interest and support. Expanding the youth safari program, planning the animal shelter—these were not just Alex's dreams. They were hers now. "I'm ready to apply for the job."

"Not just as a business partner," he warned. "This is a lifetime contract."

Kate smiled. "I certainly hope so. When do I start?"

His lips grazing hers, Alex said, "Right now."

She put her arms around him. "I'm ready," she said. Her kiss proved it was so.

Harlequin Superromance.

COMING NEXT MONTH

JAYNE ANN KRENTZ WINS HARLEQUIN'S AWARD OF EXCELLENCE

With her October Temptation, *Lady's Choice*, Jayne Ann Krentz marks more than a decade in romance publishing. We thought it was about time she got our *official* seal of approval—the Harlequin Award of Excellence.

Since she began writing for Temptation in 1984, Ms Krentz's novels have been a hallmark of this lively, sexy series—and a benchmark for all writers in the genre. *Lady's Choice*, her eighteenth Temptation, is as stirring as her first, thanks to a tough and sexy hero, and a heroine who is tough when she has to be, tender when she chooses....

The winner of numerous booksellers' awards, Ms Krentz has also consistently ranked as a bestseller with readers, on both romance and mass market lists. *Lady's Choice* will do it for her again!

This lady is *Harlequin's* choice in October.

Available where Harlequin books are sold.

AE-LC-1

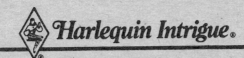

Harlequin Intrigue®

High adventure and romance—
with three sisters on a search . . .

Linsey Deane uses clues left by their father to search the Colorado
Rockies for a legendary wagonload of Confederate gold, in #120
Treasure Hunt by Leona Karr (August 1989).

Kate Deane picks up the trail in a mad chase to the Deep South and
glitzy Las Vegas, with menace and romance at her heels, in #122
Hide and Seek by Cassie Miles (September 1989).

Abigail Deane matches wits with a murderer and hunts for the people
behind the threat to the Deane family fortune, in #124 *Charades* by
Jasmine Crasswell (October 1989).

*Don't miss Harlequin Intrigue's three-book series The Deane
Trilogy. Available where Harlequin books are sold.*

DEA-G

COMING SOON...

Indulge a Little
Give a Lot

An irresistible opportunity to pamper
yourself with free* gifts and help a
great cause, Big Brothers/Big Sisters
Programs and Services.
*With proofs-of-purchase plus postage and handling.

Watch for it in October!

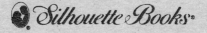

Harlequin Books®

Silhouette Books®